JACK'S GAME

ANDREW CHAPMAN

Copyright © 2021, Andrew Chapman

Andrew Chapman has asserted his right to be identified as the author of this Work in accordance with the Copyright, Designs and Patents Act 1988

All rights reserved. No part of this publication may be reproduced, stored in a retrieval system, or transmitted in any form or by any means, electronic, mechanical, photocopying, recording or otherwise, without the prior permission of the copyright owner

Published by Andrew Chapman, andrew-chapman@live.co.uk

For Rachel and Kassidy

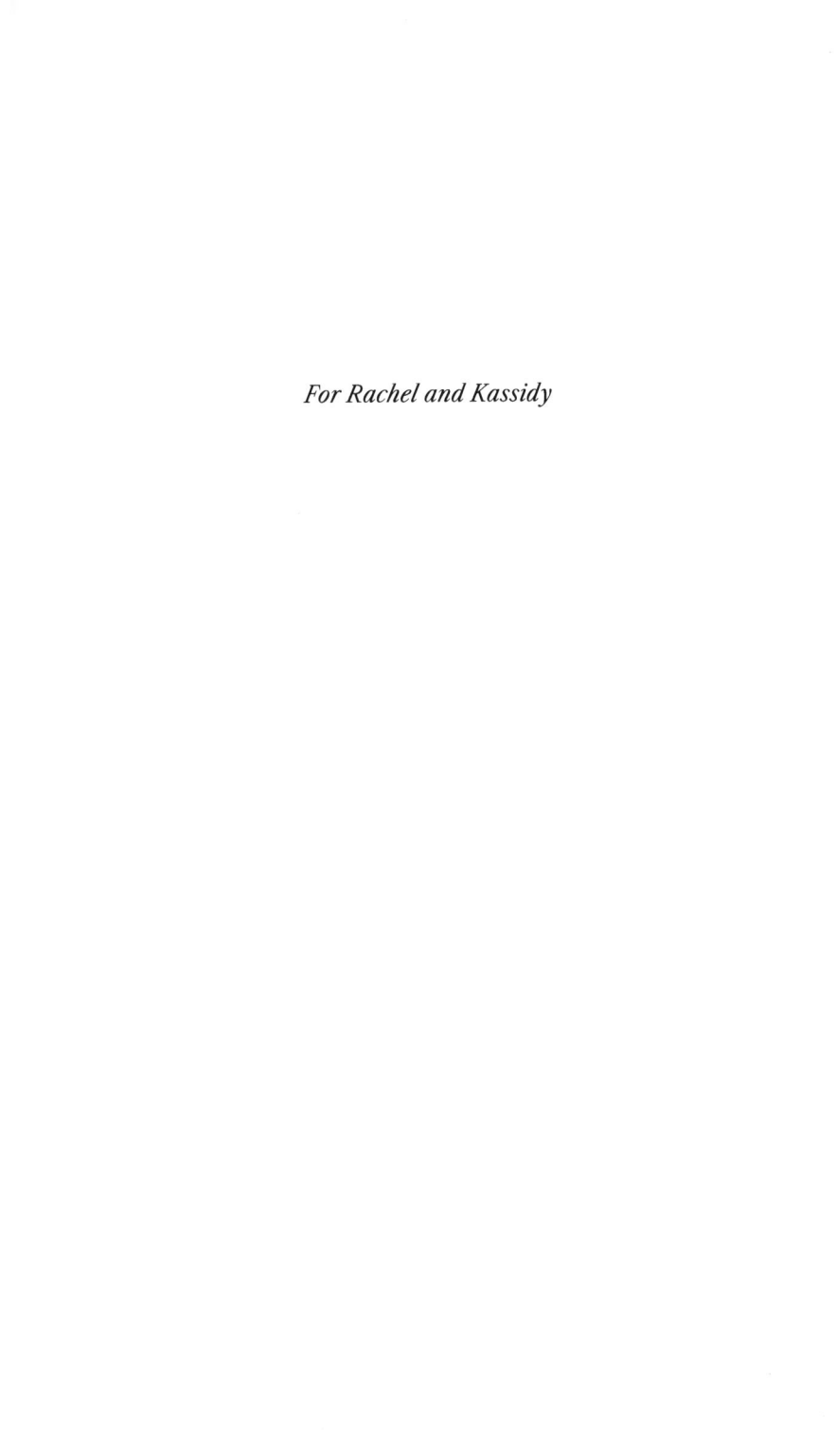

Cacophini stood in the sky and looked down at Shelley Town.

1992

A basement.

Sarah's little body had stopped convulsing. Blood pulsed out of the jagged wound above her nose. Her body was flat on the floor, belly-down, her chin against the wall, facing up at an unnatural angle.

It was dark.

Blood trickled down her ponytail and ran down her back.

William Rain stepped back and dropped the axe.

JACK'S GAME

CHAPTER 1

2002

The sun hammered through the sky. It was a belter. The hottest August on record. Slugs lay dead and shrivelled on the pavements.

Billy Rain slipped his trainers on and shrugged his backpack onto his shoulders. He left the house, picked up his red BMX, and cycled left out of the drive.

His mother, who never left the house, never had as far as Billy could recall, had sent him out on one of her many errands to get her this or that, or whatever thing she didn't have but needed right away. This morning it was cigarettes and milk.

The way the curb went down in front of the neighbour's driveway and then back up created a ramp which he had a habit of jumping off every time he left the house. If he caught it just right he could really get some air.

He rode along the west side of the green, weaving on and off the pavement, bunny-hopping off the curbs. He scared some pigeons into flight as he cycled onto the cobbled pedestrianised side of Shelley Town square and stood up on the pedals to absorb the shock of the uneven ground.

He lifted his left leg over the frame and coasted on one pedal to a stop outside the tobacconist. He stepped off and went into the shop with the back wheel still spinning on the fallen bike.

'Hey, Billy,' said the old tobacconist behind the counter.

'Hey, Mr Finnegan,' said Billy. 'Can I have a pouch of Amber Leaf and some filters, please?'

Mr. Finnegan knew Billy well. He was a big man. The streaks of grey in his beard had turned yellow from tobacco smoke. He had the air of a professor and the gut of a bricklayer.

The shop looked like it had been there forever. Under the scratched glass top of the counter were expensive lighters and pipes. There were a few pocket knives for sale there too and a long barrelled handgun. This fascinated Billy. There were rumours that Finnegan had a backroom racked with rifles and shotguns. The rumours were true, but it was nothing illegal. The place had started life as a gun shop that sold tobacco on the side. Turns out addiction sells better than bullets and he moved with the times.

Billy stared at the gun.

'You're still not old enough, Billy,' said Mr. Finnegan.

'Could you just let me hold it for a second?'

'Ha,' said Finnegan, in a way that meant *not a fucking chance.*

'Okay. But one day.'

'Alright, Billy.' Finnegan smiled and put the tobacco on the counter. 'Can I get you anything else?'

'No, that's all. Thank you.'

'How is your mother?' asked Finnegan, knowing the tobacco was for her and not for him. He wouldn't sell tobacco to any kid that walked in. Billy's mother hadn't left the house in years.

'Same as she always is, I guess.'

Finnegan nodded. 'We'll get her out of that house one of these days.'

'I don't think so. But thanks.'

'You're welcome. That will be eight pounds and fifty pence for the tobacco and filters.'

Billy put his hand in his pocket and took out the ten pound note that was loose in there. The old cash register drawer slid open with a chime and Finnegan gave Billy his change.

'Why don't you treat yourself to a sweet with that change? You never do. Kids need treats, Billy.'

'It's okay, I need to buy milk.'

'Well alright, you have a nice day. I expect I'll see you back in here before the week is out.'

'Probably. Bye Mr. Finnegan.'

Billy ran out and hopped back on his bike. He was gone before Finnegan had a chance to reply.

He lifted a hand in a half wave. 'Goodbye, kid,' he said, to the closed door.

Billy stopped at the grocers and picked up a pint of milk. He put it in his backpack, along with the tobacco that was already in there, and got back on his bike. He looked down the square back towards home and hesitated. There was something different about the weird old house on the east side of the green. Something in the garden.

He tried to ignore the voice in his head. The one that said, 'Don't go down there, Billy. You know it's not safe.' He looked away from the house and started off the way he always went. But then his curiosity got the better of him and he swerved left to the other side of the square, to the old Matterson house.

Billy stopped outside and got off his bike. He carefully laid it down, not wanting to make a noise, and stared, mouth slightly agape, at what occupied the usually vacant front garden of the property.

A garden sale.

Billy scrunched up his face in bemusement. He looked up at the house. It was a mess. He didn't think anyone lived there. He had been told to never go near the place. Everyone knew to not go there. People avoided the east pavement. Even the people next door would cut through the green rather than pass its low fence.

The paint on the walls had turned grey and peeled off in flakes the size of butterfly wings that settled on the flowerbeds and windowsills like architectural dandruff. Some of the windows were smashed and the front door hung open from its broken frame. The grass had been dead so long it looked like hay.

There was an old car in the driveway. All four tyres were flat and the brake lights were cracked. The bodywork was dented and the exhaust was rusted through and hanging off.

Billy walked closer and stopped with his knees touching

the low fence. The garden was full of all sorts of clutter. There were piles of books and faded toys. Old tools and a pile of dolls. A tall brass standing lamp leaned against a table which had a Polaroid camera on it and some 90s VHS tapes.

He walked along the fence, taking in everything. On the last table there was an open box. A wire with a plug on the end hung out of it. He could just make out the edge of a gamepad.

He looked down at a sign that had been hammered into the ground. It read, FREE TO A GOOD HOME.

Billy looked behind him to see if anyone was watching. There was a couple walking their dog on the green but they hadn't noticed him. He looked back at the sign and then up to the house. He stared at the windows, looking for some watching figure, but nobody was there. He looked back again at the box. That was definitely a gamepad.

He looked around again, to make sure no one was watching, and then leaned over to get a closer look. He got up on tip-toes and leaned forward as far as he could. He still couldn't see in the box but more of the gamepad was revealed. It was rectangular and basic, like the controller that came with the NES, the first Nintendo console. Billy leaned back again and took another look at the house. Still no sign of anyone.

He climbed over the low fence and stepped into the garden. He walked as quietly as he could and looked inside the box.

Along with the gamepad was a console. He didn't recognise the make but there was no mistaking what it was.

There was a cable coming out of the back to plug it into a television. It wasn't HDMI or SCART, or anything nearly as sophisticated, just an aerial lead. The other wire ran to the plug that was hanging over the edge. Billy reached in and lifted the console to get a better look in the box. There was another controller and six or seven games. He opened one of the game boxes. It was called Jet Set Willy. He shook it and a cartridge fell out. He picked it up. It wasn't a Nintendo cartridge, it wasn't Sega either. He had never seen one like it before.

He heard a faint sound come from inside the house and closed up the box and grabbed it with both hands.

He got over the fence and picked up his bike as fast as he could. He balanced the box on the bar between his legs and stared wide-eyed at the front door of the house for a moment, expecting some monster to thrash out towards him, but nothing came. He breathed for the first time since grabbing the box and put the bike in motion. He moved like someone escaping a hurricane with a box of hurriedly packed supplies. He was back at his house in no time.

He didn't jump any curbs or weave around the parked cars. He just got there, fast and safe. He dumped his bike in the driveway and headed straight to the big tree in the front garden.

CHAPTER 2

Billy's treehouse had been built by his dad years ago, back when Billy was a kid. It had undergone several changes since then. That was back before his dad had vanished, seemingly for good, on a prolonged business trip.

The treehouse had begun its days as a basic four-walled shed about ten feet off the ground where the tree forked in three different directions. Two other areas were added over the years. They were connected by short tunnels, like mineshafts that you had to crawl through. It felt more like home to Billy than the house did. This was Billy's domain. His mum had never been up there. His dad had even kept out when he'd been around. To Billy and his two best friends, Martha and Dirk, this was a secret place, out in the open and completely hidden at the same time. They could say anything in there and do what they wanted. It was a hideout and a den of geek.

They mostly hung out in Den One, the name they gave to the original section. The other two areas were known as Den Two and Den the Third. They had no idea why they didn't call the third section Den Three, it was always just Den the Third. It goes like that sometimes. In Den One there was a bench that had been taken out of an old coach. It was made up of three seats bolted together. The seatbelts were still there and they sometimes buckled themselves in when they were playing Mario Kart on the Nintendo 64.

The television was top-of-the-range once. Now you could pick one up for next to nothing in the free-ads. It was big and heavy and had a mess of wires coming out of the back of it with an array of old video game consoles plugged in; A Nintendo 64 (which got played the most), a Nintendo Game Cube, a Super Nintendo, a Sega Master System (the Sega didn't get played much), there was an Xbox, but that was only used to play DVDs. In the corner of the treehouse they even had an old ZX Spectrum, which was piled on top of an Atari 2600 and an old VHS player, but they mostly just stood in the corner like dusty relics in a museum.

Den Two was lined with shelves. It was a retro gamer's heaven. Every shelf was rammed with games. The right wall was full of classic films on VHS and DVD. There must have been 150 movies in there, and as many games.

Den the Third had an old mattress on the floor and not much else apart from a small beer fridge full of soft drinks, and a wooden chest full of snacks. Sometimes they all crashed out in there. Those were great nights.

Billy put the box on the grass and climbed the ladder into the treehouse. There was a makeshift pulley system attached to a thick branch by the entrance with a rope running through it. Tied to one end of the rope was a wide drawer taken from an old desk. He unhooked the rope and lowered the drawer to the ground. He climbed back down the ladder and lifted the box into it. He went back up and pulled the rope, hand over hand, until the drawer reached the top. He tied off the end of the rope and brought the box inside.

Billy sat cross-legged in front of the box and opened it slowly. There was something so satisfying about opening a box with some unknown thing dwelling inside. He took the console out and rested it on his lap. Billy, it could be said, was something of an expert when it came to gaming (his father, after all, had created one of the most successful games of the 90s, Doctor Hammer), but this was like nothing he had seen before.

There were no markings on it at all. Not even a logo. He picked it up and looked underneath. There was normally at least a serial number but there was nothing. It looked something like a Super Nintendo but not quite. It took cartridges but that didn't help much. A lot of the old consoles did. It was too new to be anything like an Atari 2600 or a Neo Geo AES. He pushed the flaps down where the cartridges go and examined it. He leaned forward and picked up one of the SNES cartridges that were strewn on the floor in front of the telly. He tried to slot it in the hole but the cartridge was too big. He put it down beside him and rummaged in the box for one of the games that came with it.

The first one that came to hand was a familiar one, Rainbow Island. Not a famous game but one he played a lot as a kid.

The box looked fairly standard but there was no mention

of the console it belonged to. He opened the box and shook out the game. It was a cartridge, as expected. A very plain object. The sticker had only the name of the game on it, no other artwork, and no other writing. Not even a copyright logo. Butterflies started to go around in his stomach. He felt like an art collector who had just stumbled across a hitherto unknown Van Gogh. He put the cartridge into the console and it fit with a satisfying CLUNK.

A sudden need to plug this baby in and find out what it was came over him. No force on earth could have stopped him. He put the console to one side and pulled wires out from behind the television, not caring what wire had come from where, such things could be figured out later when they had to be plugged back in again. He plugged the console in and scrambled to find the TV remote.

'Where the fuck is it?' he said, cursing casually, as if he swore all the time.

He pulled the coach seats forward and found the remote behind them. He aimed it at the TV and pressed the power button. It turned on. He switched on the console and tried the first four channels. Each channel turned to static.

He knew he had to tune the TV to find a games console this old but it had been a while since he'd had to do it. After much pressing of buttons he figured it out and waited as still as he could, frozen to the spot with anticipation. The tuning bar on the screen scanned slowly, for what? The right frequency? A signal? He didn't know. The static darkened and lightened as the screen worked its way through the blizzard.

The TV was searching and soon it had to find it. The expectant buzz in Billy's brain needed it. It wasn't worth thinking about this thing not working. It had to work. He had to play it. He had to.

He only realised how tense he had become when the screen suddenly formed into a picture and his tension let go.

'Yes!' he shouted, and reached into the box to pull out the controller. He untangled the wire and plugged it into the port on the front of the console. Martha and Dirk were going to freak out when they saw this.

The game started and it was the same old game he remembered. He was still good at it too. He completed the first level easily, getting to the top with a triple rainbow attack and a whole bunch of gems. The chest burst open and he collected all the fruit that came out of it. It was the normal ending to the level, nothing unusual about it.

He looked at the controller in his hands. It was a basic rectangle, like an old NES controller. A D-pad on the left, start and select buttons in the middle, and two buttons on the right. He looked at the top. No shoulder buttons. It was a very basic thing but it worked well enough.

He switched off the console and took the cartridge out. He put it back in its box and rummaged around to see what other games had come with it. He took them all out and had them in a pile on his lap. There were six in total. He went through them one by one. It was all fairly standard fare for the most part. He recognised most of them. The NewZealand Story, Contra, Double Dragon, Pac-Man, but it was the sixth and last game that gave him pause. The packaging on the game was completely black apart from the title that was printed in bold white letters on the front: SHELLEY TOWN RPG.

Billy frowned at the game and turned it over. There was nothing on the back. The box looked like it had never been opened. It still had the tape sealing it shut. He opened the box and pulled out the inner packaging. The original instruction manual was still in there and the cartridge was housed in its cardboard compartment. The cartridge too was completely black apart from those white words, SHELLEY TOWN RPG.

He put the cartridge in the console, with that satisfying CLUNK, and switched it on. The static on the television turned to black and flickered. The game title rolled up the screen and stopped in the middle. **SHELLEY TOWN RPG**. It went away and some new words appeared. **ENTER CHARACTER NAME**.

Billy pressed start and the words went away and were replaced by a QWERTY keyboard with a flashing underscore icon above it. _

Billy typed in his name by navigating the keyboard using the D-pad on his controller. The flashing _ moved along with each letter he selected. He wrote BRAIN_ and pressed start. He always used BRAIN when he had to name a character in a game, or enter his name on a scoreboard. Billy Rain. Brain for short.

The QWERTY keyboard went away. The screen went black and Billy fidgeted. He thought about pressing pause and getting more comfortable on the coach seats behind him but he found himself mentally stuck to the screen and stayed crossed-legged on the floor.

From the blackness a room faded into focus. At its centre was a sprite (that's what they called characters in games way back when). Billy looked at it, his head cocked slightly. The character didn't look so different to how he looked now. Short brown hair, a pale red t-shirt, blue jeans, a backpack. The sprite that was called BRAIN was sat on a rug in front of a television. The room it was in looked a lot like the inside of Billy's treehouse.

Billy stared at the screen for a moment. He looked up, absurdly, as if their might be a camera looking down on him. Nope. Just the inside of the wood panelled roof. He looked at the screen. He pressed right on the D-pad. The sprite walked in a swift three frame repeating animation. BRAIN walked to the entrance of the treehouse and the screen faded to black and then came back again. Now BRAIN was standing in the garden at the bottom of the tree. Billy made the character walk along the picket fence to the driveway and out to the pavement. Billy shook his head in disbelief. The game's graphics were basic but there was no mistaking it. This was Shelley Town, and that was Billy's treehouse, and Billy's picket fence.

'Billy? Billy, what are you doing out there?' came his mother's voice.

Billy froze and remembered his backpack with the milk going warm and the tobacco going unsmoked. He switched off the console, grabbed his backpack, and climbed out of the treehouse and down the ladder, his mind full of questions.

CHAPTER 3

Billy took his shoes off in the porch before entering the house. He went into the hallway where an upright piano stood, ready to play and with the sheet music open to Lady Madonna, a song his mother had been learning for over a year. She could play it perfectly but something in her prevented her from moving on to the next song. It was just Lady Madonna over and over again. Billy walked past it and went into the lounge.

As far as interior decoration went Billy's home was pretty nice. Not special really, but clean and airy. It could have been the centrefold of an upper middle class Good Homes type magazine. Everything was carefully selected and in order. The glass tops of the nest of tables in the living room were smear free. The sofa, upon which his mum was sitting upright, never in a state of easy relaxation, was like new. The dining sets in the display cabinet against the wall were pristine and never used. The curtains went from floor to ceiling, the ruffles were evenly spread. The carpet was cream in colour and perfectly spotless.

Billy took the tobacco out of his bag and put it on the coffee table next to a Laura Ashley deluxe hardback. Billy's mum didn't look him in the eye. She looked at the coffee table, although not really focused on it, and said, 'What took you so long?'

'I'm sorry, I picked up a new game and guess I forgot.'

She looked up at him. 'What new game?'

Billy paused for a moment, slightly surprised by her directness, and almost told her about the games console, and the house where he had found it, but he stopped himself. 'Rainbow Island.'

She looked down again. 'Please could you put the milk in the fridge?'

Billy nodded. 'Can I get you anything?'

'I'm ok. Thank you.'

'Ok. Shout if you need anything,' said Billy, and he turned and left the room.

'I will. Thank you, Billy.'

Eunice Rain had blonde hair that fell in curls around her shoulders. She was in her mid-forties but she could have been thirty five.

She leaned forward and picked up the tobacco and filters. She rolled a cigarette and put it between her lips. She walked over to the window at the front of the house and took the lighter out of her dressing gown pocket. She cracked the window open and put the flame to the end of the roll-up and drew in a deep breath. She exhaled and the smoke drifted out of the window.

Billy, halfway up the ladder to his treehouse, heard the

window open and turned to see his mum light the cigarette. He smiled at her. She smiled and waved back with her fingertips. Billy looked up at the treehouse. The game was like a magnet. Every part of him wanted to get back to it. To play it. To explore its virtual world.

'Billy,' came a young female voice from beyond the garden fence.

'Martha, you're not going to believe what I found. Where's Dirk?' shouted Billy, climbing back down the ladder.

'He'll be here in a minute.'

Martha was Billy's best friend. Well, she and Dirk were both his best friends really but between him and Martha they both agreed that they, Billy and Martha, were the strongest link in the trio. It was close though, they both loved Dirk. Unique and odd as he was.

She had Hopkirk with her, that ever faithful puppy. Hopkirk was a Saint Bernard. A quiet animal with big paws. He had a barrel around his neck that traditionally would have been full of whisky but his was an elaborate housing for the dog's information, should he get lost. His address was written in full; Plot A8, Three Oaks Touring Park, Shelley Town. There was also the phone number of Martha's dad and a small handwritten note that read; *Good afternoon, or morning, or evening, I hope you are having a fine day. I am not. My name is Hopkirk and I am a Saint Bernard. I appear to be lost. Would you be so kind and take me home, if it's not too much trouble? If it is too much trouble, shame on you. Look at me, how could you leave me out here all alone? I'll tell you what, take me in and give me a bowl of water, maybe a bite to eat, and call my home on the number below. Someone will come and get me. If I sit on your furniture I apologise in advance as, for all of my master's efforts, I have proven to be a poor student when it comes to my house training.*

Billy came back down the ladder and stepped off and struck a weird pose with his hands on his hips and his groin jutted forward. He pulled a face. She mimicked him, pulling the same face and the same pose.

'Blarble Garble!' growled Billy.

'Snoogle Fargle!' grunted Martha, and burst out laughing.

Billy snorted and almost got snot on himself.

'That was gross,' said Martha, walking across the garden to Billy. 'And between you and me, that is still fucking funny.'

'It's stupid. We need a new greeting,' said Billy.

'We could shake hands like business men,' said Martha.

Or we could kiss, thought Billy.

Martha swore. A Lot. She always had. Billy and Dirk were cagier about the whole thing. The odd curse had started slipping out of Billy's mouth recently but generally he avoided it. Martha 'fucked', 'shit', and 'cunted' all over the place. You ever seen a fourteen year-old girl tell a shop assistant to, 'Stop being such a retarded cunt and sell me the fucking wine.'? It's a hell of a thing.

Hopkirk sat on the floor next to Martha's feet, his tail thumping against the grass, his brown eyes staring up at Billy. Billy reached down and scratched him behind the ears. Hopkirk wagged his tail harder. 'Hello Hoppy,' said Billy.

'Hopkirk,' said Martha.

'Hopkirk's a boring name isn't it, Hoppy,' said Billy, petting the dog with more effort.

Hopkirk's tongue fell out and he started panting and wagging his tail harder. 'See, he likes Hoppy better,' said Billy.

'Sheeble Shmarble!' came a third, higher voice from beyond the garden fence.

'Dirk! You'll never guess what I found,' said Billy, and he stopped petting the dog.

Dirk ignored him. He was striking the weird pose and pulling the same face, 'Sheeble Shmarble!'

Martha and Billy looked at each other and then faced Dirk and put their hands on their hips, thrusted their groins forward, pulled their faces, and shouted (each with their own phrase),

'Blarble Garble!' and 'Snoogle Fargle!'

'What are you so excited about then you weird fucktard?' said Martha, smiling with her tongue in her cheek. Not metaphorically, tongue actually poking cheek.

'Not too sure about that particular nickname Marth, but-'

'What have I said about calling me "Marth"?' said Martha, starting her way up the ladder to the treehouse.

'That it sounds like barf,' said Dirk, going up after her.

'We'll just call you vomit,' said Billy, going up last.

They always went up in this order when the three of them were together. It was for Dirk's sake. He was the same age as Martha and Billy but about a third shorter and much scrawnier too. He had been diagnosed at the age of three with brittle bone disease. Over the years it had become second nature for Billy and Martha to put Dirk between them, for his own safety. The kid was a risk to himself. What would bruise any other person would break Dirk. The day they realised Dirk couldn't be trusted with his own wellbeing was the time he spent his saved up pocket money on a skateboard. He showed up at Billys', proud of his new deck, and Martha promptly snapped it in half and threw it in the bin. If Dirk decided to lose his footing and fall off the ladder Billy would be below him to soften the fall.

The drawer on the rope lift was lowered down and settled on the grass where Hopkirk was waiting. He sniffed at it and then nudged between the ropes and settled in for his trip upwards.

'He's getting a bit too big for this isn't he?' said Martha, looking down at Hopkirk as Billy hoisted him up.

'Yeah, we'll need a bigger lift soon,' said Billy.

The drawer got to the top and Billy lifted Hopkirk into the treehouse. Hopkirk plodded past the trio and went through the small tunnel to Den the Third where he could lie on the bed and doze until it was time to leave.

'What is that?' said Martha, taking her usual seat on the end of the three seater coach bench.

Dirk sat next to her and Billy knelt down in front of the games console.

'I got it today. I'm not really sure what it is. Any idea, Dirk?' said Billy.

Dirk, a veritable encyclopaedia when it came to gaming

history, leaned forward with his usual confidence. Any question fired at Dirk about anything to do with computers would be answered with full knowledge of the history, the system capabilities, the people behind its creation, what games were released with it, the advertising campaign around its launch, the cost price, unit sales, demise, cultural significance; there were few blind spots in his knowledge. 'It's a-' he frowned. He moved from his seat and knelt down next to Billy. He picked up the console and turned it around. 'Where did you get this?'

Billy shuffled uncomfortably and shrugged, 'I found it.'

Intrigued by Billy's vagueness Martha leaned forward and looked over Dirk's shoulder. 'A Nintendo?' she offered.

'No,' said Dirk, 'it's not a Nintendo.' He didn't want to say that he didn't know what it was. Not yet. He checked the ports that the controllers plugged into to see if it was one used on any other console. It wasn't. He pushed the flaps down where the cartridge slotted in and examined it.

'Did it come with any games?' asked Dirk.

'A few,' said Billy, grabbing The NewZealand Story from the box and handing it to Dirk.

Dirk examined the cartridge and then pushed it into the slot. 'Does it work?'

'Yeah, it all works, do you know what it is?'

Dirk put the console down and frowned. 'I mean, it could be a prototype for something but I don't know what. I've never seen anything like it before.'

Billy raised his eyebrows in disbelief, but a part of him,

deep down in his gut, wasn't surprised at all.

'You don't know what it is?' said Martha.

'I have no idea,' said Dirk.

That was a first.

'Turn it on,' said Martha.

Billy turned the television on and switched on the console. The game started with a scene of small yellow birds huddled together in front of a zoo entrance. A big blue sea lion came on screen from the left and the birds fled off screen to the right. The sea lion chased them and came back on screen with the birds trapped in a sack slung over his shoulder. He ran off screen to the left. One of the birds jumped out of the sack and watched as his friends were hauled away. The screen went black and was replaced with the words: **LEVEL 1_1, READY?**

Dirk pressed start on the remote and played the platformer for a few minutes. The small yellow bird was armed with a crossbow and fired arrows at snails which turned into fruit when they died. He got to the end of the level and rescued one of the captured birds from a cage.

'It's the classic game. Nothing odd about it. There was no copyright information, or developers name at the beginning, which is very odd, but the game plays the same. Where did you find this?' said Dirk.

Billy switched off the machine. 'The old Matterson house,' he said, and then looked at them both to see their reactions. Slack faced stares is what he got.

'You went in the Matterson house?' said Martha.

'No, of course not. I'm not crazy. I just went in the garden.

There was a garden sale and a sign that said "free to a good home" so I went over the fence and grabbed it.'

'Show me,' said Martha, standing up

Billy thought about saying no and showing them the other game instead. The one in the black box with the white words that read, SHELLEY TOWN RPG. But maybe he wanted to keep that one to himself. Just for now. Just until he had played it a bit more and gotten to understand it better. Then he would show them.

CHAPTER 4

'It was right here. There were tables set up and lamps and cameras and all sorts of things for sale,' said Billy.

The three of them were standing on the pavement looking into the garden of the big vacant Matterson house. Hopkirk hung back and waited by the fence of the neighbour's garden.

'You don't believe me do you?' said Billy.

'I don't think you're lying but there's nothing here,' said Martha.

'Then it must have been put away.'

'By who?'

'Whoever lives here,' said Billy.

'Nobody lives here,' said Martha.

'I don't like this. Can we just go back to The Den?' said Dirk, already walking away from the house.

'We could knock on the door?' suggested Martha.

'We're going back to The Den,' said Billy, going after Dirk.

'Pussies,' said Martha.

'You can do what you want. You know where we'll be,' said Billy, not looking back.

Martha watched them walk away for a moment and then

looked back at the house. The door was slightly ajar. She made a decision. She was good at making decisions. The best decisions, she thought, were the ones you don't really make. The best decisions were things you just did.

She ran to the end of the fence and pushed the gate open. She ran up the drive, past the old car, and banged three times on the front door.

'Martha, what are you doing?' shouted Billy.

Martha stood there. Staring at the door. Not swallowing. Wanting to run down the drive and far away from the house but some kind of mad pride kept her there. Billy and Dirk ducked down by the neighbour's fence with Hopkirk. A bush beyond the fence hid them from view of the Matterson house. The windows of that house looked down on them like the eyes of a tired old man, exhausted by his own hatred.

There was a breeze and the door swung inwards an inch. Martha took a step back. She stared into the house. The wallpaper was old and decayed. Where a pattern had once been there was mould. The carpet around the inside of the door was torn like rats had been clawing at it. Scrabbling to get out.

Three enormous bangs shattered the silence and every nerve in Martha's body jangled. She fell backwards and her head missed the car in the drive by a whisker. She hit the ground hard and the air blew out of her lungs. She gasped for breath and grabbed onto the smashed wing mirror and pulled herself up, cutting a jagged line across her fingers. She got to her feet and ran down the drive. The door slammed shut behind her.

'Martha!' shouted Billy, running from the safety of the neighbour's fence.

He met her as she reached the gate and grabbed her by the hand. There was another loud bang that reverberated around the green.

'Hurry up!' shouted Dirk.

Hopkirk was on all fours standing as close as he could without breaching the divide between the houses. There was another bang and Hopkirk barked involuntarily.

Billy and Martha collapsed next to Dirk. Hopkirk paced around Martha, he tried to climb onto her and lick her face. Martha let go of Billy's hand and pushed the dog away. She clasped her bleeding hand.

'I've cut myself,' said Martha.

Billy took his t-shirt off and tore off one of the sleeves. There was another bang and their attention was startled towards the sound.

An old yellow Triumph Stag moved slowly along the road. The engine was making a grinding sound. The car stopped. The driver, a middle-aged man with wire framed glasses and balding grey hair, banged on the steering wheel. He turned off the ignition, waited for a moment, and then turned the key. The three litre V8 started with a rumble. He put his foot down on the accelerator and it backfired causing black smoke to fart out of the exhaust.

Reality dawned on Billy, Martha, and Dirk, and they relaxed in their bones.

Billy laughed. 'It was just a car.'

Dirk sat down and let out a sigh. Martha laughed. 'Scared ya,' she said.

'You were scared shitless,' said Billy.

Martha turned her hand over and looked at the gash across her fingers. Blood was pulsing freely from the wound. Billy took the torn sleeve and wrapped it tight around the cut.

'Close your fist around it to stop it from bleeding too much. We can fix it better at mine,' said Billy.

He stood up and pulled Martha to her feet by her good hand.

CHAPTER 5

Billy reached up and pulled the first aid kit out of the top cupboard in the kitchen. Martha was sitting at the table looking at her wound with more curiosity than anything else. It didn't hurt too much but an aching throb had settled in. The blood had stopped gushing as the wound had congealed together.

Billy sat next to her and opened the green box with the white cross on it. It smelled of antiseptic cream. Inside were gauzes and plasters and a half empty box of paracetamols. Dirk leaned against the counter by the sink. That was close enough for him. Blood was not something he wanted to get too close to. Hopkirk was sprawled on the floor, snoozing by Martha's feet.

'That's really bad,' said Billy.

'It's just a flesh wound,' said Martha.

'All wounds are flesh wounds,' said Dirk.

Martha considered the statement for a moment and found she essentially agreed.

'Even a bullet in the head, if you think about it,' continued Dirk.

'It's unlike you three to be in the house,' said Billy's mum, entering the kitchen and putting the kettle on to boil. 'Tea anyone?' she said, opening the pot she kept the tea bags in and dropping one in a cup.

'Martha's cut her hand,' said Billy.

Eunice turned and stared at Martha. 'Show me,' she said.

Martha held up her hand. Her palm was dark red with dry blood.

'Jesus Christ, how did that happen?'

'I cut it on some broken glass,' said Martha.

Eunice looked at the cut more closely. She grimaced. 'Eesh. Do your parents know?'

'No.'

'I'm calling your father.'

Martha was about to protest but figured it was probably for the best. Eunice picked up the kitchen phone and opened the address book that she kept by it and flicked through to Perry. She found the number and dialled. The line rang a few times and someone answered.

'Hi Peter, its Eunice. I'm fine, thank you. Martha's cut her hand on some glass and- no she's ok, it's stopped bleeding, could you- ok that's great, see you soon. Bye Peter.' Eunice put the phone down. 'He's on his way.'

They stood, the three of them and the dog, in the driveway waiting for Martha's dad to arrive. The treehouse loomed in the tree behind them. The game called to Billy. A part of him was glad Martha was going. He didn't want to acknowledge it but it was there. He wanted Dirk to go to. He wanted to play the game.

'He's here,' said Martha, spotting her dad's Ford Transit minibus pull into the square.

'Why does he drive a minibus?' said Dirk.

Martha shrugged, 'He just likes minibuses.'

The light blue bus stopped in front of the drive and Martha's dad jumped out. He had long hair and a long beard, but only on his chin. The sides of his face were usually clean shaven but he had a few days' growth there today. He had a moustache that was long at the ends. He wore an old navy-blue t-shirt, brown boots, and dark blue jeans. When he smiled he smiled with his whole face. It was refreshing to see in an adult.

'Hey guys,' he said to Billy and Dirk.

'Hi Mr Perry,' said Dirk.

'Hi Pete,' said Billy.

'Let's have a look then, Marth,' said Pete, taking Martha's hand in his own.

Martha rolled her eyes at Billy and Billy mouthed the word, 'Marth' and suppressed a laugh.

'It's going to need stitches,' he said, letting go of her hand, 'Come on, little trip to the hospital and you'll be right as rain.'

'Bye Marth,' said Billy.

'Bye, shitface,' said Martha.

'Will she be okay to come out tomorrow?' said Dirk.

'She'll be alright, for sure,' said Pete, showing no reaction to Martha's use of the word "shitface".

'Until tomorrow, losers,' she said, getting into the passenger side of the bus.

Hopkirk jumped in ahead of her. Her dad got in the front and started the engine.

'What now?' said Dirk, as the minibus turned a corner and disappeared out of view.

'Goldeneye?' said Billy.

'Sure,' said Dirk.

Billy put the Goldeneye cartridge into the Nintendo 64 and switched it on. He picked up his controller and sat on the coach seat next to Dirk. Dirk had the grey N64 controller. Billy always used the yellow one, the one with the rumble pack. Every time he fired it shook in his hands.

'Music?' said Dirk.

Billy leaned over and pressed play on the CD player on the floor next to him. It was a compilation album called Big Shiny Tunes. Songs from the mid-90s. The first song was *Breathe* by The Prodigy. Billy skipped it, it wasn't that he disliked the Prodigy, they had just heard the song too many times. The next song started playing. It was *Song 2* by Blur.

Billy set the game to the Temple level, in two player, with proximity mines as the weapon of choice. He chose his character; Boris. Dirk chose Natalia. He always did, and Billy always chose Boris. That's just the way it was. Billy liked shouting, 'I am invincible!' whenever he killed another player, just like in the film. Dirk was just a pervert.

There was a trick you could do in Goldeneye where you

planted a mine on an ammo box and then collected it. The mine would disappear but still be there. It was a glitch. Goldeneye was great for glitches. That's the real reason people loved the game. It was so hilariously screwy. You would get baddies with four faces and, if you pressed the right button at the right time, you could make a sniper rifle look like a paint brush and whack people to death with it. It's the small things.

'Not proximity mines,' said Dirk.

'I am-'

'Don't say it.'

'Invincible!' said Billy, laughing maniacally.

Dirk exploded. Or Natalia did. In the game. His screen went black and Dirk pressed start to get back in the game. His eyes fell on that strange old console Billy had found.

'I'll ask my parents if they know anything about prototype consoles when I get home today.'

'Okay,' said Billy.

Dirk's parents had been game developers in the early 90s and had, between them, a greater knowledge than Dirk had on the subject. Nowadays Dirk's dad was the head researcher at a local development company. They build control systems for mobility scooters. But once he helped build one of the defining computer games of the early 90s in the UK. Billy's dad and Martha's parents had a hand in it too. That is how they all knew each other. The kids of locally, yet obscurely, famous parents. No one really cares who's behind their favourite game. They only really care about their high scores, and how much fun it was to play. But they knew. Billy, Dirk, and Martha knew. There had been a time when their parents were kinda pretty famous. But most people forget. But it was their heritage, and they were proud of it.

They played Goldeneye for a few hours. After playing multiplayer for a few rounds they took turns trying to complete levels in the main game, trying to get quick times. If you beat each level faster than a predetermined time you could unlock cheats. They got stuck on the train level for almost an hour trying to get the Silver PP7 cheat. They always got beat at the end where you have to fire a particularly well aimed shot at General Ourumov to rescue Natalia and then break through a panel in the floor with a laser watch. It was Billy who finally got it. This made Billy happy beyond reason. It was normally Dirk who completed the hard ones. It was Dirk who figured out you could complete the Archives level in record time by not using any weapons. It was the only way to not attract enemies with the sound of gunfire. It was brilliant the first time he did it. Billy could do it too after he saw Dirk do it. But it was always Dirk who figured it out. He probably read how to do it in Nintendo Power magazine, Billy thought.

They played around on a few levels with the new cheat enabled until they got bored of it and before they knew it, it was dark outside.

'I better go,' said Dirk, looking out of the treehouse at the darkening sky.

Billy remembered in that moment the game that came with

the console he found and thought about showing it to Dirk. He had completely forgotten about the whole thing while they'd been playing. No, not yet. He would show him but only after he had played the game for a bit by himself. If Dirk played it he would find all the secrets before Billy had a chance to prove that he would have been able to do it himself.

He saw Dirk out and watched him walk the short journey home. Dirk lived on the opposite side of the square to the Matterson house. Billy looked over at that creepy old building. He realised that Dirk's house and the Matterson place were directly facing each other. It was as if they were locked in an eternal staring competition. The light and the dark battling a never ending war of good and evil.

Billy hadn't had an evening meal yet. He figured he probably wouldn't. He had a half-eaten bag of Tangy Cheese Doritos in the snack chest in Den the Third if he got hungry and a bottle of Sunny Delight to quench his thirst. He didn't care if it turned you orange and had the nutritional value of toilet cleaner, it tasted great.

Anyway, who cared about food? Billy's only thoughts were of the game. He took the cartridge out of the black box, with the words SHELLEY TOWN RPG on the front in bold white letters, and held it in his hands. The plastic was cold. Something about it made him shiver. He put the game into the slot in the console and turned it on.

He sat cross-legged on the rug in front of the television and pressed start. Instead of asking Billy to input his name, like it did the last time, the game started right where he left off.

CHAPTER 6

Detective Chief Inspector Ryman parked his dark blue Ford Mondeo in the carpark of the Exhibition Centre. It wasn't a standard white police car with reflective squares and Her Majesty's royal stamp on it. No flashing light on the roof. None of that in-your-face crap. It was just a dark blue car. Of course, if he needed to pull someone over, or make his presence known, he could flick a switch and lights hidden in the radiator grill, and in the tinted rear window, would flash blue. Flick another switch and the siren would wail and bleat just like any other cop car.

He got out and brushed crumbs off his trousers. He noticed a small coffee stain on his shirt just above the belt and tried to rub it off with his thumb. It wouldn't budge.

'Fuck's sake,' he said.

He went around to the back of the car and opened the boot. He took out a hi-vis jacket, with the word POLICE printed on the back in a reflective blue rectangle, and put it on and zipped it up.

'Problem solved,' he said, not that anyone was around to hear him.

The Exhibition Centre was an old converted church. It

stood at the highest point in town, overlooking the square.

Ryman looked up at it. There was a canvas sign hung over the entrance with the words RETRO GAMING CONVENTION printed on it in 8-bit pixel lettering. The left side of the main double door opened and the organiser of the event came out. His name was Chris and he dressed like a man who skateboarded to work.

'Working late?' said Ryman. His voice was loud enough that he didn't need to shout for his voice to be heard across the carpark.

'Will be until the weekend. A lot to get ready,' said Chris, 'You coming in, or you just gonna stand there? What are you doing here anyway?'

'Need to talk to you about how busy you're going to get,' said Ryman, 'Just give me a second, let me grab the laptop out of my car and I'll be right over.'

The hall of the church was big. A lot of work had been done to convert the old building into a functioning convention centre, but the architecture itself hadn't changed much. The big circular stained glass window still dominated the far end of the hall above what was now the main stage, and the stained glass windows with arched tops still ran along the sides of the building, sending in a kaleidoscope of coloured light during the day. The building itself was big. It must have been the size of at least one football pitch, maybe more. The old pews that used to fill up the room in rows were gone. The whole lot had been sold to an antique furniture dealer for a low price. It was that or burn them, and that just didn't feel right.

Old arcade machines were huddled together in the far left corner, waiting to be organised into position. A canvas screen lay rolled up on the stage waiting to be put up over the stained glass window. Speaker monitors were already on the front of the stage and the light rigging scaffold was hung from the ceiling rafters.

A booth for the mixing desk that controlled the lights and sound was at the main entrance end of the hall. A woman with blue hair was in there moving sliders up and down fading various lights on and off, making sure it all worked. She had the stage direction sheet on her desk and was programing the basic needs for the show. It wasn't a complicated job. Probably the easiest one she had done in her career. It was just spotlighting and mics for guest speakers, and then the main tournament. She usually did the lightning for pantomimes and the occasional band, so this was rookie work.

Around the rest of the room were a few stalls for food venders and a real ale bar at the back in the far corner. There were vacant stalls set up in blocks of four so visitors could walk around each one before moving on to the next. Some stalls would be selling retro t-shirts and gaming posters. One would be selling old gaming systems and games. There was going to be a memorabilia stall. But it wasn't all retail and food. There was also going to be tech demonstrations and some developers giving early previews of upcoming games. There was a company working on some new VR tech that was looking pretty exciting. But all that was yet to fill the hall. They would be arriving later in the week to set up. That was a few days away.

Ryman and Chris walked through the hall and pulled up a couple of chairs around a stall that would, when the weekend came, be host to a nostalgia booth. Old consoles would be set up for people to play.

DCI Ryman opened his laptop and waited for it to boot up.

He looked up at the stage. He remembered when there was a pulpit up there. His own son had been christened there not so long ago.

'Some part of me thinks this whole endeavour must be blasphemous on some level,' said Ryman, looking up at the stained glass window that had in it the image of Christ on a cross. 'People are coming here to worship computer games instead of God.'

'I didn't take you for a religious man,' said Chris.

'I'm not really. Who in England is these days?'

'You couldn't get away with it in America,' said Chris, yawning.

'Tired?' said Ryman, entering his password and pressing the return key.

Chris shrugged, 'Sleep is for beauty queens and students.' Chris had dark bags under his eyes and his hair was matted and out of place.

'You look like you haven't slept in months.'

'This thing took a lot more organising than I think any of us were expecting.'

'It will all be over next week. I guess you can sleep then.'

'I don't know, if it's a success we'll be taking the whole event to other towns. Keep the whole circus rolling. We'll be filling up the Birmingham NEC if it gets big enough. There's been comic book conventions that size for years. There are enough gaming geeks out there to do the same, in my opinion.'

'Maybe you're right. Not really my field of expertise,' said Ryman. The laptop had finally loaded and Ryman opened up some emails he had saved to his desktop. 'What do you know about this documentary that's showing on the BBC tonight?'

'What documentary?' said Chris.

'I had a call from some journalist about it. Apparently the media got an early screening. Hold on, I asked her to email me some information.'

He brought up the first email and Chris leaned in to read it. 'The Untold Story of Jack Matterson. The real genius behind Doctor Hammer.'

Chris raised his eyebrows. 'Who's Jack Matterson?'

'Well, I looked into that. He was a resident in the square. I went by there today. Have you ever noticed the old house on the east side, the first house you come to? Some old shithole, falling apart at the seams?'

Chris shrugged, 'I'm not sure,' he said.

But he did, really. Some part of him did anyway. Everyone had some reason to go down to the square at some point in the week. In a lifetime he should have passed it thousands of times. The same was true for Ryman, and every other person in town, but for some reason the eyes never glance up when you walk past that particular address. You feel it, but you don't look. And then you forget all about it.

'Yeah, I must have been down that road at least once a day for as long as I can remember. I guess I just never took much notice. This Jack Matterson made computer games back in the late eighties and early nineties.'

That piece of information woke Chris up. If he was tired before, now he was fully awake. His ears pricked up and his eyes widened.

'What did he make?'

Ryman shrugged, 'I'm no expert in computers but I think it's safe to guess it was Doctor Hammer if the title of the documentary tells us anything.'

'Right. But I don't think so. I would have heard about him. He would be coming here this weekend. One of the guys who worked on the game is helping me organise the event.'

'Who?' said Ryman.

'Walter Chaplin.'

'Right, no surprise there. What about our other local gaming celebrities?'

'William is out of town. He's agreed to speak though if he can get down in time. Pete and Amelia will be here too, hopefully one of them can talk a bit if William can't get here. They'll all be doing a Q and A at the end of the night. Even their kids all have some part to play. Young Billy is hosting the tournament.'

'No kidding. But no mention of this Jack Matterson?' said Ryman.

'First time I've heard of him.'

'Alright, well, what I'm learning about him isn't good. Where he lived is just a derelict dump. Once you notice it it makes the whole square look like a slum. It's like someone's taken a great shit in the corner of a neat lawn and the shit has been allowed to grow mouldy with age and still people are picnicking next to it, regardless of the smell. I swear I'd never noticed the place but now it's all I see. I see it when I close my fucking eyes for fuck's sake. It's like a bad dream.'

Chris didn't know what to say to this so he just nodded and let Ryman continue.

'I've looked into the guy and found a bit but not much. It turns out he lived here back in-'

'Why are you telling me this?'

'What?'

'Why have you come here to tell me this?'

'Because, Chris, when the news gets out about what happened, or is going to be claimed to have happened, this place is going to be swamped. I'll be surprised if we don't get national news down here. You're having a Q and A right? You're going to have every fanboy and nerd show up from all over to find out more about what went on. You're going to need security. I guess that's why I'm really here, to make sure you're ready for this. I don't have much of a police force to spare for this shit so you've got to help me out a bit.'

'This is nonsense. We haven't even sold out yet.'

'Wait. Wait until after the documentary and then tell me how quickly your tickets sell. We can talk about what you're doing about extra security then, okay?'

'Okay, Ryman. Whatever you say.'

Ryman moved the mouse cursor and scrolled down the email. 'So, it says here, "documentary airing on BBC Two at 10pm on-" hold on, let me scroll down some more. The blurb is here somewhere. Here it is. "The documentary looks at the success of one of the biggest games of the 90s but are things really all that they seem? Who is Jack Matterson and what happened to him? We interview the developers behind the game and dig up some shocking truths. Did deceit and plagiarism lead to the disappearance of a previously unknown fifth member of the "Beatles of the gaming world"? Did Walter Chaplin, William Rain, and Pete and Amelia Perry do something unthinkable? This documentary changes everything you thought you knew about WWAP and their most famous game, Doctor Hammer.".'

Ryman finished reading and looked up at Chris. 'What a load of shit! A fifth member? You know all four of them, right? You think any of them could hide something like that? Do you think we wouldn't know? Don't you think you would know?'

Ryman shrugged, 'Nothing would surprise me.'

'Have you seen the documentary?'

'No, like I said, a journalist phoned me asking about it. I've dug around and not found much, apart from the fact that he existed and lived in the square. I guess I'll know more when I see the documentary.' Ryman looked at his watch, 'Which is in about thirty minutes.'

Ryman got up and closed the lid on his laptop. I'm going to go home and watch it.

'Ok, I'll watch it too.'

'Why are they called WWAP?' asked Ryman, stopping momentarily.

'Walter, William, Amelia, and Peter,' said Chris. 'WWAP.'

Ryman left the church and Chis sat and thought for a while. He looked up at the stage and at the projection screen rolled up on it.

'Hey Becky.'

Becky looked over from her light and sound pit. 'Yeh?'

'Give me a hand getting that screen up.'

CHAPTER 7

Billy pressed right on the D-pad and the character in the game, BRAIN, walked back into the garden that looked a lot like Billy's own garden. The treehouse was there, rendered in two dimensional pixels.

BRAIN walked up to the ladder and climbed up in a basic two frame animation. When he got to the top the screen faded to black and a new screen loaded showing BRAIN from above inside the treehouse. The television was there on the right and so were the coach seats on the left. Billy stared at the screen, his mouth hanging open.

Dirk showed Billy once how to access the sprite pallets in a game's coding and change the pixels to alter the appearance of the characters and any element in the game. You had to use an emulator on a PC but it was easy if you knew how. People changed games in that way and released them as mods. He wondered for a moment if Dirk, or someone, had altered a game that already existed to look like the local town. It wouldn't be impossible. Maybe this was a hacked ROM of Earthbound or something similar. It didn't feel like it was though. It was too well done. And besides, playing hacked games never made your spine want to curl up and die.

BRAIN walked over to the television and Billy pressed A on the controller to see if he could make it do something. Nothing happened. He made BRAIN walk to the entrance of Den the Third and the screen faded to black then faded back again. BRAIN was now standing in Den the Third. Billy tried pressing on the snack chest in there. In any other game the chest would have opened and a sword would have come out for the player to use. Or at least some health. A jewel even. But nothing happened.

BRAIN explored Den Two and found nothing there either. He left the tree house and went back into the garden. BRAIN walked up to the front door of his house but it wouldn't open. He walked around the garden randomly pressing A and B on bushes and plants but the character seemed to have no abilities or effect on anything at all.

Billy was getting bored of the game. It seemed pointless. He couldn't put it down though. It was baffling enough to keep his interest for hours, regardless of its apparent absence of gameplay.

BRAIN walked up to the closed garage doors and Billy pressed A. The garage doors opened. Billy raised his eyebrows in surprise. The game finally did something. Hurrah.

Again the screen faded in and out and BRAIN was standing in an almost empty garage. In the middle of the garage was a shovel. BRAIN walked up to it and Billy pressed A on the controller. The shovel disappeared from the floor and appeared in BRAIN's right hand.

Billy pressed B and BRAIN started digging. It made a

scraping sound but dug no hole. Intrigued at finally having something to do BRAIN went back into the garden and tried digging out there. BRAIN dug with a basic two part animation and pixelated dirt particles came up from the ground but nothing happened. You probably have to dig in the right place, Billy thought.

It started to get cold in the treehouse and Billy shivered. He sent BRAIN out into the street and walked onto the green across the road. He tried digging in a few places with no luck. He thought he'd explore the town and see if the game offered up any clues as to its objective.

BRAIN walked to the old Matterson house. He thought maybe some monsters would come out of the ground and he would have to kill them with the shovel and get some points but no luck. The house just stood there, dark and vacant, just like it did in real life.

BRAIN wandered all around the town not finding anything to dig, nothing to collect, and no one to fight. One thing was for sure, someone had spent a long time making a game that did nothing. Maybe it was some sort of university project. *Create An RPG Map Based On Your Home Town.* It was possible.

Billy shivered again. He put the controller down and reached behind the coach seats to pull out the old blanket that was kept there for the winter months.

He felt like someone was in the Den with him and he looked around. It was so dark. Darker than it should be. He looked outside. The square was light enough. It was late evening but the street lights were on. The sky was clear and the stars were out. But the inner walls of the treehouse were almost black with shadow. The entrances to Den Two and Den the Third were black squares. Dark voids. He stared into the entrance to Den the Third and the complete absence of light made him look away. He could feel the eyes of someone watching him from within the darkness. But he knew that was absurd. It was just the dark playing tricks on his mind. He lifted the blanket over his head and sat in front of the television. It was the only source of light in the room. It should have been enough light to illuminate the whole den but it did nothing but draw you in.

Billy picked up the controller and stared mesmerized at the screen. BRAIN walked aimlessly around the town.

He got to the old converted church that was now an exhibition centre. There was a dark blue car parked in the carpark and there was a banner up on the church that read, RETRO GAMING CONVENTION.

Billy raised his eyebrows. That was this weekend. His dad was supposed to be coming to town to talk about a game he had helped create back in 1992, a decade ago. Dirk's and Martha's parents were special guests there too. It was the ten year anniversary of Doctor Hammer and there was supposed to be some kind of challenger to the current high score and they've decided to turn the challenge into a tournament. Billy had been asked to introduce and commentate and he had said yes, why not? Dirk and Martha were going to be there too, of course. They would be treated like royalty there, it was going to be great. But how can it be in this game?

BRAIN tried to get in the church but it was locked. He walked around the side of the building where there was a small bungalow that used to be the vicar's house. Nowadays it was used as storage by the centre. Billy had been in there once with school and was volunteered to help set the seats up. All he could remember about it was all the chairs. There were hundreds of them, packed from floor to ceiling. 'Got to keep them somewhere,' the guy who worked there had said.

BRAIN walked to the back of the bungalow. On the floor was a flashing X. Billy smiled. Finally, something to do. He went to the X and dug. The same pixelated dirt particles came up from the ground but this time a small hole emerged, and then a bigger one, and then a bigger one still.

There was a CHA-CHING sound and something popped out and travelled to the top of the screen. It was the letter **J** in bold white type. It moved to the top left corner of the screen and a hangman game appeared with four underscores for letters to be filled in under it. But the game was set up all wrong, as far as Billy could remember from playing the game as a kid. The hanged man was already there in full. Dead. The **J** took the place of the first underscore so now it read **J** _ _ _

The right arm of the hangman disappeared. It was like the game was playing in reverse.

Billy looked at it with his lip curled up. It made no sense. He played on.

BRAIN walked back to the square. Something had changed about the Matterson house. The front door was banging open and shut. Billy jumped at the sound and gasped. The whole treehouse shook. The door in the game slammed again and the noise was so loud Billy had to cover his ears. He looked back up at the screen and BRAIN was moving by himself. Billy looked down at the controller. The left button on the D-pad was pressed down. Billy shuffled backwards and the blanket fell off him. He stared up at BRAIN. He was walking away from the Matterson house but his shadow stretched all the way back into the drive. The door was now firmly open and it was like the house was trying to drag BRAIN in by his shadow. The pixelated BRAIN walked across the green to the other side of the square. To Dirk's house.

A light was on in the window of Dirk's bedroom. BRAIN seemed to be staring up at it as he walked. Billy lurched forward and switched off the console. It was freezing to the touch and switching it off did nothing. He recoiled from the machine and then lunged forward and tried to turn it off again. He switched it on and off again and again but nothing happened. He pulled the console away from the television and the wires detached from the back of it. The game continued to play. BRAIN continued to walk. The shadow continued to stretch.

Billy picked up the console and threw it out of the treehouse and it crashed to the ground and came apart along the joint. The game continued to play. Billy grabbed the television and pulled it forward. It smashed to the floor and the screen shattered sending glass skidding across the rug.

Billy stood there panting. It was so dark he couldn't see an inch in front of his face. He couldn't see the fog that escaped from his mouth with every exhaled breath.

He couldn't see the man standing against the wall in front of him.

Billy's eyes fell onto the only thing that was visible in the treehouse. On the floor by his feet was the box for the game. The white letters that read, SHELLEY TOWN RPG, glowed in the blackness. He grabbed the game and his backpack and bolted for the entrance. He climbed down the ladder quicker than he ever had before. He knew it made no sense but he also knew one very urgent and true thing. He had to get to Dirk before, before what? Before the something in the game got to him first.

The figure in the shadows watched Billy get on his bike and ride out onto the pavement. The natural light in the treehouse started to return. The shadows ebbed away, and the man was gone.

CHAPTER 8

'Hey Walter, thanks for picking up so late.'

'It's ok, I wasn't sleeping,' said Walter Chaplin, holding his phone to his ear. 'Christ, Dirk is still up too. There's no such thing as late when it comes to the summer holidays. Know what I mean? Especially when there's a teenager in the house.'

'I'll know that soon enough I guess,' said the voice on the other end of the line.

'Right, you've got a couple haven't you?'

'Yep, eight and twelve.'

'Girl the oldest?'

'That's right. Claire, she's starting to show signs of rebellion already.'

'Yep, that'll start happening now. It's all downhill from twelve, man. They stop being kids all of a sudden. They start knowing things you don't.'

'They start speaking their own language.'

'You got it.'

Walter took a yogurt out of the fridge and turned it around. The best before date was yesterday. He opened the pedal bin with his foot and dropped it in. His wife would have killed him had she seen him do it. She figured best before dates were just a guide. He figured yogurt started to taste sour just as soon as your mind thought it was off, whether it was or not.

He picked up a half full bottle of Sauvignon Blanc and closed the fridge.

'What are you calling for, Chris?' said Walter, pouring a glass and keeping his mobile phone lodged between his shoulder and cheek.

Walter's phone was a Nokia 3310. He had become addicted to a game that came on the phone called Snake. It was so damn simple it drove him half crazy. Who knew making games could be so easy? He had spent years developing a very successful game a decade ago and it was a hard birth. It was difficult getting it to work right and harder to make it look right, and here was this basic game of a line moving around inside a square, getting bigger when it eats a single pixel, and everyone who had a Nokia was hooked. It can't have taken more than an afternoon to code.

'I'm at the Ex Centre,' said Chris. 'Ryman was just here talking about security.'

Walter left the bottle on the kitchen worktop and went into the lounge. Walter's wife, Penny, was curled up in the armchair reading a book by Elwood Flynn. A western. Walter thought she had a crush on the protagonist of those books. Some guy called Robin Castle. But that was fine. She could fancy as many imaginary people as she liked.

'Who's that?' she mouthed.

'Chris,' mouthed Walter.

'Hi Chris!' she said, and then got back to her book.

'Hey Penny,' said Chris.

'He says hi,' said Walter, sitting down on the three seater. His laptop was sat open on the middle seat. It had a PDF document open with the layout of the exhibition centre displayed. 'What about the security?'

'He's worried this thing's going to be bigger than we're prepared for.'

'Why?'

'Because of the documentary that is apparently due to air on BBC Two in about ten minutes.'

'What documentary?' said Walter, leaning forward to put his glass down on the coffee table.

'The Untold Story of Jack Matterson. The real genius behind Doctor Hammer.'

Walter missed the table by an inch and his wine glass fell to the floor and spilled onto the shag pile rug.

'Fuck,' he said, picking up the glass.

'I'll sort it,' said Penny, putting her book down and making a beeline for the cupboard under the kitchen sink.

'Why didn't I know about this?' said Walter.

'Fucked if I know. Apparently you're in it,' said Chris.

'How can I be in it? I've never heard of it?' said Walter, and then remembered an interview he had done earlier in the year.

He had been approached by a production company who were interested in making a documentary about WWAP and their historic rise to fame. They had been like rock stars back then. Ask any game freak and they could reel off a list of game development companies and what games they made, Rare, Ubisoft, EA, Namco, etc. but ask them to name the actual people who created the games and few people could. Of course there was Shigeru Miyamoto, the creator of Mario. Everyone knew that name but he was the exception to the rule.

WWAP arrived on the scene and things were just different. The game was so strange and compelling people needed to know what mind came up with it. Who were WWAP? The games company had the advantage of being the initials of the four people involved. A company like Namco could have had teams in their hundreds, who knew? But WWAP? Once people knew it stood for the initials of William, Walter, Amelia, and Peter, they were intrigued. It helped of course that they had rapport. They were interviewed on national television and were witty. They started being compared to the Beatles almost immediately and their fate was sealed.

The interviewer asked Walter all the usual questions, clarifying this, asking Walter to elaborate on stories that had come out about a recent rift between him and William, which Walter had said was just tabloid bullshit. They still spoke all the time on the phone. Not quite true but true enough. Sometimes Walter's phone would ring at 3am and William would be on the line, drunk and swearing and ranting.

The interview lasted almost an hour but the name Jack Matterson was never mentioned. Walter hadn't heard anything about the progress of the documentary afterwards. Normally there would be a courtesy call to let people involved know that an interview or documentary was airing but nothing had been said.

Penny picked up the wine glass and mopped up the spillage with some paper towels.

'Move out the way, Walt,' said Penny, spraying a chemical on the stain.

'Where's the TV remote?' said Walter, ignoring her.

'It's probably in front of the TV where it always is.'

Walter stood up and walked around the coffee table. He turned on the television and turned over to BBC Two.

Penny stopped cleaning and turned to look at him. 'What are you watching?'

'You still there, Chris?' said Walter.

'Still here Walt. I've got the big screen up on the stage to watch this thing.'

'I'll call you later,' said Walter, and hung up. He went through the list on his phone and called Pete. There was no answer. 'Where's Dirk?'

'Upstairs playing games,' said Penny.

'Good.'

The BBC announcer introduced the next programme. 'Coming next on BBC Two, The Untold Story of Jack Matterson. The real genius behind Doctor Hammer.'

Penny stared at the television. She opened her mouth to say something and stopped. What was there to say? Walter topped up his glass with what was left of the wine in the fridge and stood in the doorway between the kitchen and lounge. He downed the wine.

'Have we got any more?' said Walter.//
'There's whisky in the bar,' said Penny.

CHAPTER 9

Dirk was lying on his bed on his front, absently kicking the pillows. He had a Super Nintendo controller in his hands. It was an old console, but good games were good games no matter their age.

In a frame over his bed was the first ever poster for Doctor Hammer. If you were around in 1992 you might remember it. Maybe you saw the advert on the side of bus stop shelters. It was a huge one, six feet tall and four feet wide. It showed the main character, Doctor Hammer, jumping out of a television screen brandishing a hammer, with his famous white doctor's coat billowing like a cape. The poster was signed by all of WWAP, Dirk's dad included.

The lights in Dirk's bedroom were off. The only light came from the TV, which currently displayed the menu screen for Super Mario All-stars.

A shadow, darker than the ordinary darkness of the room, began to fill the window. The stars that could be seen began to fade and disappear until the window was just a black square. Dirk shivered. He pressed right on the D-pad and chose the first game in the collection, Super Mario Bros. The first Mario game after his iconic debut appearance as Jumpman in the 1981 arcade machine, Donkey Kong.

The game loaded. Dirk selected **1 PLAYER GAME** and pressed start.

Level one began. Mario ran forward and then stopped. Dirk pressed the right direction button but Mario didn't move. The screen flickered. Dirk pressed A and then B but Mario just stood there. The music in the background of the game sped up and then slowed right down. The music was so slow, each note drawn out, that it was eerie. Dirk put the controller down so he could get off the bed and reset the machine. Before he had a chance Mario jumped with that sound that is so familiar to so many gamers, BLOING. Dirk stared at the screen. Mario jumped again. BLOING. Dirk shuddered. Something about the glitching Mario made him feel uneasy. Mario jumped again and then the music stopped. Dirk stared at Mario.

A cold hand brushed against Dirk's feet and he lurched out of bed. He ran to the door and yanked at the door handle. It was locked. Did it even have a lock? No of course it didn't. He yanked the door again and then turned to face the room to see what had touched him. There was nothing there. Dirk let himself catch his breath. Of course there was nothing there. He glanced at the window to see if it was still closed and saw that it was. A part of him withdrew from the sheer blackness of the window pane but the conscious part of his mind couldn't quite work out what was wrong. It was just dark outside was all.

He ran across the room and jumped onto his bed and

pulled the covers over himself. Lights, he thought, just turn the fucking lights on! He leaned over to reach for the lamp on his bedside table but made the mistake of glancing at the television as he did.

Mario was staring at him.

'Wha-?'

Dirk knew full well that Mario did not have that frame of animation in the coding of the game. He knew because he had once hacked the game on an emulator himself. He stared at the inch high figure of Mario on the screen. He fixated on the two single black pixels that made up his eyes. It was like looking at the back of your own head in a mirror. It was alien and weird.

Mario blinked and then jumped straight up and down. The jump sound was gone, replaced by the sound of shoes landing softly on pavement. He jumped again and again, his feet smacking harder on the pixelated ground until cracks started to appear.

Dirk grabbed for the light switch on the lamp and flicked it. The bulb inside the lampshade exploded in a great white flash that momentarily illuminated the room and dazzled Dirk. He rubbed his eyes and blinked. The after image of the room stayed with him. It floated around his vision. A black square surrounded by blue-white light, like a photo negative.

The window, quietly but definitely, started growing wider across the wall. Dirk noticed it but put it down to the image residue in his eyes from the exploding lightbulb. He let his eyes focus on the screen again and saw Mario jump one final time and smash through the bottom of the game. There was an audible thud on his bedroom floor followed by the fast patter of tiny feet.

That iconic jump sound was back but when he heard it this time it didn't come from the TV speakers, it came from beside the bed. BLOING! A one inch high, two dimensional, Mario landed on his bed. Dirk scrambled up the sheets to escape this surely insane hallucination. Mario cut slices in the duvet as he ran. It was as if his feet were made of fine razor.

BLOING! Mario jumped again and landed on Dirk's chest. Dirk screamed.

CHAPTER 10

Billy stopped cycling when he got to Dirk's house and let his bike fall to the pavement floor. He stared up at Dirk's bedroom window. Most of the lights in the house were on but his friend's room was dark.

Billy opened the garden gate and walked up the path to the front door. He heard a scream come from Dirk's window.

'Dirk!' he shouted, and opened the front door without knocking.

Billy nearly collided with Dirk's dad on the way past the lounge door.

'Everything okay, Billy?' said Walter, stepping out of the way and holding his whisky glass up to avoid spilling it.

'Yep,' said Billy, without stopping, 'Just need to see Dirk.'

'Okay, your mum know where you are?'

Billy didn't answer. Dirk's door had a sign on it that had been there since he was young. DIRK'S LAIR. KEEP OUT.

Billy pulled the door handle down but it didn't open.

Dirk screamed again and Billy took a few steps back and barged into the door with his shoulder.

'Billy?' Walter shouted up the stairs.

Billy ran to the other side of the landing and ran hard at the door. This time if the door didn't open Billy would break his shoulder. He smashed into it and it flung open sending splinters flying from the broken latch.

Billy fell into the room. Dirk was flailing around on the bed.

'Dirk!' shouted Billy, running over and pulling Dirk off the bed by the arm.

Dirk thrashed and locked eyes with Billy. His pupils were wide and he was panting. His mouth was turned down in a terrified grimace. His cheeks were shiny with tears.

'Dirk! It's me, Billy. What's going on?'

Dirk stopped thrashing and looked down at his chest. There was nothing there. Dirk scrambled to his feet and pulled his shirt off. His chest was covered with small scratches.

'What the hell happened?' said Billy.

Dirk got behind Billy and stared over his shoulder at the television screen. Mario was standing there, at the beginning of level one. The music was playing quietly. The timer was counting down as normal. Mario was facing forward.

Dirk's breathing started to normalise.

'What is going on in here?' said Walter, walking into the room.

'The door was jammed,' said Billy, 'I thought Dirk was in trouble.'

'You okay Dirk?' said Walter.

Dirk glanced at Billy and then at his dad. 'Yeah, the door was just jammed. I couldn't get out.'

'How did you know he was stuck, Billy?'

'I was walking by outside and thought I heard him.'

Walter knew there was something the kids weren't telling him. Normal teenage behaviour, he thought. What group of fourteen year-olds didn't have their own secret and overblown melodramas? He looked at the broken latch on the door.

He sighed. 'Okay, this can be easily fixed. I'll make sure it doesn't get stuck in future, okay?'

'Okay, thanks dad,' said Dirk.

Walter might have stayed longer to interrogate the kids properly but there were other things on his mind.

'It's starting,' Penny shouted from downstairs.

'I've got to go. You two definitely okay?'

'We're fine, thank you,' said Billy.

Dirk nodded.

'Alright then,' said Walter, frowning at them before leaving the room.

Billy turned the main light on and looked at the cuts on Dirk's chest.

'What happened to you?'

'You wouldn't believe me if I told you. Just some bad dream I think.'

'How did you get all these cuts?'

Dirk tried to rationalise what had happened and thought plausibly that he had been asleep and the lightbulb had smashed and glass had gotten onto his duvet. Maybe the whole thing with Mario was just a bad nightmare and his own flailing around in bed had caused the glass to cut him. But that wasn't it. He knew that wasn't it. But what else could it have been?

'Mario tried to kill me,' he said, and then laughed at the absurdity of the idea.

But Billy didn't laugh. 'Okay. We need to get out of here. I need to show you something.'

Billy thought for a moment. 'Actually, forget that. We need to make sure Martha is okay.'

'Martha?' said Dirk.

'If something has happened to us it's possible something has happened to her too.'

'Why, what happened to you?'

'You wouldn't believe me if I told you,' said Billy.

Billy and Dirk snuck down the stairs and stopped by the open door to the lounge.

The lounge was big and the couch was in the middle of it facing the television. Walter stood behind the couch leaning on it with his elbows. He had a glass of whisky in his hands. Penny was sat on the sofa at the end with her feet tucked under her and her hand over her mouth. They were both watching something on TV.

Dirk and Billy crept past and quietly opened the front door and let themselves out. Billy pulled the door shut behind them and they stood still on the porch for a moment.

'I think we're clear,' said Dirk.

Billy nodded. 'Get the Dirkmobile.'

'I'm not doing that.'

'Get it.'

'Not a chance.'

They argued in hush tones.

'It's faster. We don't have time for this,' said Billy.

'I look retarded in that thing.'

'You are retarded, Dirk, remember? That's why we made it for you.'

'I'm not retarded, I just have brittle bones.'

The Dirkmobile was a converted bike trailer. Martha and Billy made it one Saturday while Dirk sat sulking at the side of Billy's garage. He protested then, and he protests now, but it is a clean solution to a basic problem. Martha and Billy both rode bikes. Dirk wasn't allowed to ride a bike because if he fell off he could risk breaking every bone in his body. At least with the Dirkmobile he could be towed safely behind. And safety was the key word when it came to the thing's design.

A thick inflatable rubber ring had been attached to the sides of a small trailer, making it look like an absurdly small lifeboat. A roof had been fashioned out of an old turtle-shaped sandpit lid. Wooden struts kept it in place. It had a flashing yellow light hot glued to the turtle's head that had been stolen one night from the top of a traffic cone at some unmanned roadworks. A seat had been made from a dismantled wheelchair. (An earlier experiment had involved simply wrapping the wheelchair in bubble wrap and towing that along, but initial test runs proved near fatal).

A pillow had been pushed into the back of the turtle roof for head support and a rudimentary seatbelt had been created using a long piece of Velcro they had found in a skip.

Dirk was right, it did look retarded, but it was still the quickest way to get around, at least until the Dirkmobile Mark III was under way.

Billy hooked the Dirkmobile to the tow hitch him and Martha had welded to the back of his BMX and Dirk, regardless of his feelings towards the thing, got in.

Gravel from Dirk's driveway kicked up from the wheels of the trailer and Dirk grabbed onto the side for support.

'Easy, Billy!'

Billy was standing up on the pedals using all his weight to get the bike moving. He rode off the curb onto the road and the Dirkmobile jumped around causing Dirk to jerk from side to side.

'Billy, there's no point in trying to protect me in this monstrosity if you're just going to ride like a twat anyway.'

'Sorry, Dirk,' said Billy, getting some speed up and then sitting on the bike seat and pedalling at a steady pace.

They rode through the empty square and took a short cut down the alley that ran behind the shops on the far end and came out by the train station. The crossing barriers were up and they rode straight across without slowing.

Billy squeezed the brakes and the BMX slowed to a stop in a pebble spraying skid. The Dirkmobile almost went sideways but Dirk leaned hard left and kept the thing upright.

'What the fuck are you doing?' said Dirk.

Billy turned to him. 'You know, it might be quicker if we go down the track a bit and get through that gap in the fence halfway down. It cuts out about a mile of the road. Would save us a whole bunch of time.'

'I think that's a terib-' Dirk stopped what he was saying and thought for a moment and reconsidered. 'I mean, there's no more trains tonight. We've done it at stupider times,' he said.

Billy nodded and got off the BMX. 'Okay, you'll have to help me carry the Drikmobile over the tracks.'

Dirk got out and Billy unhitched the trailer.

'Wait here a sec,' said Billy. He rode back to the middle of the crossing and turned right onto the train tracks. He cycled, the bike shuddering as it went, over the sleepers between the rails. Just beyond the other side of the small station he got off the bike and carried it a few metres to the side. He left it on the ground and went back for Dirk.

'Alright, help me drag this thing,' said Billy, holding onto the hitch and lifting it off the ground. Dirk went on the other side and the two of them pulled it back to the crossing and onto the tracks. The two wheels fit between the rails but only just.

'We have to be careful not to let the wheels touch the rails. One of them is electrified. If we touch it we'll be fried,' said Dirk.

'I heard burnt human flesh smells like crispy bacon,' said Billy, looking at Dirk as they carefully pulled it along.

'How would you know that?' said Dirk, keeping an eye on the wheels.

'I heard a couple of firefighters talking about it in the tobacconist a few weeks ago. Apparently they don't eat bacon because of it. Bacon sandwiches just tastes like dead bodies to them.'

Dirk nearly gagged imagining a sandwich with rotting burnt flesh in it. Hair matted with blood protruding from one side and the burnt end of a finger out of the other end. 'Want sauce with that?' said the imagined café owner in Dirk's mind, opening the sandwich and squirting thick brown sauce onto the mess of scalp and fingers.

'Can we talk about something else?' said Dirk, trying to shift the image from his mind.

'What business would firefighters have in a tobacconist anyway?' said Billy.

Dirk turned the Dirkmobile towards Billy slightly to stop the wheel from crashing into the rail on his side. They straightened up and kept moving.

'Maybe they didn't have much work on and needed some matches to liven things up a bit,' said Billy.

'How far?' said Dirk.

'Nearly there,' said Billy. 'So, you were really attacked by Mario?'

Dirk shrugged. 'I don't really want to talk about it.'

Back at the crossroads a dark figure stood watching them. The lights on the crossing flickered. The man was featureless apart from his eyes. You could stand right in front of that colourless human shape and the outline of his body would start to merge with the shadows. You could not discern what he was wearing or what he looked like but stare into his eyes and it was like staring at distant stars, thousands of miles away.

A terrible fear would scream through you and you'd be lucky not to die on your feet right there of fear before you even had a chance to run.

Dirk and Billy reached the end of the station and Billy looked back down the track. Billy's reaction caused Dirk to let out a short cry. Billy stumbled backwards and would have fallen if Dirk hadn't grabbed him by the arm.

'What the fuck is wrong?' said Dirk.

Billy stared down the track. There was no one there. 'I thought I saw someone,' he said.

Dirk stared down the track and looked up at the station. 'Stop trying to scare me, Billy.'

'I'm not. Let's get out of here. Grab my bike, I'll pull this.'

'Okay,' said Dirk, and stepped over the track and picked up Billy's bike.

The two of them hurried to the hole in the fence. Dirk went through first and Billy second, dragging the Dirkmobile without caring if it bashed into the sides.

Immediately on the other side was the road that ran along the woods opposite. Billy hooked the trailer back up and Dirk climbed in, as quickly as he could. From stumbling on the track to getting to the road and hooked up felt like it took twenty seconds flat. Panic does that. It slows things down at first but then it speeds things right up.

Billy was peddling hard and before they knew it they were turning right into Three Oaks Touring Park. They stopped at the barrier and Billy pressed the four digit code to open it. The barrier jerked and swung upright.

They rode in and followed the paved path around to the left. Martha's caravan was in the 8th pitch at the back of the *A* field.

CHAPTER 11

Martha and her dad pulled into the parking space next to the caravan. Pete stopped the engine and Martha slid the side door open and jumped out. She saw Billy and Dirk wheeling the BMX, with the Dirkmobile attached, into the field and she curled her lip in surprise.

'What are you two doing here?' she said.

'Bit late for a visit, isn't it?' said Pete, closing the driver's door behind him.

'I know, sorry. Can we talk to Martha for a bit?'

Billy always thought Martha's dad looked like a homeless cavalier, with his long hair and strange beard.

'She's all yours. Be careful with that hand Marth,' he said, unzipping the awning to the caravan.

'Is she back?' said Martha's mum from within the caravan.

'She's here. All sewed up. She'll be fine,' said Pete, disappearing inside.

Martha's mum came out wearing a dressing gown and wellies. 'Oh, hi boys,' she said, noticing Billy and Dirk.

'Hi Amelia,' said Dirk and Billy together.

'What did you two do to my daughter?' she said, with a smile on her face.

'Sorry,' said Dirk.

'I'm just joking. You okay, Martha?' she said, taking Martha's bandaged up hand in her own.

'I'm okay. A few stitches and a bandage. It will be fine in a week.'

'Does it hurt?'

'No, it's fine. I'm okay, mum, really.'

'Okay. Can I get you a coffee or anything? Do you boys want a coffee?'

'You don't need to fuss, mum. I'll be in in a bit.'

'Alright then, we'll be up for a bit anyway. I'll see you before bed. Don't leave the campsite this late though, okay?'

'Don't worry, I have no plans to go anywhere.'

'Okay sweetie,' said Amelia, 'Enjoy doing whatever you're doing.'

Martha's mum went back into the caravan.

They could hear Pete and Amelia talking inside. 'Wine dear?' said Pete. 'Oh, I think I can manage a glass or two,' said Amelia.

'Are we Shneeble Meegling?' said Martha, pulling a face and putting her hands on her hips.

'Might as well. No need to break tradition just because a ghost is trying to kill us, right?' said Billy.

'A what?' said Martha, taking her hands off her hips.

'Sheeble Shmarble!' said Dirk, in a grunted weird voice, jutting his groin forwards with his hands on his hips.

Billy snorted and Martha laughed.

'Okay, we are doing it then,' said Martha, putting her hands on her hips. 'Snoogle Fargle!' she rasped.

Billy rolled his eyes and put his hands on his hips. 'Blarble Garble.'

'Ghost?' said Martha.

'Can we go to Den the Fourth?' said Billy.

'Sure,' said Martha.

Den the Fourth was an abandoned Streamline Duchess Travel Trailer at the bottom of the campsite. That's what they call a caravan in America. A Travel Trailer. It was once like a chrome metal bullet, a futuristic travel machine with all mod cons. Now it was a faded grey collapsing thing with two flat wheels and dented panels. It looked like a retired burger van. It stood at the edge of what the locals on the campsite called, The Caravan Graveyard. Far out of the way of the people who lived on site. There was no light and no power.

Once a month the local raceway would come down and take whatever caravans had been dumped there for their monthly caravan destruction derby but they knew not to take the Streamline. For one, it seemed like a damn shame to destroy it, but mostly the guys down the raceway knew Martha and when she told them one day to take it at their peril they listened. She had that effect on people.

There was no electrical power at Den the Fourth. This wasn't a place for gaming and movie nights, like the treehouse. This was where they came to talk and play cards. They played truth or dare there sometimes. They don't talk about it but once, a few years ago, they had played spin the bottle together there. On that night, the unmentionable night, Martha had become Billy's first kiss. The thing that was talked about less, was that Billy had become Dirk's.

Martha unlocked the padlock and opened the door. Most of the inside had been stripped out. The only thing left was the bench seats that faced each other at the front of the trailer. The kitchen had been ripped out and the bed in the back was just a hollow frame.

They had made a table between the benches out of pallets, topping it with a patchwork of chessboards they had picked up at a local car boot sale. The biggest chessboard was hinged at opposing edges and opened up in the middle. They kept tealight candles and matches in there.

Martha sat down and Dirk and Billy sat opposite her.

'Well?' said Martha.

'Is your hand okay?' said Billy.

'It will be fine. What's this "ghost trying to kill you" business all about? And, before you start, it already sounds like a load of old shit.'

Billy opened the chessboard and took out three candles. He struck a match and lit them.

He sighed. 'I need to tell you about that game I found.'

'The console?' said Dirk.

'No, there was a game that came with it. I didn't show you earlier. I don't know why.'

'Ooh, what game was it?' said Martha. 'Ghouls 'n Ghosts? Did that game shit you up? Or was it Castlevania? That's a scary one.'

'Ha ha. No. It's nothing like that.' Billy paused. 'There was a game called, Shelley Town RPG.'

Billy told Martha and Dirk about the game and what had happened in the treehouse. The letter he had found behind the old vicarage and the four letter hangman game that started with the letter J. He told them about the game playing itself and about throwing the console out of the treehouse and smashing the television. He told them about the darkness and the cold.

Martha listened dubiously at first but saw the terror in Billy's eyes as he described the event.

'You're making this up,' she said. 'Are you just trying to scare me?'

'It's true,' said Billy.

'You smashed the console?' said Dirk.

Billy nodded.

'So what happened when you got to Dirk's?' said Martha.

Dirk tensed up and told his story, staring at one of the squares on the chessboard. Of course, he couldn't see the chessboard, his attention was focused inward on the memory.

It was the first time Billy had heard the whole story of what had happened in Dirk's room and his nerves jangled with unease. His gut felt loose and he didn't know if he was going to fill his pants with diarrhoea or throw up. Thankfully he did neither.

'Show me,' said Martha, when Dirk had finished.

Dirk unzipped his hoodie. There were small blotches of red staining the shirt beneath. He undid the top three buttons of the shirt and pulled it open. On his chest were dozens of fresh cuts. Small beads of blood had formed on the deeper slashes.

Martha gasped and stared at the mess of red lines. 'Does it hurt?'

'A bit,' said Dirk, and he sniffed. A tear breached his eyelid and rolled down his cheek. His breathing became erratic and he started crying in jerking fits.

Martha jumped up and threw her arms around him. She squeezed him tightly, not caring if his bloody chest would stain her top. 'It's okay, Dirk,' she said.

She looked up at Billy. 'If this is a prank-'

But before she finished Billy started to well up too. Hugs weren't going to fix this mess, she thought. She let go of Dirk and stood up.

'STAND UP!' she shouted.

The shock of her voice startled Dirk out of his upset. He had been in a small dark place in his mind. It felt like escaping it would be impossible. There was only the uncontrollable sobs and endless dark fear. Martha's voice cut right through him. It was the verbal equivalent of being smacked across the face, like how men used to slap hysterical women.

Martha wasn't the touchy-feely type. She could just about manage consoling Dirk for this out of character slip, but two of them? Give me strength, she thought (in her mother's voice).

'Didn't you hear me?' she said.

Billy and Dirk stood up.

'So let me get this straight. You brought a haunted console with a game that is set in Shelley Town and the main character is you, it glitched and you freaked out. Right? And then you, Dirk, were attacked by Mario but were luckily saved by Billy, who had decided to come to your rescue because a shadow in a game made him think you were in trouble? Right so far?'

'When you say it like that it sounds stupid,' said Billy.

'And I suppose you can't prove any of this because you smashed the console?'

Billy shrugged.

'What if I could fix it?' said Dirk.

'Wait, I can prove it,' said Billy.

He unzipped his backpack and took out a book-sized black box and dropped it on the chessboard-topped table. Dirk and Martha looked at it.

'There,' said Billy. 'Proof.'

Martha picked up the box. 'Shelley Town RPG,' she read.

'Let me see,' said Dirk.

Martha handed it to him and Dirk opened the box and pulled out the cardboard inlay.

'Where's the game?' he said.

'Still in the console,' said Billy.

Dirk removed the instruction manual and checked to see if there was anything else in the box. It was empty. He put the box down and turned the instruction manual over in his hands. On one side were the words, SHELLEY TOWN RPG, and underneath that was the word INSTRUCTIONS. The other side was just black. He went to flip through the pages but found there weren't any. Instead the manual was one large folded piece of glossy paper. He unfolded it and laid it out on the table, pushing the box and inlay onto the floor as he did.

One whole side of the outspread document was black apart from one corner which served as the cover when folded. Dirk turned it over.

The three of them leaned in. The light from the candles illuminated it from one side.

'It's a map,' said Martha.

CHAPTER 12

Becky pulled open a bag of Doritos and offered the open end to Chris. Chris reached in and came out with a handful.

'Hungry?' said Becky.

'It's the closest thing to an evening meal I've had in a week,' said Chris.

The canvas screen had been set up on the main stage and Becky had managed to link the projector to a television. They could have just watched the documentary on the TV but where's the fun in that? If you have access to a big screen and a hefty sound system why not use it?

They were both sat on swivel chairs in the sound and light booth. Becky had her feet up on the console. Chris had more respect for Becky's gear and was sat with his right foot resting on his left knee. Becky took her feet down and reached under the mixing desk where she kept a small fridge full of drinks. When the show gets going there's not much chance to have a break so a fridge full of, in this case, beer and energy drinks, had become a part of her usual set up.

She opened the fridge and took out two bottles of Becks. They were plastic bottles with screw tops, the kind they had started selling in nightclubs to reduce serious head injuries. If the youth of Britain could be said to be truly good at anything it was getting drunk and beating the shit out of each other. Removing glass from the situation must have saved thousands of lives. But that's not why Becky opted for the plastic bottle. She used them because they were quieter and easier to open than a glass bottle or a can.

'Cheers,' said Chris, opening the beer.

'No worries, dude,' said Becky.

Becky put her feet back on the mixing desk. She leaned forward and moved two sliders up the deck. The speakers in the hall got louder. She set the sliders just right and leaned back again. She opened her beer and shoved a handful of Doritos in her mouth.

The documentary was just beginning.

DCI Ryman had changed out of his uniform, which now lay crumpled on the floor by his bed. He was now sitting on his wide leather chair with a strong black coffee resting on the top of a Marshall amp next to the arm rest. A banged-up old Gibson Les Paul was in its stand next to his ancient cathode ray television. He once had dreams of being a rock star. Some part of that dream still existed. These days, pushing forty, overweight, and not overly endowed with talent, he resigned himself to the occasional late night of whisky and rough blues riffs played loud through his amp. But tonight wasn't about that. Tonight was about watching a documentary, drinking coffee, and taking notes on a folded piece of A4 paper.

The documentary started with a head-shot taken out of a

school yearbook. The picture was of a sixteen year-old kid turning away from the photographer with a hand covering his face. The caption under the photo read, *"I'm not giving you a f***ing caption."* – Jack Matterson.

'Jack Matterson went to school at Shelley Town Comprehensive.' The narrator began. 'He had the highest grades in school but, as far as we've been able to discover, no real friends. He left school at sixteen and, against his parent's wishes, decided not to apply for any colleges or further education. Instead he hid away in his parent's basement and played with computers.'

On the screen now was a picture of the Matterson house in the square, but instead of the dilapidated dump it is now it showed a neat and well-kept home with white walls and a nice garden with trimmed hedges and handsome flower beds. In the drive was a brand new car.

'His parents, regardless of their disappointment, encouraged his interest and before long he had built his own home computer from parts he had ordered from specialist magazines. This was in the late seventies, don't forget, before terms like *Personal Computer* and *Operating System* were in common use. The idea of owning your own computer would have seemed utterly absurd. Most computers, that people were aware of, took up entire rooms and few people knew how to operate them.'

The picture cut away to some home video shot by Jack's dad on old 8mm film. The clip was short and there was no sound. The image was grainy and flickered. The scene was of

Jack's mum in the basement joking around with her wedding dress, holding it against her body and doing a twirl for the camera. On the floor next to her was a box with the words, Wedding Bits, written on it with a black marker pen. There were other boxes around, and some old suitcases, Christmas decorations stored away, the usual things you find in basements.

The camera followed Jack's mum around and then paused. In the background a young man could be seen hunched over a computer monitor with a screwdriver.

'We believe this video was taken in 1982 and is the only video footage that exists of Jack Matterson. Just a few frames, caught by accident, by his dad. Sadly this was also the last time Jack's mother would be seen on film. Just a few weeks later both of his parents were dead.'

Ryman raised his eyebrows at this and made a note. It seemed tomorrow, just to satisfy his own curiosity, he was going to have a laborious day looking through decades old, badly filed, police records. People were going to be asking questions and he wanted to be as prepared as possible.

He knew he was a slob. Ryman didn't really care about that sort of thing. Too many people, he thought, seemed to believe that success had more to do with your ability to purchase a tie than actually being good at something. Ryman was much smarter than he looked. Where there weren't discarded whisky bottles covering the carpet around his flat there were piles of books. He had a habit of going around the charity shops and buying heaps of them on any subject, whether it seemed boring or not. He believed ignorance was a great thing. He thought stupid people had a more complete knowledge than most because they had no idea just how much they didn't know. The more you learn the more aware you are of how much you don't know. You become more aware of your own ignorance. Ryman spent much of his spare time trying to close the gap, but of course it just gets bigger. The more you know, the more you realise you don't know, and so the gap gets bigger still. The hunger for knowledge becomes an addiction. A desire that can never be fulfilled.

People were always surprised by him. This fat dirty slob somehow managed to make his way up to DCI and he seemed to really know his shit. He could converse with anyone and know enough about their own pet subject to make a connection. It made interrogating people easier. Make a connection. Become a friend, at least on the surface level. That was the key to getting information out of people. It was always about information. Knowledge. The gap gets bigger and eventually you fall into it. That's how you end up surrounded by empty whisky bottles and piles of books.

In the exhibition hall Becky and Chris both opened fresh beers.

'This shit's getting interesting,' said Becky.

'Shut up, I'm listening,' said Chris.

On the huge canvas screen the 8mm video footage went away and now there was an old woman standing in her doorway. Her name came up in white letters at the bottom of the screen. Mary Higgins. The documentary maker must have asked a question that was cut out in the edit because the woman just started talking.

'Oh, it was a terrible thing that. They were such a nice couple. Their boy was a bit funny mind, not "ha ha" funny, more like, well, how would you put it? You wouldn't want to leave him alone with any of your pets, if you know what I mean?'

The door opened and an old man, her husband, squeezed in next to her. The words, Harry Higgins came up in white at the bottom of the screen. 'Don't say things like that Mary, they'll think the poor kid was a psychopath.' The woman nodded at the camera when he said "psychopath" and the man continued, 'You can't blame the kid for going a bit strange after his parents died in such a tragic way, can you?'

'I think it was him that did it,' said Mary.

'What exactly did happen?' said the female documentary maker from behind the camera.

Mary looked to her right at the house next door. The camera followed her gaze. It was the Matterson house, all run down and rotting. Mary started speaking and the camera returned to her.

'They were found dead in the basement. My Harold was the one who started to suspect something was up, didn't you, Harold?'

'I wish you wouldn't talk about it like it was so much gossip, Mary. They were real people.' He looked at the house and then towards the camera. He didn't look directly into the camera, like his wife did, but at the documentary maker herself. 'I hadn't seen them in a few days and normally I would say good morning to John, the boy's dad, on my way out to work. He started on his way to work at the same time as me. I think he had some high up job at the developing place. It's not there anymore but there used to be a factory out by the campsite. I think it's a gym now. What were they called? Silvertone? They built cameras and had a department developing film. He had some hand in that. A smart guy, I thought. I noticed the car hadn't moved for a while and the curtains were closed in the day so I went and knocked on the door. When there was no answer I walked right in, that wasn't so odd back in those days, people were more friendly then.'

'He found their bodies in the basement, no wounds or anything, just stone dead,' said Mary.

'Let me get there myself, Mary,' said Harold.

'So where was Jack Matterson when you found the bodies?' asked the documentarian.

'The poor kid had locked himself in his room. He hadn't eaten and was about as scared as a boy could get.'

'We think it was him that killed them don't we, Harold?' said Mary.

'Well, I'm not sure about that. The police said he was just in shock. The coroner said it was monoxide poisoning that got them.'

'It was all over the papers,' said Mary.

'So what happened to Jack after that?'

'I'm not really sure. We didn't see much of him did we,

Mary?'

'I checked in on him now and then but he was old enough to look after himself. I think he must have had some kind of counselling. The mortgage was paid off so he inherited the house and whatever savings his parents had. He just hid away for a while,' said Mary.

'Until he met that girl,' said Harold.

The footage of Mary and Harold went away and was replaced with a picture of a fairly attractive young brunette.

The narrator said, 'Jack met Hillary in 1984, two years after his parent's death, which was judged by the coroner and the police to be an accident. Hillary was working at the Silvertone factory where Jack's dad had worked. On the second anniversary of their deaths a plaque was put up on the wall to memorialise John Matterson and the extraordinary work he did. Jack went along. It was his first known social outing since their deaths. Nobody knows the details of how they came together but it is assumed they met on that day. Soon they were dating and not long after that they were engaged. They lived a private life and not much is known about the relationship. In 1988, a few years into their relationship, they had a baby daughter which they named Sarah after Jack's mother. Hillary, sadly, died during childbirth. And so, this private and socially anxious young man, no doubt still mourning the loss of his parents and now dealing with the fresh loss of his fiancée, had to raise a daughter by himself. It was around this time that he met William Rain, Walter Chaplin, and Amelia and Peter Perry. Who would, just two years later, become known the world over as WWAP.'

A new picture faded into frame. It was taken at a children's nursery. Amongst the parents were William and Eunice, Walter and Penny, and Peter and Amelia, and their young children, Billy, Dirk, and Martha. On the far right of the picture, Jack Matterson sat off from the rest of the parents with a young daughter on his lap. He had dark bags under his eyes and a bandage on his left wrist.

Walter watched the documentary from behind the couch. Penny looked up at him. 'How much do you think they know?' she said.

Walter sighed and shrugged his shoulders. 'I guess we'll find out soon enough.'

CHAPTER 13

'What do you think the crosses represent?' said Martha.

'Treasure?' said Dirk.

'I don't think so,' said Billy. 'That one there is where I found the first letter in the game.' He pointed at the black X behind the old vicarage.

'Why would a game tell you where everything was in the manual?' said Dirk.

Billy shrugged.

'Let's go there,' said Martha.

'Go there?' said Dirk, his eyes wide.

'I don't think that's a good idea,' said Billy.

'Why not? You want to find out what this is all about, don't you? I don't believe all this haunted game crap but something obviously scared you or you wouldn't be crying like fucking babies.'

Martha got up and opened what used to be a wardrobe but now served as their larder. There wasn't much in it. Three rolled up sleeping bags. A couple of cans of peas (which wouldn't be eaten in a thousand years, even if starvation was staring her in the face and all she had on her person was one of those cans of peas and a tin opener. They all agreed that peas tasted like playdough and shouldn't be consumed by humans. People will just about eat anything, dirty animals. If the peas were in there for any reason at all it was to protect adults from themselves). The larder was running bare at the moment. Martha made a note to herself to stock it up and picked up the half-drunk two litre bottle of cheap cola and three plastic cups from a stack that leaned against the wall of the larder. They were the kind of cups you get piled up next to water coolers.

Martha sat back down and poured the drinks. She picked up her cup and sipped. This whole getting drinks for everyone business was really just to give herself time to think without the morons butting in. She put the cup down and looked at Billy.

'Let's say, just for argument's sake, that you really are being haunted by a computer game. You said you think you saw it at the train tracks, right?'

'I think I did,' said Billy.

'So why hasn't the ghost followed you here? He's obviously not tied to the game otherwise how would he have got to Dirk's house to fuck with him?'

'Maybe he travelled down the wires or something, that's why it was Mario that attacked me and not a ghost,' said Dirk.

'That wouldn't explain the train tracks,' said Martha.

'But maybe it does,' said Billy. 'Think about it, let's say it needs wires to get around. It could get to the train tracks easily, and if it hasn't followed us here maybe it's because we're in the woods. Nothing's plugged in here,' said Billy.

'Not in this banged up old den anyway,' said Martha.

'What do you think then? That the ghost came from the Matterson house in the game and for some reason is trying to scare us to death? Where did the game come from?' said Dirk.

Billy imagined a Scooby-Doo like ghost maniacally programming a computer game and smiled. 'Sounds pretty dumb doesn't it?'

'Here's what I think,' said Martha, squeezing her empty plastic cup and chucking it into the dark end of the caravan. 'We sleep in here tonight. Tomorrow we take a look at this game.'

'I smashed the console,' said Billy.

'Dirk can fix it,' said Martha.

Dirk nodded. 'I think I could do that.'

There was a THUD and a long scrape at the door and all three of them jumped. 'What the fuck is that?' said Dirk.

Billy froze and his ears pricked up.

'Are you two serious?' said Martha, standing up.

'What are you doing?' said Billy.

Martha opened the door and Hopkirk bounded in and jumped up on Billy and licked his face. Billy pushed him away and Hopkirk jumped on Dirk and licked him too.

'Get down, Hopkirk,' said Martha. The dog got off Dirk and trotted over to Martha, panting and wagging his tail. 'I'm going to take him back and get dad to call your parents to let them know you're staying here tonight.'

'He scared the crap out of me,' said Billy, with a relieved laugh.

The caravan door opened and Hopkirk jumped in.

'Hey boy,' said Pete, scratching the dog behind the ears.

Martha leaned into the caravan but didn't enter. That would mean taking off her boots. 'Hey dad, could you phone Dirk and Billy's parents and let them know they're sleeping here tonight?'

'Sure. You sleeping in the den?'

'If that's okay?' said Martha, putting on a big charming grin.

'Of course. I'll call them as soon as I'm done cooking.'

'Bit late for dinner,' said Martha.

'Yes, I fancied a little day trip to the hospital earlier, so things are a bit delayed.'

'Oh yeah,' said Martha, remembering it was her fault dinner was late. 'Hospital trips are fun,' she said.

'If you say so, Martha. Will you be eating with us?'

'I'm okay. We've got food in the den.' A lie, but Martha was in the habit of skipping the occasional meal if she could. She thought people ate too much. Three times a day? That's way too much. Big breakfast and forget the rest, that was Martha's motto.

Martha's mum was sitting in the awning reading. 'Alright mum?' said Martha, closing the caravan door.

Amelia looked up from her book (The Broom of the System by David Foster Wallace) and smiled. 'Hi honey,' she said, and returned to the novel.

The awning was not like most awnings. When they first gave up bricks and mortar for the simpler life, their friends thought they were nuts. But when they saw what Pete and Amelia had done with the place it all started to make sense. The awning was huge. There were two book cases rammed with literature and reference books. The ceiling had been lined with vintage fabric maps. There was a globe bar between two large leather chairs, (one of which was currently occupied by Amelia. Glass of wine in one hand, a book in the other, and her spectacles on the tip of her nose). There was also a two-seater leather couch which was mostly the domain of Martha. There was a patchwork of Afghan rugs on the floor and the floor itself was a properly carpeted wooden affair held up on joists. From the outside it looked like a normal caravan and awning but when you walked through the zip-up door you were transported to something between a Victorian gentleman's study and a library. It was like a TARDIS. Pete was a novelist these days and Amelia was an artist. In the past Pete had written game concepts and created the story and the world of Doctor Hammer, and Amelia had created the character art and scenery. She even designed the box art. WWAP was, and still is, a big part of their lives. But now, with money in the bank and almost no outgoings, they lived the life of retired intellectuals. In one corner there was an old dark-wood desk with a Tiffany banker's lamp on it and a stack of papers next to a desktop computer (the printed-off first draft of Pete's current novel in progress, waiting for its first proof read).

'I'll be at the den if you need me,' said Martha.

'Okay, sweetie,' said Amelia, without looking up.

'Everything cool?' asked Billy, when Martha got back to Den the Fourth.

Martha closed the door behind her and gave the double thumbs up. 'All sorted,' she said. 'Come on, help me get the bed together.'

They took the seat cushions off the benches and arranged them in the wooden frame where the bed had been. They got their sleeping bags out of the wardrobe and placed them on the bed, alternating top and tail. Dirk and Billy always slept with their heads on one end with Martha's feet between them.

Dirk and Billy stripped down to their underpants and balled their clothes up to make pillows. They climbed into their sleeping bags and rested their heads. Martha got into her bag fully clothed and then squirmed and wriggled around. Eventually she pulled a bundle of clothes out and put them under her head. Dirk and Billy looked at each other. There was a look in their eyes that said, 'Do you think she took everything off?'

'I know what you're thinking, perverts,' said Martha.

'We're not thinking anything,' said Billy.

'Billy was thinking about your boobs,' said Dirk.

'Dirk!' said Martha and Billy at the same time, and they all laughed in that catching way that only seems to happen to kids at sleepovers.

They calmed down. All three of them were staring up at the ceiling. Dirk laughed again, his cheeks were hurting from it. 'Sorry,' he said, and sighed.

'Do you guys really believe there's a ghost out there trying to get you?' said Martha.

'I don't know what happened,' said Billy. 'It all feels like a bad dream right now. Like it wasn't real, you know?'

'We'll figure it all out tomorrow,' said Martha.

'Can I be honest with you guys?' said Dirk.

'Sure,' said Martha.

Dirk rolled over. He could just make out Billy's face in the dark. 'It doesn't matter,' he said.

'Go on, what is it?' said Billy.

Dirk shrugged. 'It's just, I don't know what happened today. But I can tell you this. I've never been so scared in all my life.'

CHAPTER 14

Pete had a brand new Nokia 7650. He slid it open and saw he had a missed call from Walter. He must be wondering where the kids are, he thought. He pressed call and put the phone to his ear. With his free hand he picked up a steaming bowl of chilli and took it out to Amelia in the awning. He put it down on the drum box that served as a coffee table and Amelia put her book down.

'That smells great,' she said picking it up. 'Spoon?'

The call went to answer machine and Pete hung up and put the phone in his pocket.

'Ah, yes. A spoon might be handy. Hold on.'

Pete went back into the caravan and came out with a spoon. Amelia was holding her wine glass upside down and pulling an exaggerated sad face.

'Shit, no wine?!' said Pete, dropping the spoon.

'No wine!' cried Amelia.

'Don't move, I can fix this,' said Pete, and leapt into the caravan. He leapt right back out again with a cold bottle of Sauvignon Blanc and knelt down in front of Amelia. She raised the back of her hand to her forehead and pretended to swoon. 'It might be too late,' she said.

Pete filled up her glass, stood up, and bowed. Amelia stared at her glass in amazement.

'My hero!' she said, in a ridiculously high voice. She took a great gulp, holding it like a chalice, and then put it on the floor.

'Anything else my dear?' said Pete.

'I'll have you if it's on offer?'

'I'm all yours, right after the chilli.'

'Oh, I see what's more important,' said Amelia, folding her arms.

'You haven't tasted it.'

Amelia rolled her eyes and leaned forward to try it. 'Where's my spoon?'

'Oh, I dropped it, hold on.'

Pete picked up the spoon and cleaned it off on his t-shit and handed it to her.

'Thank you darling,' she said, and dipped the spoon in the chilli and tasted it. 'Yeah, you're right,' she said, eating with her mouth open, 'The sex will have to wait a bit.'

'You're so beautiful,' said Pete.

Amelia nodded and put another spoon of chilli in her mouth and opened it to show Pete in the hope of grossing him out. They acted like this a lot, they always had. It was probably the reason Martha had always behaved older than she was. She felt like the adult of the family. Someone had to be.

Pete's phone rang. Walter's name was on the screen. 'Just have to get this,' said Pete.

'Walter,' said Pete.

'Are you watching this?' said Walter.

'Watching what? I don't have a TV.'

'Of course you don't.'

'What is it?' said Pete.

'Jack Matterson, the real Genius behind WWAP. It's a documentary.'

'Is this a joke?' said Pete.

'If you had a TV right now you could tune in to BBC Two and catch the end of it. We need to talk about this. I'll need to try and talk to William somehow.'

'You've got his mobile number haven't you?' said Pete.

'Yeah, but he doesn't answer.'

'I can call him.'

'When was the last time you spoke to him?'

Pete thought for a moment. 'It's probably been a good year. He might answer to Amelia if I get her to call. What did the documentary reveal? How did they even find a connection?'

'Someone at the nursery found a picture of us all together with the kids and apparently some clever bastard at the BBC heard about it somehow and decided to look into it. A real WWAP freak and gamer nerd had noticed similarities between some old indie game Jack had made and ours. He looked into the coding and found similarities. They saw we all lived on the same block and voilà, conspiracy. A documentary was commissioned. And do you know what? We were all in it. Interviewed.'

'What? I've never even heard of it,' said Pete.

'Remember that Rise of WWAP thing we were all interviewed for?' said Walter.

'Yeah,' said Pete.

'It was really for this.'

'They didn't ask me anything about him.'

'Nor me.'

'So how much do they know? Do I need to hook up the caravan and get the fuck out of here?'

'They only know that Jack,' Walter paused and Pete heard him swallow and then heard the sound of a glass being put down on a table, 'That Jack and his kid disappeared. They leave the documentary with a big open question, 'Why hasn't anyone in WWAP ever mentioned him?''

'Okay, so now what do we do?' said Pete.

'We get together in the morning. Not tonight. Tonight I'm going to polish off a big bottle of whisky and fuck my wife.'

'Thanks for the info,' said Pete.

'We'll meet in the morning,' said Walter. 'I'll call you and let you know where. Probably here. Actually, just come here at eight, okay?'

'Okay. We'll be there at eight. Oh, and Walter, Dirk is crashing here tonight,' said Pete.

'Dirk's upstairs with Billy.'

'No, they're both here with Martha. I'll call Eunice and let her know where Billy is too,' said Pete.

'There's no controlling those kids these days is there? They just go where they want.'

'I think it's nice. They feel at home at whichever house they're at. They'll make sure Dirk is okay, they always do.'

'I know. No worries where that's concerned. We've raised

some good kids there, Pete.'

'We sure have. See you at eight, Walter.'

'Alright. Call me if Dirk has any problems.'

'Will do.'

'Bye, Pete.'

The phone went dead.

'Be where at eight?' said Amelia.

Pete put his phone in his pocket and sat down on his matching chair next to Amelia. 'Not eating?' she said.

'Lost my appetite. We're going to Walter's in the morning. We need to talk about Jack.'

'We need to what?' said Amelia.

Pete told her about the documentary and everything Walter had said over the phone. When he was done she put her half-finished bowl of chilli down.

'I think I just lost my appetite too,' she said. 'What are we going to do?'

'We should have known it would come out eventually,' said Pete. 'Have you got any tobacco? I've run out.'

'In my bag,' said Amelia, motioning towards her bag on the floor next to Pete's desk.

'You mind if I smoke in here?' said Pete, getting up.

'No, I think I'll join you.'

CHAPTER 15

'Where have you been?' said Eunice, standing at the open lounge window that overlooked the front garden and the green beyond it.

Billy was riding his bike into the driveway towing Dirk behind him in the Dirkmobile. Martha rode in around them, Hopkirk running alongside, and leaned her bike against the garage wall.

'We stayed at Martha's, I thought you knew,' said Billy.

'I was worried sick,' said Eunice, 'Why didn't you call?'

'I'm sorry, Eunice,' said Martha. 'My dad was meant to call you. He said he was going to.'

'Well he didn't. I tried calling Walter and Pete but both their phones went straight to answer phone. I've been sat up all night. I almost called Mr Ryman.'

'I'm really sorry, mum,' said Billy. 'Hold on guys, I'm going to go in and talk to her.'

'We'll be right here,' said Martha.

Billy went in the house and closed the door behind him. Eunice closed the window and disappeared from sight.

'Do you think he's in trouble?' said Dirk.

'He'll be fine,' said Martha.

'Look, there's the console,' said Dirk, walking over to the treehouse.

The console was on the grass at the bottom of the ladder. The game was still in the slot, a black cartridge with the words, SHELLEY TOWN RPG printed on it in bold white lettering. Dirk and Martha looked at it. Hopkirk sniffed at it and growled.

'It's just a game, Hoppy,' Martha said to the dog.

Dirk picked up the console.

'There's nothing wrong with it,' he said.

'I thought Billy said it had split in half when it hit the ground,' said Martha.

Dirk shrugged. 'There's not even a scratch on it.'

'Come on, let's plug it in,' said Martha.

Martha climbed the ladder to untie the rope that ran through the pulley system but stopped when she got to the entrance of the treehouse.

'Well he wasn't lying about the TV,' she shouted down to Dirk. 'It's completely fucked.'

'How are we going to play the game?' said Dirk.

'I think Billy's got an old TV in the garage. Let's clear all this shit up and bring it in.'

'How are we going to get the old one down?' said Dirk.

'Well, first of all,' came Martha's voice from the treehouse. 'You need to get yourself and Hopkirk well out of the way.'

'What do you mean?' said Dirk. 'Oh, I see.'

The old television lurched out of the entrance of the treehouse and stopped before it fell out. Martha leaned over and looked down. 'All clear?' she said.

Dirk grabbed Hopkirk by the collar and dragged him to the safety of the driveway. 'Martha, we can just tie the rope from the lift around it and lower it down slowly with the pulley.'

'Nope,' said Martha, and pushed it out of the hole.

In reality the fall took less than a second but for Martha and Dirk it seemed to fall in graceful silence, turning as it plummeted, for a tense and elongated age. It collided with the ground and the plastic frame around the screen (which thankfully was already smashed on the treehouse floor) sprang off and flew towards the drive. Dirk grabbed Hopkirk and huddled over him. The frame soared over his arched back, causing his shirt to ripple, and lodged itself in the bush that ran alongside the driveway.

'You okay?' shouted Martha.

'Yes, but maybe let's not do that again.'

'Okay, sorry, Dirk.' She smiled guiltily. 'Was pretty cool though, right?'

Billy noticed the garage door was open when he came out of the house. He looked over to the treehouse. Dirk and Martha were just finishing up tying the television, which had indeed turned out to be in the garage, to the pulley rope. Hopkirk looked down at them from the entrance of the treehouse, panting. A long slither of drool hung from his open mouth and dripped to the floor, missing Dirk by an inch.

'What are you doing?' said Billy, joining them.

'Replacing your TV,' said Dirk.

'How's your mum?' said Martha.

'She's okay. You know what she's like. Worries too much.' Billy noticed the old TV by the wheelie bins at the end of the drive. 'How did you get it down?'

'Don't ask,' said Dirk.

'Anything I can do?' said Billy.

'Yeah, get up there and pull this thing up,' said Martha.

They got the new TV into the treehouse and put it where the old one had been. It was much smaller than the old beast of a telly but it would do. Martha had swept up the glass and tidied the place up.

'Wow, you guys work fast,' said Billy.

'It was all her,' said Dirk.

'Fucking Wonder Woman, right here,' said Martha, puffing her chest up and striking a pose.

Billy caught himself looking at her body and turned away. He picked up the console and looked at it. 'You already fixed it?' he said, glancing at Dirk.

'No. There was nothing wrong with it,' said Dirk.

'That's impossible, it had completely come apart. The cartridge was cracked.'

'It wasn't. It was sat in the grass just as it is. Not even a grass stain.'

'We shouldn't do this,' said Billy.

'Come on, I've worked too hard getting that fucking thing up here to not play it,' said Martha, gesturing at the television which was now turned on.

The screen was displaying a snowfall of static, echoes from the big bang, or so they had been told in school.

Billy stared at the blackness of the game cartridge. It was so dark you almost couldn't see the shape of it. It was just a flat rectangle cut out of the foreground. It made him feel sick.

'It's evil,' said Billy, without thinking about what he was saying.

'That's a bit dramatic,' said Martha. 'Give it here.'

She took it off him and felt an icy shiver run up her arms. She dropped the console on the floor and stepped back from it. 'What the hell was that?' she said, shaking her arms. The coldness moved back down to her finger tips and disappeared.

'What happened?' said Dirk.

Martha stared at it. 'I don't know,' she said. 'It just, I don't know. It made me cold.'

'I told you, we shouldn't do this,' said Billy.

'It's just a fucking game!' shouted Martha. 'This is stupid.' But she couldn't bring herself to pick it up again.

'Fine, you want to do this, we'll do it,' said Billy and he picked up the console and took it to the television.

Martha watched him, a look on her face like Billy was about to put a wet knife into a toaster, but she said nothing.

Billy messed with the wires, got them plugged in, and set up the TV. Nobody said a word.

It was insane to think anything was going to happen. It was a bright day in the middle of the summer holidays. Hauntings don't really happen, especially not when it's so bright out. Ghouls only come out at night, right? And besides, ghosts weren't real, and if they were they didn't make computer games.

He turned on the game but this time, instead of going straight into the game, the name input screen came up. It said, **PLAYER TWO: ENTER NAME**, and there was the QWERTY keyboard and the flashing underscore _.

'How does it know there's a player two?' said Martha.

'I don't know. And the controller isn't working anyway,' said Billy, pressing all the buttons.

Dirk looked in the box the console came in and found two more controllers in there.

Billy frowned. 'They definitely weren't in there before,' he said.

'Well, they are now,' said Dirk. 'Do you want to plug them in?'

Billy shrugged. He didn't want to. Not really. But he knew that he would. This whole thing felt inevitable. He plugged in the controllers and gave one each to Martha and Dirk.

They all used the same names in games. Billy always used BRAIN. Martha always used MIRTH and Dirk always used DARK, which Martha and Billy found funny.

'Why DARK?' Martha had once asked him.

'Because it's better than DORK,' Dirk had said.

Martha entered her gamer name, MIRTH, and pressed the start button. The screen went away and the same screen popped up. **PLAYER THREE: ENTER NAME**.

Dirk entered his name, DARK, and pressed start. The screen faded away and the game started.

'Are you shitting me?' said Martha.

On the television was a top-down view of the treehouse. In the top left corner of the screen was a hangman game with the first letter filled in. The letter J and then three blank spaces. In the treehouse were the characters of MIRTH, BRAIN, and DARK. Hopkirk was there too, a pixelated Saint Bernard with a barrel around his neck. Martha looked down at Hopkirk. The dog was huddled up against her, sat on his own tail, visibly shaking. He looked up at her with big wet eyes.

Martha looked down at her clothes and back up at the screen. 'We're dressed the same.' She said, and looked at Dirk and Billy and at their doppelgangers in the game. 'It's us. Exactly as we are now,' she said.

'I don't want to do this,' said Dirk.

'So turn it off,' said Billy, knowing it would probably be impossible.

Dirk leaned forward and flicked the switch. Nothing happened.

'Let's just do this,' said Billy. 'You wanted to do it, so we're going to do it.'

No one did anything for a moment. They just sat there in silence staring at the screen. Thoughts were running through Martha's mind, trying to find a rational explanation. Nothing came to her other than the thought that whatever was going on she'll be the last person foolish enough to be afraid of a game. She held her controller firmly and moved MIRTH to the entrance of the treehouse. The screen faded to black and reloaded in the garden. BRAIN, MIRTH, DARK, and HOPKIRK stood in a group in the garden next to the tree.

Billy and Dirk turned their heads and looked at her. She shrugged. 'If it wants us to play we'll play. Where's the map?'

Billy opened his backpack and pulled the manual out. He opened it and laid it out on the floor.

'Where's the next X?' said Martha.

'The old factory,' said Billy, pointing at the mark on the map.

'Okay,' said Martha. 'Let's go.'

CHAPTER 16

A mist crawled low over Bodmin Moor in Cornwall like a cloud too tired to stay up. The sky was bright blue but the ground was wet. The Jamaica Inn was quiet. It was an old building. Once it played host to smugglers, now it was a tourist trap. It was famous for its ghosts and for Daphne Du Maurier, who wrote a novel with the same name as the Inn. A plaque on the floor in the bar marked the spot of an infamous murder. In room three, William Rain had his head in a toilet.

He coughed and his stomach tightened. His mouth yawed open and thin acidic bile ran off his tongue. He spat into the puke filled bowl and pulled the flush. He closed his eyes and the room span around. If he had been standing he would have fallen. He had already fallen once this morning and landed badly on the side of the bath. He opened his eyes and grabbed onto the sink to pull himself up, one arm held tightly around his ribs. He swilled some mouthwash around his mouth and gargled it. It didn't make much of a difference to the taste but it helped a bit. The feeling in the back of his throat that made him want to dry heave was gone.

A shower would fix him. He turned and looked at the bath. It had broken glass in it.

'Alright,' he said. 'Maybe later.'

It was no surprise there was broken glass in there. He couldn't remember how it got there but it wouldn't take too much imagination to figure it out. Some drunken accident. Maybe he fell last night too.

He blinked and a memory caught him for a second. A hangman game on his mobile phone, but the memory was gone just as fast as it was formed.

He turned around and limped into the bedroom. The room was nice, or it had been, right now it was a bad mess. The bed was unmade. The duvet was, well who knows where that was, it wasn't on the bed that was for sure. The ashtray on the bedside table was overflowing. He stared at it. His mind wandered and he imagined himself in a barren wasteland, walking forever through the ashes, no trees to shield him from the hard acid rain.

He snapped out of it.

There was a television hung on the wall at the end of the bed. Under it was a dresser cabinet that was powdery from a baggie of cocaine that he had pulled open a bit too hard. A cloud of the drug puffed up from the split bag and settled evenly. Some of it on him, most of it on the cabinet. That was right before he started throwing up. William looked at the chair in the corner. It was still dripping from that first gush of vomit. The sight of it made his stomach turn. Luckily there was nothing left to come out.

He walked over to the French doors, carefully avoiding the bottles on the floor, and slid them open. He stepped out into the humid morning air. The duvet from the bed was damp on the wooden patio floor. Empty beer cans were on and around it. There was a plate on the duvet too, with a half-eaten roast dinner, now stale and hard.

Still holding his ribs with his right hand he awkwardly withdrew a packet of cigarettes from his pocket. He shook a cigarette out, letting the pack fall to the floor, and put it in his mouth. He found his lighter in his left pocket and lit up. He stood there, watching the cars on the road about half a mile away, beyond the moors directly outside the inn. They drove with their fog lights on, carefully slowing down when other cars approached coming the other way.

Just let them crash, William thought. That would wake him up. Nothing gets you going like witnessing a head on collision. No, changing his mind, drive safe. I'm not that guy.

He finished the cigarette and flicked it onto the grass.

I should sleep, he thought, but then remembered that he couldn't. There wasn't time. He had to be somewhere. He frowned and went back into the room. He looked around and then got on the floor and looked under the bed. His Motorola phone was halfway under. He reached and his fingertips touched the flip-phone. It was tacky, like it had a thin coating of syrup on it. He flinched at the sensation and then reached further and grabbed it.

Still kneeling on the ground he looked at the device. It was completely covered in something dark and red. He shivered and a memory from the night before filled his vision, of blood seeping out of the seams of his phone. But before that there had been a hangman game with four empty spaces. He got the word right with his first guess. JACK. He remembered staring at that name, a feeling of horror falling over him. A coldness ran through his bones and his skin goose pimpled. The phone started to feel heavy in his palm and dark red blood started to bead along the edges of the screen and then covered it entirely. The blood had come slow at first but then faster until it was cascading over his hands.

William came out of the memory and carefully opened the phone. It was tacky with dry blood. He wiped the screen clean with his thumb but the phone was dead. He tried switching it on but it didn't work.

He dropped the phone. Another memory was triggered and he looked at the hotel phone on the bedside table. He had called someone. There was a red handprint on the receiver.

Walter. He had called Walter. The phone had rung a few times and then Walter answered and just started ranting about some documentary. William hadn't had a chance to speak. He remembered Walter cursing the name Jack Matterson and then William had hung up. Yes, that was it.

Wanting to move away from the memory he stepped backwards and slipped on an empty wine bottle. He fell and landed hard on his elbow.

'Ah, fucking fuck!' he shouted, and kicked the bottle into the wall. The bottle didn't smash. It just bounced off and landed on the floor where it span a few times and stopped.

The bottle was pointing towards the door.

'Yeah, I think you might be right,' said William. 'It's time to get the fuck out of here.'

He looked at the bottle like it might answer and then stood up, using the bed to help his ascent.

He had been holed up in this room for too long now. Hiding, or running away, he didn't really know what he was doing there. One day he just had to get out of Shelley Town. Chased out by his own bad conscience. He had locked himself in a dark box, shut in by alcohol and drugs.

He found his shoes and put them on, not tying the laces. He shrugged his coat over his shoulders and held his ribs and torso tight. One arm holding the pain from his ribs, the other keeping his stomach still. He walked out onto the moors and headed for the road.

CHAPTER 17

Ryman pulled a box out of the archive room and judged it to be half full, by the weight of it. He carried it through the station where there was a bank of six desks. His office was on the other side of the room. He saw by the log on the box that it had been taken out recently.

'Who's been looking through this?' he said, to the only other person in the department. A constable named Arnold Sky.

'What is it?'

'Files on a guy called Jack Matterson, you know anything about it?'

'I take it you saw the documentary last night? Some journalist was digging through it a few months ago. I had no idea it had anything to do with the WWAP lot.'

Ryman nodded but didn't bother carrying on with the conversation. He often didn't. Conversing with people on the verge of gossip was a waste of time. Especially people like Arnold Sky. He carried the box to his office and closed the door behind him.

There was a cup of coffee on his desk and a chicken wrap he had made at home that morning. He had already cleared a spot for the box. He put it down. He had a bite of the wrap and dropped it back on the desk. He opened the box and took out everything that was in there. Pushed the box onto the floor and dumped the files where it had been.

He opened the first file. It was all about the death of Jack Matterson's parents. The interviews mostly focused on Jack's reaction to the tragedy. His parents had died of monoxide poisoning due to a faulty gas heater in the basement. The kid had been found a few days later, a bit messed up, but he was a screwy kid anyway. There was a document from a psychiatrist that suggested the boy might have Asperger syndrome which explained his unusual behaviour, and besides, no one acts normal when faced with the lifeless corpses of their parents.

They put his unwillingness to cooperate down to the mild autism that was his Asperger's. His inability to maintain eye contact, and his obsessiveness about small and unimportant minutia of the current bit of computer hardware he had been tinkering with around the time of their death.

He was given counselling but only attended two sessions which proved unproductive but the diagnoses of Asperger's was confirmed.

The second file was thin and contained just a few documents regarding the death of Jack's fiancée during child birth. A psych analysis judged that Jack was fit to parent the child alone. These things always did. Social will never take a kid unless there was abuse involved and the child was too young for that to have happened. You have to be really mentally deficient to lose custody of a kid just because the mother is dead.

The next file was much bigger. In 1992 Jack Matterson and his daughter, Sarah, vanished. He had last been seen with William Rain. This was before that name was famous and the interview was short. There was no suspicion of murder or wrongdoing. William had worked with Jack in solving a fiddly bit of code in a game they had been working on, or so William said. He said Jack had been talking about moving to America to find work in the quickly growing tech industry in California.

Also in the file were copies of two plane tickets with Jack and Sarah's names on them.

The next page had a passenger list from the flight which showed that they hadn't boarded.

There was a big question mark made in a red ballpoint pen that had evidently been made by the investigating officer at the time. Or maybe it was the journalist, if she was incompetent enough to mark a police file.

The investigation went down a few dead ends and then just petered out. No conclusion. His bank account hadn't been used. He hadn't showed up anywhere. The case was picked up a few times with bits of evidence that went nowhere. The case remains unsolved. The name William Rain cropped up again in 1993. By then his name would have been known across the country. The others were interviewed too but they told the same story. He was a local guy who knew a bit about coding and helped out on some of the tricky stuff. They met at their kid's nursery. When he vanished they didn't find it particularly out of character. The good natured local police kept quiet about the link to a missing person partly out of respect but mostly because there was nothing to connect them to his disappearance other than the fact they had known him.

Ryman's coffee had gone cold. He took a sip and spat it back into the cup. He left his office to fill it back up again.

Constable Sky was sitting cross-legged on his desk. He was holding a copy of The Sun newspaper. He saw Ryman and started reading aloud.

'WWAP happened to Jack Matterson?' he said, reading the headline. He laughed. 'Tell me that's not the worst pun you've ever heard?'

'Shut up, Sky,' said Ryman. 'Get off your desk.'

Sky got off the desk and followed Ryman to the kitchen. 'Have you read this shit?'

'No. And I don't intend to. That's not journalism, it's a comic book at best.'

'Why don't they just phone us and ask?' said Sky.

'They did. I just didn't give any comment.'

'Oh yeah, "local police refused to comment", that's you then?'

Ryman ignored him and poured his cold coffee down the sink.

'Make me one, Ryman,' said Sky.

Ryman took a mug off the draining board and put it next to his. He filled them both up from the jug and put sugar in his own. He took the half pint of milk out of the fridge and topped up both cups. He took his and walked out of the kitchen. Sky picked up his cup and said, 'Cheers,' absently while reading the last paragraph of the article.

'What's the plan then?' he said, dropping the newspaper in the bin and following Ryman out.

'I'm going to go talk to them, unofficially. See if I can gleam anything important. There's something strange about all this but from what I can tell this Jack Matterson was a strange guy. I'll take a look at the Matterson house too. You ever been there?'

'Have I fuck,' said Sky. He was only twenty and his childhood memories of stories about the place being haunted still held some weight.

CHAPTER 18

Pete pulled up outside Walter's house and turned off the engine. Walter opened his front door.

'Hey, Pete,' he said.

'Walt,' said Pete, locking the minibus.

'Why do you drive that thing?' said Walter, letting Pete pass.

'Plenty of room for the kids. Shoe's off?'

'Yeah, or Penny will bite your head off. You only have one kid. She doesn't need eleven seats.'

'Tell *her* that. It was her idea to buy it. That was the deal, you know? We wanted to move to a caravan, in return she would get to choose the family car. To be honest I thought she was going to choose some stupid sports car. But she didn't. She thought about it a while and came up with that thing. She could give you a thousand reasons why an eleven seater minibus is the best vehicle in the world. She's a hell of a persuader. And she's always right. Hey, Penny.'

'Hey Pete, where's Amelia?' said Penny.

'She got out down the road, she'll be here in a minute.'

'Will she want a coffee?'

'Probably.'

'I don't need to ask *you* do I?'

'Nope,' said Pete.

'Two spoons of coffee and three sugars?'

'Yes please, Penny.'

'Fucking hell Pete, that shit will give you a heart attack,' said Walter.

Pete shrugged. 'And if that happens I'll go down to two sugars.'

Amelia knocked on the door and let herself in. 'I picked up some bits from the bakery,' she said, holding up a bag stuffed with pastries and cakes wrapped in paper.

'Coffee, Amelia?' said Penny.

'Yes please, Penny.'

Penny took the bag of cakes off Amelia and took them into the kitchen. Amelia had her coffee black. Penny didn't need to ask. That was one of those bits of trivia that everyone knew about WWAP. The main character in the game got a health boost when he drank a cup of black coffee. When asked why in interviews they said it was because Amelia drank about fifteen cups of the stuff a day. That wasn't true now, she only had about three, but she still had it black.

'Come on, we'll go out to the garden,' said Walter.

Walter had installed an American themed bar in his back garden. The bar had working beer pumps with a cooling system. There were optics along the back wall fully stocked with whisky, vodka, and gin.

This morning though there was a wooden shutter over the bar, padlocked shut. There was a fire pit that also served as a barbecue to the left of the bar which had a low wooden bench curved around it.

There were two pub benches side by side in front of the bar with a huge canvas umbrella between them that was wide enough to provide shade for both when it was hot.

Walter sat down at one of the benches and Pete and Amelia came and sat opposite him. Penny came out with coffee and then ran back inside and came back out with the cakes and pastries arranged on a plate.

'You don't know anything about the documentary then?' said Walter.

'Only what you told me. Should we be worried?' said Pete.

Walter shrugged. 'Who knows? I can't say it hasn't gotten to me. I was hoping that was all behind us.'

'Where's William now?' said Amelia.

'God knows,' said Pete.

'He called me last night but sounded pretty out of it,' said Walter.

'Out of it how?' said Pete.

'Out of it like he used to be.'

'Is he using again?' said Penny, remembering a particularly dark time after the success had brought wealth into their lives and William had gone off the rails.

'I think he's been like it for a few months,' said Walter.

'I heard he was in London having meetings with a publisher about doing an autobiography,' said Amelia.

'I think that might have been a front. I checked the area code he called from. He's in Cornwall.'

'What's he doing there?' said Penny.

'I imagine he's getting shitfaced and not much else,' said Walter.

Walter picked up one of the pastries with the idea to eat it but found he had no appetite and put it back down.

'So what about this documentary do we need to know?' said Pete.

'It didn't have much to say really. Some hard core gaming nerd-'

'Let me stop you there,' said Amelia, 'We are all hard core gaming nerds, are we not?'

'I wasn't being derogatory. That's what he was. This guy was digging around the coding of that game Jack made before we met him-'

'How the hell did they find that?' said Pete.

'Everything is on the internet these days, Pete, fucking everything. It was in a collection of ROMS for an emulator. Anyway, the game was good and had some similarities with our game so he checked it out. As you know programmers have a sort of fingerprint. Just like if you found a book with no cover by your favourite author you would recognise the style, you know?'

'Of course we know, come on Walter, get on with it,' said Pete.

'So he thought he had an early unknown game by us on his hands and got excited. When he looked into it he found out it was by Jack, and where did Jack live? Shelley Town. And voilà, conspiracy. So they look into Jack, find out he mysteriously disappeared and the conspiracy deepens. That's about the bulk of it. You can bet people will be asking questions. A lot of fucking questions.'

Everyone nodded at that.

'So what do we say?' said Pete.

'The truth,' said Walter.

'Not a fucking chance,' said Amelia.

'I don't mean the whole truth. We tell the truth up to the point where he disappeared. We just keep to the truth we've always told to the police. We knew him, he helped out, and that was it.'

'That's not the truth though is it?' said Penny.

'It's truth enough,' said Walter, glowering at his wife.

CHAPTER 19

MIRTH, BRAIN, and DARK, (and the computer-generated Hopkirk) arrived at the old factory. A pixelated sun hung in the sky. There was an X hovering over a spot around the side of the building. BRAIN walked up to it and started digging. There was a CHA-CHING sound and the letter **A** popped up and floated to the top left side of the screen. The second letter of the hangman game was filled in with two spaces left.

'We should go there,' said Martha. Dirk and Billy looked at her. 'We should go there and dig,' she said. 'Maybe that's what this is all about.'

Dirk looked at the map. 'There's two other X's. What do you think the word is?'

Martha shrugged. 'Jack? What else can it be?'

'Jazz?' suggested Dirk.

'Jamm,' said Billy.

'Jam only has three letters,' said Martha.

'What do you think we'll find if we go there?' said Billy.

'Maybe it's buried treasure,' said Dirk, but without the enthusiasm you would expect from a kid with his hands on a treasure map.

'Probably nothing. What harm could come from looking?'

said Martha.

'Maybe some psycho buried landmines there,' said Billy.

Martha laughed. 'But maybe it *is* treasure. Imagine that.'

'Should we keep playing?' said Billy, and pressed left on his controller to start the journey to the next X on the map. There was a noise like a whip cracking and a spark flashed between his hands. He dropped the gamepad and scrambled to his feet. 'Shit, it burnt me.'

Everything went dark, as if a light had been turned off. The treehouse became a black box in the middle of the day. Martha and Dirk dropped their controllers and stood up. Thin wisps of smoke floated up from Billy's gamepad on the floor. A painfully loud feedback loop started screeching from the speakers and the screen started flashing violently.

'What's happening?' said Dirk, stepping backwards.

Billy raised his hands and looked at the scorch marks on his palms. Martha turned and watched as Dirk edged backwards towards the entrance of the treehouse.

His face was twisted with fear. He was staring into the flashing screen. The strobing effect made every movement staccato, like film slowing down. Like every second frame had been spliced out.

Hopkirk started barking at the television. It was like there were a hundred paparazzi taking pictures with flash bulbs.

FLASH A freeze frame of Hopkirk with his mouth open, drool flung forward, a bark between pictures. FLASH His mouth closed, his ears thrown up. Another bark. FLASH His face in a snarl.

Billy staring at his hands. FLASH FLASH FLASH Billy's hands halfway back down, his head turned to face Dirk.

FLASH Martha in a sprinters starting position. FLASH She's halfway to Dirk.

FLASH FLASH FLASH Dirk's left foot steps off the breach.

FLASH FLASH Martha's hand outstretched, her body diving towards him.

FLASH Dirk's foot discovering the thin air outside, the shock of the fall revealing itself on his face.

FLASH FLASH Martha thumping into the treehouse floor, her arm reaching over the edge, Dirk's hair blown forward, his back arched, his arms grabbing to find purchase.

FLASH Hopkirk, with his mouth wide open, teeth showing, ears back, launching towards the entrance.

FLASH FLASH Billy is halfway to the door.

FLASH FLASH. Billy on top of Martha, reaching out of the treehouse.

FLASH Hopkirk suspended over them, mid leap.

FLASH FLASH FLASH FLASH The impact of a body hitting the floor with a yelp.

'Hopkirk!' shouted Martha, two hands clasped around Dirk's ankle.

Dirk was tangled in the rope lift. Billy grabbed onto his other leg and stared down at Hopirk. 'Shit. You okay, Dirk?'

'Not really,' Dirk groaned.

'Pull him in here quickly,' said Martha.

They pulled him into the treehouse by his feet, the rope feeding through the pulley, keeping his upper half supported.

The television had stopped flashing and it was light again inside. As soon as Dirk was in, Martha climbed down the ladder to Hopkirk. She leaned over him and put her arms under his body.

'Oh thank God, he's alive,' she cried.

She picked the dog up and sat him on her lap. She checked his legs and ribs but there seemed to be no breaks. He got his breath back and life came back to his eyes. Martha held him tight and massaged him around the neck and ears. She put him down to see if he could walk and he fell over. He got up and walked slowly and with a limp on his back left leg. Maybe he broke something after all.

'Dirk! What were you thinking?' she shouted up to the treehouse.

'I don't know, I'm sorry,' said Dirk. His whole body was trembling.

Billy grabbed the map off the floor and stuffed it in his backpack. 'Come on,' he said.

'It wasn't my fault,' said Dirk. 'I didn't mean to fall out and I didn't mean for Hopkirk to jump out after me.'

'I know,' said Martha. 'What the hell happened up there? Can you explain it?' she turned to Billy.

'No. I don't know what's happening. I mean, I don't know what happened. I don't know what's happening or what's going to happen. But now you've seen it. It's haunted, you see? Something's wrong with the game, or the house I got it from,' said Billy.

'Right, the Matterson house. And what was the name of the guy who lived there? You remember? Jack. Right? It was Jack Matterson. Him and his daughter disappeared. It was a big mystery and then everyone just forgot all about it. Nobody talks about it. Don't you think that's weird? The house just sits there and no one even looks at it,' said Martha.

'So what do you want to do?' said Billy. 'You still want to dig?'

'Yes,' said Dirk.

'Wow, look at you all brave all of a sudden,' said Martha.

'Hey, there's no need for that,' said Billy. 'Everyone's scared, just cool down a bit.'

Martha almost replied with a series of screamed expletives but controlled herself. She let out a long breath and turned her attentions back to the dog. He was walking better now. He had shaken his head a few times, like he was trying to shake off circling stars or tweeting birds, like in an old cartoon. 'What do you say, Hopkirk. Wanna go digging?'

Hopkirk looked at her with his tongue hanging out. Clearly fine. Somehow he got lucky and only winded himself. Martha looked into those big wet eyes of his and saw Dirk reflected in them, standing behind her. She wasn't really mad at him. She was just scared, more scared than even they were, maybe. The truth is they were all about as scared as each other. They wanted to turn their backs on this whole thing and run away from it. But they knew they couldn't. They knew they had to see whatever this was through to the end. Sometimes the train you're on can't be derailed no matter how hard you try. You can delay it, sure, but you can't stop it. They knew that, not in thought, but in feeling. Deep in their bones.

'Alright, let's go there now then. Let's see what's buried,' said Martha.

They had loaded a shovel onto the back of the Dirkmobile and set off towards the old church that was now the town's exhibition centre. Billy rode his bike, towing Dirk behind him, and Martha rode with Hopkirk keeping up the pace beside her. They got to the church and hid their bikes around the side of the vicarage. There were a few people coming in and out of the church carrying stuff in and setting things up.

A lorry was parked up by the entrance. The tail-lift was down and a man was struggling to rock an arcade machine forward enough to get a sack truck under it. The machine rocked back towards him and almost reached its tipping point. Another guy came out of the church and ran to help him. They got the thing steady and shunted it onto a sack truck and the two of them leaned it back and wheeled it safely inside. This small show was enough to draw the gaze of the few other people milling around and allowed Martha, Billy, and Dirk to sneak past unseen.

Now they stood at the back of the vicarage. Billy had the map open in front of him. Hopkirk was sniffing at the ground.

'It should be right here,' said Billy.

'So, who's going to dig?' said Martha.

Billy looked at Dirk and Dirk shook his head. No way was that going to happen. Billy folded the map and put it in his back pocket. He picked up the shovel and shoved it into the ground. He put his right foot on the spade and pushed down. He dug for a while, the others not saying anything, and then he stopped.

'I think I found something,' he said.

He dropped the shovel on the floor and moved some dirt with his hands.

'It's a shoe box,' he said.

'So pull it out,' said Martha.

Billy leaned forward and pulled the box out of the dirt. He stood up with it and turned to face Martha and Dirk. Hopkirk, still limping a touch, walked behind Martha's leg and growled, low and deep.

'Do we open it here, or what?' said Billy.

'Open it now,' said Martha.

'I don't feel like there's going to be any treasure in there,' said Dirk.

Billy looked at Dirk and then down at the box. He swallowed and carefully removed the lid. Inside was a folded over piece of thin paper. The kind of paper you get in shoe boxes. There were four black spots on the paper. They looked like ink blotches, or spreading mould.

'Maybe it's shoes?' said Dirk.

Billy pulled the paper back and they all gasped. He dropped the box and what was inside fell out. Fingers touched Billy's foot and he lurched away. The thing on the floor, the rotting dead object that had lolled out of the shoebox, was a decaying human hand.

CHAPTER 20

DCI Ryman pressed the doorbell and looked up at the treehouse in the garden. Man, he wished he had one like that when he was kid. He didn't even have his own room when he was a boy, let alone a thing like that.

The letterbox clattered causing Ryman to jump, not enough to scare him but enough to put all his senses on high alert for a moment. A woman's voice came out of the slot. He noticed the fingers holding the flap open, with perfectly painted pink nails.

'Who is it?' said the voice.

'Mrs Eunice Rain? It's DCI Ryman.'

She paused, not replying. The letterbox closed softly. He heard the catch go and then the door handle moved down. The door clicked open and Eunice Rain stood before him. A thing of pure beauty. A single throb echoed through his groin. It was an unintentional reaction but it was completely unavoidable too. She was wearing only a laced nightie and her figure was extraordinary.

'I'm a, excuse me, I,' Ryman never found expressing thoughts a particular challenge but the words just wouldn't come. 'Is your husband home?' he flushed. 'You can put something on if you like Mrs Rain?'

She smiled and her eyes ran all over him. He was overweight, sweaty, and unshaved. 'What do you want officer?' she said.

'Is William home? I need to ask him a few questions.'

'No. I don't know where he is. He went on a business trip a few months ago and never came back. I don't think there ever was a business trip. The coward just left and couldn't tell me to my face. Billy doesn't know though,' she said, glancing up at the treehouse, assuming he was in there, 'You should come in so we can speak privately.'

Ryman nodded, agreeing, but thought he might have to fight this woman off. He wasn't about to get involved with the wife of William Rain. It would be like fucking Yoko Ono while John was still alive.

He followed her into the house. Eunice went straight to the living room and Ryman allowed himself a look at her. She walked like she had a bell on her hip. Her waist was slim and her ass was perfect. By the way the silk moved he could tell she had nothing on underneath. Her skin wasn't quite white, and wasn't quite tan either, it was that healthy shade of cream you don't often see. He imagined the fabric lifting up, just a bit.

He forced his imagination away from her and looked at the pictures on the wall in the hallway. Most were colour but some were black and white. They were photos of WWAP during various seminal moments of their career. There was one of all four of them, big grins, three sheets to the wind, and

Bill Murray (looking sober and tidy by comparison) to the right of them holding out a glass of champagne in a salute to the photographer. There was a photo of William shaking hands with Tony Blair. Another photo showed them on stage at Glastonbury in 1995 with Oasis. Pete was playing a guitar in step with Noel and the other three were singing into the microphone with Liam Gallagher. That was one hell of a decade for them, Ryman thought. He had forgotten just how famous the notorious residents had once been.

The last picture he came to was an older black and white photo. It was of a small room with three desks squeezed in. There were computer parts everywhere. There were drawings pinned to the wall of early character designs from the game that would one day make them famous. Amelia was there at a graphic design desk, hinged at a 45 degree angle, drawing something with great concentration (Big Ben with arms and legs). Pete was sat next to Walter at a computer. Pete had a pad in his hand and was pointing at the screen with a pencil. Walter was looking at the screen with his hand on the mouse. Beyond them William was sat in front of a computer but was looking beyond the monitor. He had a hand raised like he was in the middle of an argument with someone. At the edge of the photo, in William's eye line, was another person. It wasn't clear at first but there was definitely someone there. The edge of someone, just the shoulder and arm, the rest of him was out of shot. Ryman looked at the hand. It was wrapped in a bandage. He had seen that bandage before in a photo from a nursery in the documentary.

'Jack Matterson,' he said.

'Jack Matterson?' said Eunice, leaning against the wall next to the picture. 'Where'd you hear that name?'

Ryman looked at her. She was wearing a dressing gown now and had it wrapped up pretty good. Not even any cleavage on show. Probably for the best, he thought. Ryman pointed at the figure in the photograph. 'Right there,' he said.

Eunice looked at the arm and curled up her lip. She shrugged. 'Don't know. I wasn't there.'

Ryman ran an eye across all the pictures again. Eunice wasn't in any of them. 'Why aren't you in any of the pictures?' he asked.

'For the same reason Linda McCartney isn't in any of the Beatles pictures,' she said. 'I wasn't in the group. You hear to talk about Jack? Because I've got nothing to say about that. I wasn't there, I didn't know him. I don't know anything.'

'Anything about what?' said Ryman, probing.

'Him and his daughter disappearing. That's what happened, right? They vanished.'

Ryman nodded. 'That seems to be the gist of it.'

'Why are you bringing it up now?' she asked.

'Because of the documentary.'

'What documentary?'

'You didn't see it?' said Ryman. Of all people, he figured anyone close to WWAP would have been all over it.

'I don't really watch TV,' she said.

'What *do* you do?' he said.

'Not much. Kill time.'

'You know what they say about that. You can't kill time without injuring eternity. Who was it that said that? Henry Thoreau?'

'I don't know,' said Eunice, looking at him blankly. 'What does it mean?'

Ryman shrugged. 'I don't really know.'

Ryman looked at the picture again. It was no surprise that it was there. He already knew they had a connection. But something was wrong. It felt to him that if he could just find the right string to pull this whole thing would unravel.

'This is my favourite picture,' said Eunice, pointing to a colour photo of the four of WWAP being interviewed by Parkinson. 'I was standing off stage watching them. I think that was the day the nation fell in love with them all.'

The picture came to life for her. She was right there again, just off stage.

Parkinson waited for the applause to quiet down. Something William Rain and the rest encouraged for as long as possible by bowing several times. Eventually they took their seats and smiled at Parkinson.

'Well, that was quite an entrance. I guess there's no need to introduce you. I will anyway. WWAP, ladies and gentleman.' The applause started again and William stood up and did one quick bow and sat down again. The audience calmed down.

'So this game. I'm not much of a gamer myself but the nation seems to have really become obsessed by it. Their imaginations have been well and truly captured, wouldn't you say? You can't turn a corner without seeing a poster or a television advert, or some kid wearing a Doctor Hammer t-shirt. Kids are being sent home for wearing doctor's coats to school, can you believe that?'

'It's pretty crazy,' said William.

'Now, my first question, this Doctor Hammer, he's a doctor?'

'That's right,' said Walter.

'Why does he use a hammer?' Parkinson leaned back and put a finger to his chin.

'Why does Mario throw fireballs? He's a plumber,' said William.

'That's very true,' said Parkinson.

'Why does Doctor Who use a screwdriver?' said Walter. 'Maybe all doctors secretly harbour a desire to do handiwork.' There was a glint in Walter's eye. They all had it at that time. Like they were all grinning childishly at the same unspoken joke.

'I can't remember why we decided on a hammer, we just wanted to make a game that was fun to play,' said Pete.

'We were all a bit high, weren't we?' said William, looking at the others.

'I don't know what he's talking about,' said Walter. 'Don't believe anything he says.'

'Out of our heads,' said William.

'I suppose it would explain a few things. Now, I find this interesting, I've heard it said that Doctor Hammer was the first game that had a satirical premise. What do you say to that?'

'I don't know,' said Walter. 'People have speculated about the games meaning, we were just trying to make each other laugh, I think. I guess we were poking fun at the establishment a bit.'

Parkinson nodded and looked down at his notes. 'The final boss was Big Ben with robot arms and legs,' he looked back up at them. 'Are you telling me that didn't represent the government?'

William laughed. 'Maybe, I don't know.'

'Amelia, you haven't said much,' said Parkinson, raising an eyebrow.

'I just drew their ideas,' said Amelia, smiling at the others, her hands held together in her lap.

'I heard it was your idea to make the damsel in distress an eighty year old woman?'

'We were just breaking stereotypes,' she said, and suppressed a laugh. 'Plumbers and princesses, it's all nonsense. At least a doctor trying to save an old woman makes sense.'

'Yes, I suppose that's true. Well, I did have a go on it earlier, back stage-'

'Did you love it?' said William.

'I'll be honest, I haven't played too many games in my time. I managed to make the little man-'

'Doctor Hammer,' said William.

'Yes. He walked forwards a bit and then he fell down a hole.'

'Yeah, it's good to jump at that bit,' said Pete.

Parkinson laughed. 'So the game's been out for over a year now and it hasn't really budged from the number one spot. Are you planning to make a sequel?'

All of WWAP looked at each other waiting for someone else to answer. Walter took the helm. 'Probably not. It would be silly trying to compete with our own success.'

'Difficult second album,' said William.

'We're all working on other things,' said Pete.

'I have an art show coming up,' said Amelia.

'An art show, what kind of art, paintings?'

'Portraits,' said Amelia, with a shy smile.

William laughed. 'They're not portraits. She paints famous people's feet, like some kind of nutter.'

Amelia shrugged.

'Do you get people in to sit for that?' said Parkinson.

Amelia nodded.

'She had Joe Dolce in. Remember him? He did that song called Shaddap You Face,' said Pete.

'David Bowie let me paint his feet too,' said Amelia.

'Do you want to paint mine?' said Parkinson.

'Sure,' said Amelia.

'Alright, that's my evening planned. WWAP ladies and gentleman,' said Parkinson, standing up and gesturing to his guests.

The audience applauded and Parkinson shook hands with them all.

Eunice smiled and looked at Ryman. 'You want coffee?'

'Sure,' said Ryman.

'Take a seat in the lounge and I'll be right out. Sugar and milk?'

'Yeah, two sugars and a good inch of milk, thanks.'

Eunice smiled and walked to the kitchen. Ryman headed to the lounge. He caught a glimpse of Eunice as he walked past the open kitchen door. She was reaching up to the top shelf of an open cupboard. She was on tiptoes.

She was cute.

Ryman took a deep breath and carried on walking. It was hard to think around her. God, was he getting a crush? At his age? That's ridiculous.

When she came out with the coffee he avoided looking at her. He asked questions and got the same sort of answers as were given in the police record by the WWAP members. She didn't know much, and didn't seem too interested. Ryman looked at the window, at his coffee, at his notepad, anywhere other than at her. He didn't want to see her big blue eyes. He thought he might get sucked in. Thought his heart would crack in his chest. God, was he blushing? He felt like he was blushing. He asked everything he wanted to ask. He noticed his knee was bobbing up and down at one point. That was some kind of anxiety thing he hadn't done since he was a kid. Fidgety legs.

She was looking at him sort of strange. He was nervous. He knew that she knew he found her attractive. He had turned into a stammering teenage boy inside, struggling to find the words to talk to a pretty girl.

In the space of a brief encounter he had fallen in love with her. It was madness. Get a hold of yourself, man, he thought.

'Okay, I think I've got everything I need,' said Ryman, and he looked at her.

She smiled. His gut went. Nudging him. He ignored it.

CHAPTER 21

They stared at the thing on the floor. Dirk held his hands over his mouth to stop himself throwing up.

'That's disgusting,' he said, through his fingers.

'No points for guessing who's hand that is,' said Martha.

Billy looked at her. 'What do we do with it?'

'I don't know. I'm not sure I want to know what's buried in the other three places,' said Martha.

'We should call the police,' said Dirk.

'And tell them what?' said Martha. 'That we've got a haunted map that shows us where body parts are buried?'

'What do you think we should do?' said Billy.

'Feed it to the dog?' said Dirk.

Billy and Martha looked at him. His mind was darker than they ever gave him credit for. Hopkirk looked up at Dirk and took a few shuffling steps backwards. 'I think that answers your question,' said Martha. 'You sick fuck.'

Billy picked up the shovel and put the spade against the rotten hand. He looked around and found a short chunky stick. He used it to nudge the hand onto the shovel.

'Can you turn the box the right way up?' said Billy, looking at Martha.

She did and Billy dropped the hand into the box and closed the lid.

Billy loaded the shovel back onto the Dirkmobile. Dirk got in. Martha was on her bike watching. Hopkirk stood beside her. The shoebox was on the floor.

'You're going to have to hold it,' said Billy.

'No way! Are you kidding?' said Dirk.

'Where else am I going to put it?' Billy picked up the box. 'Just imagine it has a pair of trainers in it. Okay?'

Dirk closed his eyes tight and put his hands on his lap, palms up. He felt the box being placed on them. He felt the weight of it. Imagined the hand. Thought about the fingers moving by themselves, opening the lid, crawling out like a sick spider.

He thought he felt it move and he flinched. The box fell off his lap and got jammed between his legs. The lid opened a crack and a finger poked out. The nail was dull yellow and the skin was dark brown, almost black. Dirk jumped out of the trailer and started breathing rapidly.

'I... think... I'm... having... a... a...' he couldn't catch his breath.

Martha leapt off her bike and ran over to him. 'It's okay, just breathe.'

On the back of the Dirkmobile was a canvas pouch with a buckled flap. The Dirk survival kit. Billy opened it and took out a paper bag.

He ran over to Martha and gave her the bag. She put it into

Dirk's hand and ordered him to breathe into it.

He put it to his mouth and the bag inflated and deflated about as fast as it could without splitting.

'It's okay, Dirk,' said Martha, with warmth in her voice. 'Just breathe.'

Martha had an arm around Dirk. His breathing began to slow and soon he was calm.

'That hasn't happened in a while,' said Dirk. He took a deep breath. 'I can't do it. I'll just walk.'

'Okay, we'll go slow,' said Martha.

Billy watched. There was not much more he could do. He had learned a long time ago that Martha was best at relieving the panic attacks. If he got involved too it was too much for Dirk. It made him feel claustrophobic and prolonged things.

'Come on,' said Martha. 'Let's head back.'

Billy rode out front, the shoebox on the seat of the Dirkmobile. Dirk walked alongside Martha with Hopkirk on the other side. Dirk stared at the box the whole walk home.

They got to Billy's driveway just as DCI Ryman was leaving the house. They all stopped and looked at him.

'Thank you for the coffee, Mrs Rain. And listen, if you hear anything about this Jack Matterson do call me won't you? I wouldn't be surprised if you get some reporters down here before the gaming convention starts. And let me know if William shows up.'

'Okay. Hi guys,' said Eunice, waving at Billy and his friends.

Ryman turned around and saw the kids. 'Hey, enjoying the

summer break? Been digging?' he said, spotting the shovel covered with fresh dirt.

Martha shrugged. Billy and Dirk didn't say anything.

'I hear you're all getting involved with the convention this week?'

'A bit,' said Billy.

Ryman stepped off the door step and walked up to them. 'Everything okay?'

Dirk glanced at Martha.

'Everything's fine. We've just been playing in the woods,' she said.

'Looking for treasure,' said Dirk.

Ryman noticed the muddy shoebox in the back of the Dirkmobile. 'Looks like you found something too.'

And then something happened to Ryman, something that happened often. It was something he had learned to acknowledge. His gut went. Something like a single flap of a butterfly. It was a nudge. It said, *this is important Ryman, say what's on your mind.*

'I don't suppose the name Jack Matterson means anything to you kids?'

Billy looked at Martha and she ever so slightly shook her head.

Billy got off the bike and walked around to the Dirkmobile and picked up the shoebox. Martha and Dirk stared at him.

Billy looked down at the box and opened it.

'I think this might be his,' he said.

They sat around the kitchen table with the muddy shoebox on a newspaper to save the tablecloth from getting dirty. Eunice sat quietly during the whole thing. Ryman listened carefully while Billy gave an edited version of events. Sometimes Dirk and Martha added something but Billy took the reins back quickly when they did. He didn't mention any ghost stuff. He said he found a map in the front garden of the Matterson house and said they decided to see what was there. He didn't mention the game. He didn't mention Mario attacking Dirk. He didn't mention the dark figure at the railway tracks.

By the afternoon, clouds had started to appear in the sky. By evening, flashes of lightning lit them up. Thunder rolled over like a slow bowling ball. Police tape had been put up around the four areas where the Xs were on the map and forensic teams were excavating. Ryman stood back, supervising, with Arnold standing next to him holding up an umbrella. Rain pelted down on them.

They watched patiently as Scene of Crime Officers in white forensic overalls dug up the fourth and last location. The dirt had turned to mud and it sloshed off the shovels and ran back into the hole. It went like that in England. Too many days of good summer and you were punished with a storm.

Martha, Billy, and Dirk stood in the street opposite the Matterson house, where the fourth X was, and watched the team of officers lift a box out of a hole they had dug in the front garden. It was much larger than the shoe box. Big enough to fit a whole torso in, Billy thought.

'Do you think we did the right thing?' said Billy.

'*We* didn't do anything,' said Martha, and thought for a moment. 'But probably, yes. What else could we have done?'

'Do we have to stand here and watch this?' said Dirk. 'I'm getting soaked.'

Hopkirk looked up at Martha, as if to second Dirk's point. He was trembling and water dripped from his sodden coat.

'Come on, let's go back to mine,' she said.

'I'm going to go home,' said Billy.

'Yeah, me too,' said Dirk. 'I haven't eaten yet and I think I just want to sleep.'

'Alright, I guess that's probably best, right? Tomorrow?' she said, and she had a look in her eyes that Billy hadn't seen before. She didn't want to be left alone. She was afraid.

'Do you want me to come with you?' said Billy. But he didn't want to. Not really. He was exhausted and felt like this thing was over now. The police had the ball and they could retire off the court and forget the whole thing.

Martha saw the slack in Billy's shoulders, the unwillingness in his eyes that contradicted his words, she could read his body language. He was just being kind, and there was nothing wrong with that. As lies go it's the kindest of them all. She was almost selfish in that moment. She wanted to tell him yes. She knew that he would be able to comfort her, just by being there. But her nature got the better of her and she answered him and not his words.

'It's okay, you go. You must be knackered, right?'

'You could say that,' said Billy.

'Snoogle Fargle,' said Martha, without the posture or the pulled face.

Billy smiled. 'Blarble Garble,' he said, in just as serious a tone.

Martha turned away and Hopkirk walked a few feet ahead of her. Dogs don't need to be told what the plan is. It was home time so that was where he would walk, unless instructed otherwise.

'Sheeble Shmarble,' said Dirk.

'Bye Dirk,' said Martha, and she walked through the square after the dog.

CHAPTER 22

William Rain still clutched his ribs with his right arm and his stomach with his left. He had been walking for, who knows how long, two hours? Five hours? It could have been a week, his feet sure felt like it. But he can't have gotten that far, the scenery hadn't changed much. If there's one thing to be said about the moors it's that there's a fucking lot of it and it all looks the same. He looked around. Maybe this wasn't even the moors anymore.

The fog had cleared and the heat from the sun felt like how old spaghetti westerns looked. The thirst! Man, had he ever been so thirsty? He should have planned the trip better. Got some walking boots and a pack. Or a car, or a bike, or a taxi. But no. He had to walk. He had to be straight when he got there. Walk it off. That's the key thing. He had left everything at the Inn, even his wallet. It was too late to turn back by the time he had realised.

He stopped in to a petrol station to get some water and only realised he couldn't pay when he got to the till. He left the drink there and went and drank from the tap in the gents. It was a few hours before he got to the next petrol station and this time he made the decision to steal. He made that decision slowly but by the time those automatic doors slid open he was resolute.

The drinks were in the aisle right in front of the entrance, next to the sandwiches. No one was around. No attendant, no customers. Just him. He got lucky. He grabbed a bottle of water and a sandwich at random and walked right back out. It was easy. He looked back over his shoulder when he was a few hundred yards down the road and watched a car drive into the forecourt and stop at a pump. No one was chasing him.

He kept walking until he reached a turn in the road and the petrol station was out of sight. He sat on the grass verge and ate his sandwich and drank the water. He kept hold of the bottle figuring he could top it up in the toilets at the next services.

The evening came and clouds formed overhead. Rain started to fall. He came to a village and stopped in a bus shelter. In time a bus came. It hissed to a stop and the doors opened.

'You getting in?' said the driver.

William shook his head.

'That's not a bed mate, get a job,' said the driver.

William got up. He walked on. He came to a pub and went in.

'I need a room,' he said, when he got to the bar.

'We're not a hotel,' said the barman. 'You buying a drink?'

'Can you stick it on a tab?' said William.

'You got money?' said the barman.

William didn't say anything.

'If you're not buying anything you can't just take up room at the bar.'

'I'm not homeless,' said William.

'I didn't say you were buddy, but if you're not buying we've got nothing for you.'

'Can you fill this up?' said William, putting his bottle on the bar.

'Sure,' said the barman, and filled it up with tap water.

'Thanks,' said William.

The barman looked at him. 'You having a bad day?'

William shrugged. 'I need to be somewhere. All I've got is my feet and this bottle. It's a long walk.'

'Where are you heading?'

'Shelley Town.'

'Fucking hell, mate, you're not kidding. There's still not much I can do for you.'

'I just need to sleep for an hour or so, get my strength back, you know?'

'I'm sorry, man, that doesn't change the fact that this isn't a hotel. I've got no beds.'

'Can I sit here until the rain stops?'

The barman sighed. 'Sure. I guess there's no harm in it. You don't seem like the type to cause trouble.'

'I'm not,' said William. 'Thank you.'

People came to the bar and ordered drinks. A couple of loud drunk girls. Then a gobby twenty year old lad. 'Oi mate, give us a beer and two Jägerbombs. What crisps have you got?

No cheese and onion? What kind of pub is this? Alright just the drinks, how much is that? You're havin' a laugh, I thought it was two for a fiver? It's still happy hour now. Come on mate, it was like two minutes ago. Alright, whatever you say. Here, keep the change. Fucking prick.'

'And you were worried about *me*?' said William, when the lout was out of the way.

'The booze makes them that way. There's a prick to profit ratio. The more alcohol they buy, the more money I make, and the more of a prick they become. It's knowing when to cut them off. That's the key.'

'You're like Frankenstein to their monster.'

'It's aliiiive!' said the barman, jokingly.

'It's druuuunk!' said William, in return.

'Here, what's your drink? You can have one on me.'

'You've changed your tone,' said William.

'Well, some homeless looking guy comes in and you automatically assume he's on something, or after something. You know how it is. You seem honest enough.'

'And now you're offering me a free drink. Maybe I was playing the long game.'

'That's a good point. Maybe I should kick you out after all? What will you have?'

'What's the cheapest beer you've got?'

'Don't worry about that, they're my taps. What's your drink?'

William looked at the pumps. 'An IPA would be good.'

The barman pulled the ale and put the glass on a beer mat

in front of William.

'So why are you walking all the way to Shelley Town?'

William put his hands around the beer and looked into the foamy head. He imagined himself curling up and falling asleep on those soft bubbles. He closed his eyes and put the glass to his lips. He sunk back a quarter of the pint and put the glass down again.

'I'm talking at a convention on Saturday.'

'Oh right, a convention huh? What kind of convention?'

'A gaming convention,' said William.

'Really? You don't strike me as a gamer,' said the barman, looking at William.

William thought for a moment. 'The truth is, my phone started bleeding and I had a terrible feeling that if I didn't get back soon something bad was going to happen to the people I love the most. Or maybe it was just a bad hallucination. I mean, I have been doing a lot of drugs recently. You know what else, I think someone I killed a decade ago is haunting me.' But he didn't say any of that. How could he?

Instead he said, 'I made a game that was pretty big a while ago.'

'What game?' said the barman.

'Doctor Hammer,' said William.

The barman stared at William. 'Look at me,' he said.

William looked up.

'Holy shit, you're William Rain,' said the barman.

'Alright, keep it down.'

'Sorry. I, I can't believe it. William Rain in my pub? What

happened to you, man?'

'What's your name? You know mine, it only seems fair that I should know yours too.'

'Curt,' said the Barman.

'Curt, I want to thank you for this beer. I'm going to drink it and then keep walking. I don't really have time to sleep anyway, if I'm honest. Got to keep moving. I'd appreciate it if you didn't tell anyone you saw me here. The papers have a way of finding out these things. They'll get a picture off your CCTV of me looking the way I do right now, and I just don't want that. Is that okay?'

'No problem Mr. Rain.'

'It's just William. But thank you.'

'Hey listen, I'll tell you what. Stick around here for a bit. I won't draw any attention to you and after I'm done here for the night I can drive you. It's only about three hours by car, I can get you there and be back in time to open up again tomorrow. It's no problem.'

William thought about it. 'You sure it's not a problem?'

'You're William Rain, it would be an honour.'

'Then I'd be a fool to say no. You don't need to take me the whole way. I don't want to burden you.'

'It's really no problem. You hungry?'

'I could eat.'

'I'll get the chef to fix you something.'

CHAPTER 23

The rain came down hard on the crime scene. The box was lifted out of the hole and dropped onto the ground beside it. Ryman and Arnold ducked under the police tape and stood in front of it. Arnold held an umbrella over them both.

'Open the box,' said Ryman.

One of the Scene of Crime Officers, Rachel, wearing white protective clothing, bent down and removed the lid. A clear plastic sheet covered a dark shape within. She pulled it back.

'Oh shit,' she said, putting her hand to her mouth. 'Who the fuck would do this?'

Ryman knelt down, not worrying that the wet ground soaked through his trousers. He took a latex glove out of his back pocket and put it on his right hand. The torso was soft with rot. The head, the left hand, and both legs were missing. Of course, the left hand had already been found by the WWAP kids, half wrapped in old bandages and covered in scars. He lifted the body slightly to get a closer look at the severed neck. There were two gashes in the lower part of the neck and a six inch gash in the chest. The collar bone was split along its length by another cut. The decapitation itself looked like it was made by at least two blows of an axe. There was a step where the first cut had reached. Ryman rested the body back down and looked it over.

'Sky, hold the umbrella more this way, rain is getting in,' said Ryman.

Arnold leaned forward with the umbrella, stopping the rain that had been splashing off the lower half of the torso.

There was a jagged wound next to the belly button. Possibly made from a broken glass or bottle. Ryman had seen a similar wound on a young guy after a bar fight. The hand looked like it had been removed with a single blow of an axe but the legs looked like they had been sawn off.

'I think more than one person did this,' said Ryman.

'Why's that?' said Arnold.

'They used a saw on the legs and an axe on the neck. The decapitation was clumsy but the legs are pretty clean.'

'Maybe he started with the saw and found it too hard so switched to an axe?'

Ryman thought for a moment. 'Maybe,' he said. He stood up and shook his head. 'Why did they bury the body in four different places? Why not dig one hole? The risk of being caught would have been so much greater.'

'You're pretty sure it was more than one person,' said Arnold.

'The gut says so. Always listen to your gut.' Ryman looked at the white-clad officer who had been standing on the other side of the box during Ryman's examination. 'Get this and the other parts down to the morgue.'

Rachel nodded and got to work.

The legs had been found in the second location, buried in a box that had once contained a vacuum cleaner. They were stacked toe to stump to make them fit and were then wrapped in a clear plastic sheet. In the third location the head had been found, wrapped in newspaper and buried in a large paint tin. There was no way to identify the head by its features. The eyes had decayed and the gunk that came out of them had dried against the sports pages. When the paper was removed what was left of the eyes came off with it. The mouth was split at an angle from a frantic (off target, Ryman thought) axe wound. The damage to the teeth made identifying the body by dental records impossible.

Ryman had checked the finger prints on the hand Billy had given him but the skin slid off at his touch. The only hope was a DNA test, and that would only work if they had the DNA on record. The Matterson house would have to be searched. Maybe they would find a hair brush with a few hairs tangled in the bristles.

'What now?' said Arnold, as he watched Rachel and another officer heft the box into the back of a police SUV.

'I'll get the forensic pathologist to do a full autopsy in the morning. The coroner has already contacted him. He'll find out what the cause of death is. See if there are any hair fibres, or anything else, from the attacker. I need to find out who made the map. Someone wanted the body to be found.'

'Maybe the killer wants some publicity,' said Arnold.

It was possible. Ryman took the map out of his jacket pocket and opened it up. He frowned at it. A few hours ago it was like new, glossy even. Now it was faded and rough around the edges. He opened it up and it came apart at the seam. A section fell away and deteriorated almost immediately in the wet mud.

'What happened to that?' said Sky.

'Maybe the rain soaked through my jacket,' he said. But his pocket had been dry, he knew that. But what other explanation was there?

He folded what was left and put it back in his pocket, which was indeed dry.

'Are you going to talk to the WWAP lot?'

'Yes. But not now. I want to see what the pathologist says first. Come on, let's get out of the rain.' William Rain popped into Ryman's mind. His gut was nudging him again. 'You know what, why don't you go with one of the guys to the morgue and let me know everything gets their safely. What's her name on the right?'

Arnold looked over. 'Rachel, I think.'

'Rachel,' shouted Ryman, and the officer looked over. Ryman beckoned her.

Rachel walked over. The bottom half of her white PPE trousers were spattered with mud. 'What's up?' she said.

'Constable Sky is going to accompany you to the morgue. I want everything taken down in one trip. Not one box at a time, got it? I don't want anything left unattended in the vehicle.'

Rachel nodded. 'You got it."

Arnold looked at Ryman to see if he was joking. 'You want

me to carry boxes of rotting corpse into a morgue?'

'Just let me know when it's done.'

CHAPTER 24

Walter Chaplin had been standing at his lounge window watching the police at work. His house, Dirk's house, was directly opposite the Matterson house. The houses seemed to watch each other. Eternally suspicious.

Between the houses a slew of police cars were parked haphazardly along the road on the other side of the green, blocking it off entirely. He was holding a whisky glass in one hand and was putting out a cigarette in an ashtray on the window sill with the other.

Pete was sat on the couch with his elbows on his knees, fidgeting. Amelia and Penny were sat with him, drinking wine and chain smoking.

'How did they find it?' said Pete.

'That's not important. They have and that's all there is,' said Walter.

He watched Ryman split away from two other officers and get into a car and start the engine. The headlights turned on, illuminating the Matterson house. The way the shadows fled up from the porch roof and windowsills gave the house a terrible grimace. If you squinted you could imagine it was a face recoiling with horror from the wound in its chest that was the hole in its garden. The car reversed and straightened on the road and the house fell into darkness. Walter turned away from the window.

'Now what's going to happen? Are they going to trace it back to us? And then what, we all go to prison?' said Pete.

'How the fuck should I know?' said Walter.

'Maybe it's only right,' said Pete, looking up at Walter. 'I mean, we killed someone. And you know what's strange, none of us have even spoken about it. We've carried on living happy lives like nothing even happened.'

Walter sighed and sat against the window sill. He took a sip of his whisky and put the glass down next to him. 'I know it doesn't make up for it but I've given a lot to charity. I've lived a modest life, haven't you?'

'You know I have. I live in a fucking caravan for God's sake. But it doesn't change a thing. You can't buy redemption. We took the success. We smiled and laughed on television. We received awards. We acted like good people doing great things. Not like a group of people who brutally killed someone and then benefited from it!'

'He wasn't human.' Walter walked over and sat on the coffee table in front of Pete. 'We've never spoken about it because we couldn't understand it. Do you know how many times I've played that night over and over again in my mind? Or how many times I wanted to ask you guy's what you thought happened? To compare notes. To try and comprehend what it all meant? Because I don't really understand what happened. I'm still confused now, ten years later.'

'I'm not talking about Jack. We had no choice but to do what we did. I'm talking about his daughter.'

'That was a fucking accident and you know it!'

'Maybe it was, but it was still wrong. It should have never happened, none of this should have happened. We should have sent her away properly, you know? Given her a proper burial. It wasn't her fault.'

'I know. And I agree. But we can't change that now. We did what we had to do.'

Pete leaned back on the couch and looked up at the ceiling. 'What if it was Martha, or Dirk? And you remember what that thing said, right before everything stopped?'

Walter's head dropped. He stared at the rug under his feet. For a moment his mind went back to when they had bought it. He remembered him and Penny at some old antique rug place in Christchurch. It had cost a fortune. It was the first expensive thing they bought together. A big cream rug. He remembered they were a bit tipsy from a liquid lunch and were giggling like kids in love, even though they were pushing thirty and had a young son of their own. That fragile boy, Dirk. There was no darkness then. Their thoughts never went back to all that blood and carnage that led to their success and wealth. They just enjoyed every moment. The only person who was really affected, in any real way, was William. He had lots of good times but the darkness was definitely in him. When it got too difficult he turned to drugs and drink.

Walter shook his head. His memory flashed to that bloody

night in Jack's basement. He saw Sarah, Jack's four year old daughter, dead on the floor, bleeding from the head.

Walter looked up, dragging himself out of the memory. 'Of course I remember.'

CHAPTER 25

Dirk had come in earlier and headed straight upstairs. The adults downstairs had heard the shower go and then the hairdryer. Dirk liked using the hairdryer. Most kids would just use a towel. But not Dirk. Dirk liked to stand in front of the mirror, the hot air blowing his hair back. He imagined a blue sky behind him. The sensation of falling. Dirk Chaplin, Sky Diver. But he didn't do that today. He dried his hair without even looking at his reflection. Just a part of the shower routine. No fun to be found here.

He felt like all the good times in the world had been grabbed from him by that decaying hand. He saw it when he closed his eyes. He could almost see it when his eyes were open. He shut off the hairdryer and went to his room.

No food, he couldn't stomach it. No games too, just in case. He tried reading but his mind kept wandering. He decided to just lie in bed and daydream for a while and hope sleep came along sooner rather than later.

Maybe he could daydream around the hand. He was good at daydreaming. He had a hell of an imagination. That was part of the problem really. That's why the image of the hand wouldn't leave. He lay on his back and stared at the ceiling. The rain against the window sounded like so many tapping fingers.

The hand floated a few inches in front of his face. He could see the chipped and yellowing fingernails in grim detail. The back of the hand was covered in scars that almost looked like writing. An old piece of bandage stuck to what was left of the wrist. He scrunched up his eyes and tried to think of something else. He imagined Billy and Martha kissing. He smiled and nearly laughed. That wasn't his plan, not at all. Why would he want to see that? But a distraction was what he was after and this one would do just fine.

He was sort of jealous of the relationship Billy and Martha had. Even though they treated him the same he still felt like the sick fragile friend. There to be looked after. Never quite a solid equal. They were both fit and healthy and could ride their bikes fast and get ahead of Dirk, who was usually left running to catch up some way behind. That had changed a bit he guessed when they made the Dirkmobile but that was all a part of the same problem. The two best friends held back by the invalid.

They were bad thoughts, and unfounded ones too, he knew that, but he thought them nonetheless. He would never be the valiant love interest in any situation, he felt that pretty strongly.

He fancied Martha. She was beautiful. He'd had a crush on her for as long as he could remember and that day they played spin the bottle and he got to kiss her was one of the best days of his life. He suspected that after that night Billy and Martha had sometimes got away from him on their bikes so they could make out without him seeing. Maybe it was just paranoia. But maybe it was true.

His daydream, a memory, was set in Den the Fourth, down at the bottom of Martha's caravan site. It was night and the scene was lit by tealight candles. The three of them were sat cross-legged on the floor. Billy span the bottle and it stopped, pointing at Martha. She smiled a wicked daring smile and leaned forward. Billy hesitated and then leaned in and kissed her quickly on the lips.

'Really, Billy? Is that all you got?' said Martha.

'What do you mean?' said Billy.

'You're supposed to use tongues, I'm not your mother.' Billy flushed red with embarrassment. 'Come on kiss me like a man.'

'Like you're a man?' said Billy.

Dirk and Martha laughed. 'No, like you're a man, dumb-ass.'

'Oh, right, yeah, I was just joking.'

They all fell into childish hysterics. Martha calmed down first and leaned forward again. 'Come on funny man, kiss me with your tongue.'

Billy stopped laughing but kept on smiling. 'Are you sure?' he said.

'Look, you're going to regret not doing it when I spin the bottle and it lands on Dirk. Then you'll get to see what you missed out on.'

Now it was Dirk's turn to blush but, and fair play to Dirk, he played it like a man. 'I'll show you how it's done,' he said.

'Wow,' said Martha.

Dirk laughed nervously. 'What?'

'I'll hold you to that,' she said, and turned to Billy. 'Come on, Billy, are we going to do this or not? Humpty Dumpty is ready to drag me off to his cave and you're acting like a mouse at a cat conference.'

'A mouse at a cat conference?' laughed Billy.

'It's the best I can do at short notice,' laughed Martha.

'You're like a floppy disk trying to be a hard drive,' said Dirk.

Martha and Billy looked at him, 'What was that supposed to mean?' said Martha, laughing.

Dirk shrugged, 'I don't know. The mouse one is better. Kiss her, Billy.'

'Yeah, come on, let's do this. My first kiss and your first kiss, together.'

Billy nodded and swallowed. 'Okay, you ready?'

'I'm ready,' said Martha.

They leaned into each other and their lips met. Billy opened his mouth and his tongue slipped into hers. Her tongue rolled around his tongue and they made muffled noises. Dirk stared at them with his eyes wide. It was the first time he ever felt a real pang of jealousy. He figured he would get his turn but it probably wouldn't be like that. For a start, when he did get his turn to spin the bottle it landed on Billy. It was gross but they made out with each other quickly to get it over with. Really they wanted to get back to Martha's turn. She went next and spun the bottle. It landed on Dirk.

'You ready for me Dirk?' she said. Dirk shrugged. 'Well if you don't want to-' said Martha.

'I do,' he said, and he leaned forward and closed his eyes.

He felt her lips touch his. They were so soft. They parted and he felt her tongue go into his mouth. His tongue touched her's and then it was all over. She pulled away and clapped.

'We've all had our first kisses,' she said.

Dirk smiled but his heart sank. He watched Martha and Billy. The way their eyes met and then darted away. Then they were both looking at him and smiling. Like they were avoiding looking at each other.

Dirk shrugged. 'Why don't you two just stay here and make out and I'll go home.'

'What? No, stay. What's wrong? Come on let's play truth or dare,' said Martha.

'Yeah, what's wrong? Didn't you find that fun?' said Billy.

Dirk shook his head. These idiots don't even know they love each other, he thought.

Dirk opened his eyes. The decaying hand had disappeared. He tried to not acknowledge that fact, knowing it would come back just as soon as he did. He closed his eyes and rolled over onto his side. He daydreamed again, this time about a time him and Martha and Billy, and the dog, had gone into the woods to collect sticks to make a fire. Nothing special happened that day but the daydream led to an actual dream and Dirk fell asleep.

CHAPTER 26

1982

A young Jack Matterson, sixteen years old, was sitting on his bedroom floor. He wore a grey jumper, light blue jeans, and multi coloured striped socks. A vinyl disk was turning on a record player in the corner of the room. It was Queen's Greatest Hits. He had only bought the album a few weeks earlier but he thought the grooves must be just about worn out already from the amount of times he had listened to it.

He had a computer magazine open on his lap and was reading an article about Steve Wozniak, one of the founders of Apple. It said that Wozniak used to be a phone phreak. It was an early kind of hacking. He built a thing called a blue box that could hack the telephone exchange letting him make calls to anywhere, even calls to other countries, for free. The automated system used different tones to connect calls. The blue box simply mimicked the tones. Wozniak had once used the blue box to call the Vatican and requested to speak to the pope (pretending he was an American politician) luckily the pope was asleep and couldn't come to the phone. Apparently there was a guy called Engressia who could do it just by whistling.

JACK'S GAME

Jack laughed when he read that and turned to the next page. He loved this stuff. Anything to do with computers, and the history of computers, got him right in the gut. On the next page were instructions on how to create a programme using a coding language called BASIC. The page of instructions taught you how to create random coloured polygons. Last month it had taught you how to make the computer make weird sounds. But this was better. Way better.

Seven Seas of Rhye blasted out of the speakers in two corners of the room. He got up and sat at his desk where he had a brand new Acorn computer. His parents had got it for him for Christmas just a few months earlier.

He typed the code in carefully. It took almost an hour and he had to flip the record a few times to keep the music going. Eventually he got to the end and pressed RETURN. There was an error. It hadn't worked. He corrected the line that was wrong and pressed RETURN again. This time it did work. The screen filled with polygons. 'YES!' he shouted and jumped up from his seat. He danced around his room to Don't Stop Me Now.

He dreamed of being able to make games like the ones he had stacked up next to his computer. He had ideas. Great ideas. He wanted to build his own computer too. There was so much he wanted to try. The progress was slow though, and it infuriated him.

It took so long to learn to make a basic shape, how long would it take to know enough to make a game? Years? He wanted to do it now. The slow pace of learning drove him crazy. He could feel it in his bones. It had to be faster. He had to be able to do it now. He wished he could just plug a disk into his mind and download all the knowledge.

He lifted the needle off the record and closed the lid. He left the computer running so he could start the programme over again without rewriting the code later. For now he had to go out. He had heard a rumour about a guy called Robert Johnson. He was a great blues guitarist and the story goes that way back when, he had sold his soul to the devil at a crossroads and in return the devil gave him the ability to play the guitar like no one else. He went from strumming like an amateur to playing impossible riffs that needed fingers ten inches long.

Jack ran downstairs. Jack's dad, wearing a shell suit and moustache, was showing Jack's mum the new 8mm camcorder he had picked up.

'Going out,' said Jack, walking between them.

'Okay, son,' said Jack's dad, not taking his eyes off his new toy.

Jack walked out of his house, wearing socks and no shoes (who has time for shoes when ideas need exploring?) and turned right towards the square. It was clear to some that something was different with Jack Matterson. Autistic maybe. It was suspected he had Asperger's Syndrome at the very least. He went into the tobacconists and headed to the back of the store where Mr Finnegan sold old vinyl.

Mr Finnegan watched him from behind the counter. After a while he got up and joined him.

'What are you after, Jack?' said Mr Finnegan.

Jack didn't look at Mr Finnegan. He just stared forward, not wanting to make eye contact.

'Robert Johnson,' said Jack.

'Robert Johnson? Good choice. You know they say he sold his soul to the devil.'

'I know,' said Jack.

'Alright, let me see what I got.'

Finnegan flicked through the albums and picked one out. He knew he had it in stock. He knew every record in the store. There were hundreds of them. Some in piles, some arranged by genre, some alphabetically, some by year of release. It was a mess of a system but Finnegan knew where everything was.

Jack took the record out of his hands and walked back down the store and waited at the counter. Finnegan followed him. He was a strange kid, that Jack Matterson.

Jack paid and left the shop. He went straight back home and put the record on. The first track was called Red Hot and seemed to be about apples. Jack listened and waited for the next track to start. The next song was called Crossroad Blues. Jack's ears pricked up. He listened to the whole song but nothing was given away about how exactly Robert Johnson had summoned the devil. He stood still and listened to the whole album through, both sides. When it was done his whole posture sagged.

He had an idea after a while that maybe Finnegan knew a bit more about Robert Johnson, so he went back to the tobacconist.

'How did he do it?' said Jack, when he got to the counter.

'Do what?' said Mr Finnegan, raising an eyebrow.

'Sell his soul?'

Finnegan smiled. His neat brown beard raised up, giving him the look of the devil, Jack thought. Finnegan leaned forward.

'The story is he went to the crossroads and met a black man there. The black man was the devil.'

'But he must have done something. You can't just go to a crossroads and there he is.'

Finnegan leaned back. 'Well, I don't know how Johnson did it, but I heard you need to bury a picture of yourself in the dirt, smeared in your own blood.'

Jack nodded and walked right out of the store. Finnegan let out a surprised laugh. 'It won't work, kid. There's no such thing as the devil.' But the door closed and Jack didn't answer.

If Robert Johnson could sell his soul to the devil to play the blues then he could do the same to be a great programmer. He would play the keyboard like a guitar. King of QWERTY, he thought.

The young Jack Matterson went down to the basement where he had a workshop set up with broken bits of electronics that he liked to fiddle with, trying to work out just how they worked. Jack's parents were down there. Jack's dad was filming Jack's mum with the 8mm camera. She had taken her wedding dress out of a box and was holding it against her body. Jack sat at his desk and reached over the broken shell of a computer monitor. Somewhere on the desk was a

Polaroid camera. He was sure of it. Jack's dad followed Jack's mum as she danced around the basement. Jack was captured in the background of the footage. Years later that piece of film would be used in a documentary about his life, and his unexplained disappearance.

Jack found what he was looking for and ran back up the basement stairs with it.

He went to his room and held the camera out, facing him. He pressed the button and the camera flashed. An undeveloped Polaroid flopped out of the slot in the front.

He had pursued interests with driven single-mindedness before but this was different. He was so full of energy and determination it frightened him a little. He was frantic. He shook the Polaroid so it would develop quicker and watched as the image of his face emerged from the blackness as if from a clearing fog.

He smiled and put the photo down on top of the record player. He grabbed a screwdriver from beside his computer and pressed it into the palm of his hand. It didn't cut right away so he rubbed it forcefully up and down his open hand, scraping the flesh away. Blood started to rise up through the broken skin and flow freely. He picked up the Polaroid and smeared his hand across the photo. He held it in both hands and smiled.

CHAPTER 27

The police SUV pulled up at the hospital and Arnold Sky and Rachel Sinclair got out. Rachel was now out of the white PPE she wore over her clothes. Her auburn hair was tied back and she was wearing dark trousers and a light blouse.

They went to the back of the vehicle and opened it up.

A doctor, Joanne Freemont, white hair, short with age, and placid with years of good bedside manner, was waiting for them.

'Checking into Rose Cottage,' said Rachel.

'Rose cottage?' said Arnold, helping to lift the delivery out of the back of the vehicle.

Jack Matterson's body parts had been loosely arranged in the correct order and zipped up in a black body bag and placed on a stretcher. It was much lighter than Arnold had been expecting. The lightness of it sent a shiver through him.

'That's what you call the morgue, right?' said Rachel, looking over to the doctor.

'Only when we're around the patients,' she said.

'Well, we've got one here for you,' said Rachel.

Joanne smiled curtly. 'We only call them patients when they're still alive.'

'Where's the pathologist?' said Arnold.

'I don't know, it's not my area. Now hurry up, I've got patients to see. Alive ones. I've left the morgue unlocked for you. Do you know the way?'

'No,' said Sky.

'Second door on the right and down the stairs. Just follow the signs. I'll be down shortly to lock it back up again.'

She held the door open for them and they thanked her as they passed. They were holding an end each. It was like moving furniture, thought Arnold, and that helped ease his nerves.

'Can't you get these with wheels?' said Arnold.

'We'll manage,' said Rachel.

It was cold in the morgue. Rachel pushed the door open with her foot and entered backwards.

'Where are the lights?' said Sky.

'Hold on,' said Rachel. She lifted her knee and held her end of the stretcher against her hip, holding it up with her left hand, and patted the wall next to the door with the other. She found the light switch and flicked it. The light didn't come on. She flicked it a few more times. 'No lights,' she said.

'Well that's just fucking typical,' said Arnold.

'Come on, it's not so dark in here.'

There was enough natural light to see by as it turned out. It wasn't light, you wouldn't say that, but you could find your way around.

There were two metal beds, more like steel tables, with rims to trap spilled blood. Between them was a unit on wheels with an array of sterilized surgical tools on the surface and a tall hinged lamp attached to one end. The back wall of the morgue was lined with square doors. Refrigerated pigeon holes for corpses. Arnold looked at them and imagined the empty lifeless bodies inside. Their pale eyes with wide unfocusing pupils. He thought of clammy toes with paper tags tied to them. He saw their chests cut open. He imagined them coughing to life and crawling out of the cold dark cabinets.

'Let's get this done and get the hell out of here,' said Arnold.

'You scared?' said Rachel.

'This place makes me nervous. Who would want to work down here?'

'Come on, we'll put it on this one.'

They carried the stretcher to the table on the left and Rachel pulled a lever and legs unfolded from under it. They lifted it a few inches and the legs snapped into place.

'I thought you said this thing doesn't have wheels?' said Arnold.

'You can't wheel it down stairs. What would we have used them for?'

'You just like being difficult don't you?'

'Are you ready?' said Rachel, holding onto two corners of the body bag.

Arnold nodded and held his end.

'On three,' said Rachel. 'One, two, three.'

They lifted the body and dropped it onto the surgical table.

A dark patch formed in the room behind them. It grew

quietly into the shape of a man. Far away, in the blackness of the thing's head, two stars shone, like pin pricks in a black sheet. The hair on the back of Arnold's neck stood on end. His body goose-pimpled all over and he felt a coldness fall over him. He locked eyes with Rachel. They both stood still, not wanting to look at the thing that had appeared just over their shoulders. If they looked it would become real.

It moved closer. It was like a shadow had come away from the wall and stepped into the room. Arnold had become so stiff his neck was aching. He nodded at Rachel, almost unnoticeably. Rachel nodded back. They let go of the body bag and stepped away from it. Arnold turned and walked to the door. He couldn't run. If he ran it might follow him. He walked hard. Rachel stared forwards and followed Arnold out, without looking at the thing and without making a sound. Their breathing had become still and adrenaline had filled their bodies. There was a primal thing happening. A need to get out. Fight or flight. A deafening internal voice reverberated around their bodies. 'GET OUT!' it shouted. It was not a supernatural voice. It was their own. And it was loud.

As soon as they made it through the door, into the light of the corridor outside, they ran. Arnold tripped on the stairs and Rachel ran past him. Arnold was up just as quick as he had fallen, and they were out of the hospital and into street. Rachel pulled open the driver side door of the SUV and got in and started the engine. Arnold jumped into the passenger seat and slammed his door shut.

They both started breathing heavily and Arnold had to stop himself from throwing up. 'Drive!' he shouted.

Rachel nodded, the unspent adrenaline running riot in her veins. She breathed hard inward and thought she might burst into tears.

The car stalled and she fumbled the keys. She got the engine started again and the wheels span on the wet road. They got a few roads away and pulled over. She turned the engine off and looked behind her, out of the rear window. Her eyes were wide. Her pupils dilated, taking in as much light as possible. There was nothing there but road.

'What was that?' she said, turning to Arnold.

'I don't know?'

Rachel looked forward. 'There was something terrible in there with us.'

Arnold put his head in his hands.

Rachel hit the steering wheel. 'There was a man in there. Or the shape of a man. Like, just a void. I felt like my heart was going to explode in my chest.'

'What do we do? Do we tell Ryman? 'Hey Ryman, you should know there's a ghost in the morgue."

Rachel shook her head and leaned back. She stared up at the sunroof. It was still raining but he could see the stars through gaps in the clouds.

'There were stars,' said Rachel.

Arnold looked at her. 'Stars?'

'In the morgue. I could see stars in the dark. I think I could see people. Thousands of them. They were screaming.'

Joanne Freemont opened the doors to the morgue and looked in.

'Are you down here officers?' She froze. 'Can I help you?' she said.

Of course, it was an absurd thing to say. Can I help you? The words just came out. It was a reflex question. Joanne stared at the man in the morgue. Her face went as pale as her white hair. He was facing away from her. He was naked. His back was rotten. Part of his spine was visible where the skin had decayed and fallen away. His left hand was badly scarred. It looked as if his legs weren't quite connected to his torso. She stared at his rectum. It was moving. Something white and pulsing pushed out of it and fell to the floor with a splat. She gasped. They were maggots.

The man turned around. If she was able to she would have run but she couldn't. Paralysed by fear is a term she had heard but never experienced before. It was true. Fear can steal away your mobility. The best she could do was tremble.

His eyes were gone. There was a yellowish residue on his cheeks where the vitreous that had once filled them had dried. His mouth was hanging half open where it was cut at an angle with the blow of an axe.

He stepped forward with eerie deftness. Dr Freemont began to whimper. He stopped in front of her. She had smelled rotting flesh before, but this was stronger. The stench that struck her had a physical punch. It was a scent with a sharp edge. It could cut right through you. There was a lighter tone running through it though. Something chewy. She gagged. It smelled like almonds. Or like pus. That's what it was. The nutty scent of gangrene.

He raised his hand and touched her face. Her mouth opened and a horrified sound escaped her. She was shaking now. She tried to scream but her vocal cords strained but made no noise. She had forgotten to breathe out. It happens.

The tips of two of his fingers touched against her eyeballs and they rolled back in her head. She felt his thumb go between her teeth and press against the roof of her mouth. She came to her senses then and went to jerk her head away but it was too late. The man pushed her back against the closed doors and forced his fingers into her eye sockets. The pressure in her eyes was relieved with the sound of grapes popping and that was the last thing she would ever hear, and the last thing she would ever see. He closed his fist with amazing strength and the front of her skull cracked. His fingers met his thumb inside her head and he pulled back, like he was scooping pulp from a pumpkin. Her top row of teeth, her nose, and the lower half of her eyes sockets came away with the sound of cracking bone and tearing fabric and blood tumbled out of the hole that was left. She fell forward onto him and blood ran down his chest. He stepped backwards and she slumped to the floor. Jack stared at her lifeless body and dropped the remnants of her face.

He turned back the way he was facing, before Joanne Freemont had interrupted him, and looked at his reflection in the floor to ceiling mirror on the far wall.

One thing was certain, he couldn't walk around inconspicuously. He turned and looked down at the woman. She was wearing a white doctor's coat. He removed it from her, violently breaking her arms in the process, and managed to get it on without too much trouble. He opened a drawer in the unit between the two mortuary tables and found a surgical mask. He put it on, tying it with a clumsy but tight knot behind his head.

CHAPTER 28

1982

Jack Matterson, sixteen years old, walked along a deserted country road between two wheat fields. In his right hand was a blood smeared Polaroid. The sun was high in the sky and the air was dry.

He was a few miles out from Shelley Town and had been walking for almost an hour. You never had to go far in England before you reached the countryside and it was the best place he could think of to find a deserted crossroads, away from all the people in town.

It wasn't long before he found exactly what he was looking for. He walked out to the middle of the unpaved road and kicked at the gravel and dirt. He looked down all four ways and saw that no one was around. He listened for the sounds of vehicles in the distance but heard only a single bee buzzing around the edge of the wheat field. He knelt down and moved some dirt with his hands. He placed the picture in the shallow hole and covered it up. He took a step back. Nothing happened. This wasn't entirely surprising to him but a part of him really thought it would work. Really thought it would be that simple.

He sat down in the middle of the crossroads, his legs crossed, and stared at his trainers. 'Fuck.' He said, under his breath.

His mind went to the computer on his desk. He imagined the polygons he had coded appearing at random on the screen. How would he ever understand how it all worked well enough to make his own game? It was never going to happen. It was too hard and would take too long.

He stayed like that for a few hours. No traffic came. The sun burned the back of his neck. His thoughts came to Robert Johnson and his pact with the devil. How come he got so lucky?

'Am I not good enough for you?' he shouted, and a gust of wind blew past him. Jack got to his feet. 'What? Are you afraid of me?' he shouted. He walked to where his picture was buried and stamped on it. 'Show yourself, Devil!' he screamed.

The air blew around him causing a few of the smaller stones to roll across the road.

The hair on the back of his neck pricked up and he stepped back a few paces.

'Is that you, Demon?' he shouted. 'You can have my soul!'

The wind billowed around him causing his clothes to ripple and his hair to blow around wildly. 'Is that you?' said Jack.

The road in front of him warped unnaturally. It was like he was suddenly looking at the crossroads through a fishbowl full of moving water. A gap opened up in front of him and for a moment he could see stars. Right there, in the middle of the foreground. It was a patch of stars. And then it was gone. Jack stared. He took another few steps backwards and watched.

It happened again and all the air around him fled towards the hole. It was like someone had opened the door in an aeroplane while it was flying. The gap in the air opened wider and wind rushed past him. He could see it turn to white as it rushed through the black hole. There was a sudden creaking sound and the walls of the hole grew massive and Jack fell and landed on his back. He leaned up on his elbows. His jumper was billowing around him and his hair was blowing around his face. His eyes opened wide. There was something impossible and terrible inside the void.

There were thousands of screaming men and women and children. They were all crammed into a pen. Like in a pig farm. So many of them. Squeezed in shoulder to shoulder. The light from Jack's side of the hole in reality illuminated their features. So many screaming and crying people.

And then he noticed the two long objects beyond the pen. At first he thought they were black burnt out towers, or trees, or something. But then one of them moved. It was a leg. Jack leaned forward and looked through the gaping hole. The legs went up as far as he could see and disappeared into blackness. It didn't need explaining to Jack who the legs belonged too. It was Satan himself, surely.

The charcoal black leg bent at the knee and then came down hard and stamped on the people in the pen. The ground shook and Jack fell back again. 'No!' shouted Jack. He turned onto his hands and knees and started to crawl backwards.

Absurdly, the scene reminded him of a story he had heard about Mick Jagger. There was a rumour going around that Mick got a kick out of getting as many chickens as he could into a pen until no more would fit and then he would stamp on them, hands on hips, pouting.

Jacks eyes fell on the face of a pretty little girl with her hair in pigtails. She was right at the edge of the pen. She could see Jack. Her eyes were pleading. She was bent forwards reaching out towards him. The foot came down again and smashed her hips. She went down hard on the fence post and her face crumpled inwards. Blood flooded out of her mouth and nose and her body flopped to the ground. Her hair floated in the blood and turned red.

The toes of the foot curled as if enjoying the sensation of split skin and cracked bones. Jack could hear the grinding of skulls and spines.

It wasn't the world Jack had imagined when he thought of Hell. It was something far worse. The whole ground shimmered black with the flow of blood. The horizon blended with the black sky. Deep in the black, maybe a million miles away, were dark wisps of purple smoke, like forming galaxies. Closer, bodies hung in the vacuum of space. Time had been slowed down for them. Jack remembered reading about the effects of the human body in the vacuum of space. It was torture. He imagined all those people. The souls of people, he thought. Feeling the blood boil in their veins.

Jack's heart started beating hard. Dark thin figures were crawling through the blood towards him. Their fingers were pointed like sharpened sticks.

Another gap opened next to him and a man, tall and thin, grinned out at him.

'Hey hey, you nearly summoned the devil himself, kid,' he said, as he stepped out of his world and into Jack's.

Jack thought he saw the man's feet dripping with blood. The toes broken. The tips flayed and sharpened like pencils. But by the time the foot touched the ground it was wearing a clean and polished shoe.

The man smiled and the hole to Hell closed. The air blew for a moment longer and then settled.

Jack cautiously got to his feet. 'I can't believe this worked,' he said.

'Well it did. Scary right? All that violence? Did you like what you saw?'

Jack shook his head. The man that stood in the middle of the crossroads was grinning. Not a charming grin but a malicious one. His teeth were straight but sharp looking. He was grossly thin and wore a tweed suit with a matching waistcoat. His shoes were brown leather.

'Alright then, you scabby little shit-fuck. What do you want from me?'

Jack swallowed. 'I want you to grant me a wish.'

'A wish? I'm not a fucking genie. I kill babies for fun. You know, just this morning I scraped out a child's eye ball with my teeth. She screamed while I did it. I could taste her tears.'

'I thought if you summoned the devil at the crossroads you could make a deal with him.'

'You can do that if you want. Make a deal with me. You can have whatever you want. In return I get your soul and then I can rape you and torture you for all of eternity. It's a good deal. Let's shake hands now, what do you want?'

'I don't want to make that kind of deal,' said Jack.

'It's the only deal I got kid, now fuck off so I can get back to my hobbies. I've got a granny to skull-fuck.'

'I'll tell you what I want. And you're going to give it to me. I want to become the best programmer that ever lived. I want to know how to code like I know how to breathe. I want that but I don't what I saw happening to all those people happen to me. Instead I want all the power you have. When I die, I want to be free.'

The man laughed so hard it sounded like painful screams. 'But if you get all that I won't have the pleasure of peeling the skin from your face and feeding it to you.'

'Tell me what you want in return, Devil.'

'My name isn't Devil, *human*, it's Cacophini.'

'I'm Jack.'

Cacophini looked at Jack and thought for a moment. 'I'll tell you what. If you're willing to nominate a loved one to take your place I would consider it.'

'You can take my parents.'

'Holy shit, kid, I only wanted one.'

'You can have them both.'

Cacophini nodded.

'So you say you want to be able to code. You want to make programmes for computers, right?'

'Yes.'

'And you're willing to give up both of your parent's souls for that? You realise that means both your parents will be tortured and mutilated and fucked and hanged and every terrible thing you can think of and could never imagine will happen to them. Not just for a few years but forever. Millions of years of pain.'

'I don't care.'

Cacophini let out an involuntary laugh. 'Wow.'

'And when I die I want to be safe and I want power.'

'You're a strong headed kid, Jack.'

'What's the deal?'

'Okay. Both your parent's souls and the soul of everyone you ever come to love.'

'Done,' said Jack, and put out his hand.

'We don't shake hands here, Jack. The deal is made.'

There was an almighty boom, like thunder had emitted from the middle of the crossroads, without the flash of lightning, and the demon, Cacophini, was gone.

Jack's left hand started to hurt. He looked down at it. Cuts were slashing into his wrist and all around the back of his hand and forearm. He gritted his teeth and managed to not scream with the pain. He watched as the cuts came together to form words in a language he didn't recognise. The fresh cuts started to burn and blacken, stopping the bleeding, and sealing the words there forever in a scar that would look, to the casual onlooker, like a badly healed burn.

CHAPTER 29

Curt's car was a gold 1977 Ford Capri with a black bonnet. It was his pride and joy.

'I restored it myself,' said Curt.

William Rain nodded. He was in the passenger seat. The comedown from the drugs and alcohol of the night before was still heavy in him. His stomach ached and his ribs hurt. The few beers he'd had in Curt's pub had levelled him out a bit but not much.

'I say we've got a three hour drive. We should be there by half four.'

'Thanks for the lift, Curt,' said William.

'Hey, no worries, man. So, if you don't want to speak about it that's cool, but what happened to you? You look like someone kicked the shit out of you.'

'I fell. Hit my side on the edge of a bath tub.'

'I bet that hurt.'

William nodded.

'William Rain in my car. I still can't believe it.'

William didn't reply. He looked out of the window and watched the road pass by. It was dark and still raining.

'Sorry, man. It's not every day this sort of thing happens,

you know?'

'Sure.' William closed his eyes. Come on, he thought, get yourself together. 'I'm really grateful for the lift. It would have taken quite a while to walk the whole way.'

'It's really no problem.'

'I'll reimburse you for the petrol. I'll send some money to the pub. Hell, I'll probably bring it down myself.'

'You don't have to do that. It's really no problem. You know, that Doctor Hammer game. That was my whole childhood that game. I loved it. Me and my friends used to stay up all night trying to beat each other's times.'

'You know it's strange, this whole time competition thing, we never intended, or thought, that would be a thing people tried to do. I can't even remember why we put that timer in the game,' said William

'My friend did it in seventeen minutes. We sent a picture of the end screen to Digitiser on Teletext and they published the record. It was cool. Do you know what the record is now?'

'Six minutes and twelve seconds,' said William.

'Holy shit, that's quick.'

'The current record holder is going to be at the convention I told you about and there's a whole bunch of people lined up to challenge him. Do you want to know a secret?'

'Sure.'

'Walter's son, you know who Walter is, right?'

'Of course.'

'Walter's son completed the game in six minutes flat.'

'Holy shit!'

'Right? It's amazing.'

'Why didn't he take the record?'

'He figured he had an unfair advantage.'

'Being that his dad helped make the game?'

'Exactly.'

They drove for a while. William watched the rain in the beams of the headlights.

'You know, you should stick around for the convention. I'll introduce you to the others.'

'Really? I would love that.'

'Then it's done.'

Curt smiled. 'Man, I don't see my childhood friends much anymore but they are going to fucking die when they hear about this.'

William smiled. He never quite got used to people acting that way around him. Like just meeting him was a major event in their lives.

'So have you got a radio in this thing or what?' said William.

'Getting bored of my conversation?'

'Just like to listen to music.'

Curt turned on the radio. The song that came on nearly made William's heart stop.

'Hit the road Jack, and don't you come back, no more, no more, no more...'

William caught his breath and switched off the radio.

'Everything okay?' said Curt.

'Yeah, I don't-' he swallowed. 'That song makes me feel sick.'

'Why?'

'It doesn't matter.'

They ate road for an hour without speaking much.

Curt started tapping his fingers on the steering wheel. He turned to ask William a question and then stopped.

'Something on your mind?' said William.

Curt shrugged. 'There was this thing on TV last night.'

'I didn't see it.'

Curt nodded and drummed his fingers again. 'I was just wondering-' he looked at William. 'What did happen to Jack Matterson?'

'I don't know.'

William put the radio back on. It was an old-timey sounding song. There was a chorus of children singing, *'Grocer Jack, Grocer Jack, Is it true what mummy said, you won't come back? Oh no no.'*

'No!' said William, his nerves shaken. He switched off the radio but the station changed instead. *'I was booorn in a crossfire hurricane-'* William hit the off button again.

'I like that one, Jumping Jack Flash, right? The Rolling Stones.'

'Stop the car,' said William.

'Alright, man, there's a services coming up, look.'

Curt pointed to a sign that read, Services 1 mile.

William looked at the sign. But it had changed. It just said JACK in big white letters.

'Stop the car!'

'What's gotten into you, man?'

'Please, Curt, just pull over into the hard shoulder. I'll get out and walk.'

'What did I do?'

'You didn't do anything. I just need to get out.'

Curt pulled over and William got out of the car.

'Come on William, it's raining, you'll get soaked. Get back in the car.'

He watched William walk in front of the car, through the headlight beams. He walked into the motorway and crossed over to the central reservation.

Curt opened the door and got out of his car. 'What's going on?'

'Head back, Curt, I'm going to walk from here. I need to clear my head.'

A car flew passed doing seventy, a foot away from Curt, and he stepped back against the car in fear of getting his feet squashed. He looked right and waited for a gap in the traffic.

'William, stop walking,' he shouted. He squinted through the rain. He could hardly make out William's silhouette against the oncoming headlights from the other side of the motorway.

It looked like there was a chance to cross after the next car passed but Curt misjudged the gap and walked out in front of a van.

William stopped when he heard the sound. There was a dull thud followed by the sound of screeching tyres. A loud and long horn blast and then the smack of metal on metal. He stood there staring forward for a while. He was conscious that cars had stopped passing him on the left. His breathing had slowed right down. He turned around and looked back the way he had come.

The motorway was blocked. A van had swerved into the middle lane and hit a Citroen Picasso. Both cars came to a stop in the fast lane and two more cars joined the pile-up. Cars were slowing to a stop as far back as he could see. Curt's Ford Capri was stopped in the hard shoulder. The driver's side door was open. Curt was nowhere to be seen. He had stopped shouting William's name.

William's tongue caught in his throat and he held his hand to his heart. He began to cry and started walking backwards, away from the bad scene. He turned around and ran. It wasn't really a run. It was more like an agonising limp. He carried on for about fifteen minutes, long enough that the accident was small in the distance behind him. The grass in the central reservation had become a muddy swamp. Running in it was hard. He tripped on a discarded carrier bag and fell on his front. He lay there in the mud and sobbed.

CHAPTER 30

Ryman drove back into the square and stopped outside Billy Rain's house. He had been driving aimlessly around town waiting for the police vehicles to clear the scene. Driving around gave him time to think. The convention was tomorrow. William should be back in town soon. The guy is probably innocent, there was nothing to suggest otherwise. But Ryman's gut had been nudging him. Pushing him towards William's house. Or maybe it wasn't his gut. Maybe something else was urging him towards that place. A woman with eyes that said, 'Make love to me,' with every kitten-like look.

He rang the doorbell.

Eunice Rain was wearing PJs. Soft white bottoms and a light pink top that revealed her shoulders and neckline. There was an inch of midriff showing. Her top clung to her firm body. Her nipples made perfect buttons in the fabric. Buttons that needed to be touched. She answered the door and stood there with her shoulders back, almost girlish in her stance.

She would say, if you asked her, that her flirtatious body language was entirely accidental. The truth was people seemed to do whatever she liked when she had her shoulders back and her breasts forward. If she acted coyly and slightly stupid then they did even more for her. You didn't have to fuck a guy to get what you want, you just had to toy with them. Girls that opened their legs to move up were just sluts with a business plan. The truth is you can manipulate your way up by nursing a crush. As soon as you put out, all your power is gone. That's how you end up in the gutter. The best way to get what you want with sex is to never actually fuck anybody.

But that was all in her past. The body language sticks with you though. And truth be told, the crush might be the other way around this time. She looked at Ryman. His shoes were dirty with mud. He still hadn't shaved. His hair was wet and had been combed back with his fingers. There was a small coffee stain on his white shirt, the top two buttons of which were undone.

'Back again, Mr Ryman?' she said, looking him up and down.

'Is Billy still awake? I have a few more questions about the map,' he said. And he supposed he did.

'He's in bed.'

'Okay, sorry to bother you. I'll try again tomorrow.'

'Have you eaten?' she said, stopping him as he turned away.

He turned to face her again. 'I guess I could eat. I wouldn't want to put you out or anything.'

'Not at all,' she said, and held the door for him to pass.

'Do you like music?' said Eunice.

'What have you got?'

She opened a black CD case, put the disc into a brushed steel stereo and pressed play. She looked at Ryman with her eyebrows raised.

'Pink Floyd?' he said.

She smiled. 'Good. That would have been a decider.'

'A decider for what?'

She shrugged. 'Do you drink?'

'What have you got?'

'What have you got?' she said, mimicking him. 'You got yourself a nice catchphrase there. I've got beer, wine, whisky, and blackcurrant squash. Personally, I'm in the mood for whisky.'

'What have you got?' he said, and smiled.

'You ever tried Jura?'

'I don't believe I have.'

'Then you must try it.'

She disappeared to the kitchen and came back with two whisky glasses, a small jug of water, and a rectangular glass bowl full of ice. She put it on the coffee table and fetched the bottle of whisky from the alcohol cabinet.

She put an inch of Jura in each glass. 'Water?'

'I'll take it the same way as you,' he said.

She put a dash of water in both glasses and handed him a small metal pair of tongues. He raised an eyebrow at her.

'Never touch another man's ice,' she said.

He put an ice cube in his glass and went to get a second. She stopped him. 'Only one.'

'I didn't realise there was so much etiquette involved in

drinking,' he said.

'How do you normally take it?' she said.

'I use a whisky glass. Put a couple of ice cubes in and fill it with whisky. I've never put water in it before.'

'The water breaks the whisky,' she said.

'What does that mean?'

'It just makes it smoother. Try it.'

He did. 'Holy shit, I've been doing this all wrong.'

'It's good right?'

He nodded. 'Do you mind if I smoke?' he said.

'Oh thank god, yes. I'll get an ashtray.'

'I thought you invited me in here for dinner?'

'Good point. Hold on.'

'She ran off to the kitchen and came back with an ashtray and a bowl of nuts. 'Dry roasted okay?'

'You read my mind.'

She sat down next him and put the peanuts down. She picked up her glass. Her sudden closeness sent a rush right through him. Her leg touched his. She didn't seem to notice it and didn't move away from him. He was very conscious of it himself and didn't want to move in fear that she would become aware of it too and move away.

She rolled a cigarette and lit it. She turned to face him and sat cross legged on the couch with one knee planted firmly on his thigh. 'So what's your story, Ryman?' she said, and blew smoke in his direction.

Ryman rolled a cigarette and looked sideways at her. 'I don't really have much of a story,' he said.

'Everyone's got something,' she said. 'Is there a Mrs Ryman?'

'No. It's just me.'

'Girlfriend?'

'Not in a long time.'

'William hasn't touched me in years. I have a vibrator. But that's all the action I get.'

'May I say, Mrs Rain, you're very candid for someone who is notoriously agoraphobic.'

'You know you can call me Eunice. I wasn't always that way you know. I think William's fame, all the paparazzi, made me a bit of a shut-in and it just stuck. It went on for years, you know? It makes me nervous thinking about going outside. It's self-inflicted in many ways. I'm not really agoraphobic, I just don't go outside. Do people think I'm weird?'

'No, not at all. Everyone knows Billy, you know. Everyone likes him. He's a good kid. I know he buys alcohol and cigarettes for you, even though he's underage. Finnegan came to me about it and I gave him the okay.'

She smiled. 'You're a sweetheart,' she said. 'Here, let me top you up.'

She leaned over him to take the glass out of his right hand and her breast brushed against his arm. It sent a tingle through him. It ran across his shoulders and down his spine. All that mattered in that moment was him and her. It occurred to him that she probably had no idea what kind of effect that slight touch would have on a man. He was flying. He wanted her. But that doubt came in and dampened things. Not much, but enough to stop him from leaning in and kissing her neck. As far as he knew this was just a late night drink with the local cop, no suggestion of sex intended. It was all in his head. She was just one of life's accidental flirts. Innately charged with sex and completely oblivious to it.

She topped their glasses up. 'Do you mind if I light another cigarette? I sort of chain smoke when I drink. Especially when there's music on.'

'Go ahead.'

He watched her. She rolled a cigarette and her lips moved along with the lyrics coming out of the speakers. He racked his mind for something to say.

'It's a crazy business with that hand Billy dug up.'

'You're not kidding. I saw you all out there digging more things up. What was that? The rest of the body?'

'We think so. It's likely. I'm waiting on the autopsy report to confirm. Is Billy okay? It must have been quite a shock.'

'I think he's fine. To be honest I don't think he would say even if he wasn't. Got to protect mum, you know? They think I'm weak.'

'They?'

'Him and his dad. The rest of WWAP. Everyone.'

'Are you weak?'

'In some ways I guess, who isn't?'

'If I'm weak it's only in my will power. Alcohol, cigarettes, and, well, I guess that's it.'

'No, go on. What else are you weak for?'

He looked at her. 'I didn't come here to speak to Billy.'

'So why did you come?' she said, and she smiled and laid back on the sofa. She moved her left leg so it was resting on his knees. Her legs opened and he could see the outline of her most intimate area against the soft fabric of her PJs. She wasn't wearing any underwear. None on top and none downstairs.

'I don't want to misread the situation Mrs Rain.'

'It's Eunice. And I don't think you're misreading anything. Why did you come?'

'You know, I normally go with my gut and don't ask questions. My gut tells me you're flirting with me. My head tells me you're married and even though you and William seem to be having difficulties there are things to think about. There's Billy. I wouldn't be able to give you what you're used to. I wouldn't be able to provide for you.'

'I'm not looking for provisions.'

'So what are you looking for?'

She crossed her arms and took her top off in one easy movement and tossed it behind her. Her breasts hung there, glorious and perfectly matured.

She shrugged. 'I don't know what I'm looking for. What do you think I need?'

She put her thumbs under the elastic of her PJ bottoms and slid them down over her hips, past her knees, and kicked them off. They landed on Ryman's lap. She was completely naked. The music was playing. The lights were on. Ryman, fully dressed and this beautiful thing just lying there like some out of place angel.

'I'm feeling like the odd one out here, Ryman,' she said.

He un-buttoned his shirt and dropped it on the floor. He stood up so he could take off his trousers. He didn't take his eyes off her the whole time. She smiled and watched him undress. He took off his socks, no elegant way of doing that. She laughed. He stood there just wearing his boxers. He didn't look so bad really. With his clothes on he looked like a bit of a slob. He had a strong chest and his belly sort of suited him. She thought he was manly, especially when compared to William.

'Are they staying on?' she said.

'They're coming off,' he said, and off they came.

He stood there, completely naked.

She looked at him and smiled with an endearingly coy glance. He knelt on the couch and moved over her. His lips touched hers and she turned her head sideways away from him.

'Hold on, Ryman,' she said, putting her fingers to his lips. 'It's a bit early for that sort of thing isn't it?'

'What do you mean?'

She looked him in the eye. 'I mean, now things have gotten interesting we should have another drink.'

She slipped out from under him and Ryman let himself fall onto the couch. He watched her walk to the alcohol cabinet. Her naked body like something out of a movie, or a teenager's wet dream. She picked up a bottle and turned to face him. 'Are we sticking to whisky?'

He smiled. He was quite happy to drag the night out. 'Are we getting dressed again?' he said.

'No, why on earth would we do that, don't you like what you see?'

'I've never seen anything I liked more,' he said.

'Good.'

She opened the bottle, some expensive old Scottish whisky, and put it to her lips. She took a swig.

'That's a good one. Finish your drink so I can top you up,' she said.

He did what he was told. She walked back to the couch, her body moving with the music. She filled up the glasses and put the bottle down.

There was no way this was happening. Ryman was dreaming. This sort of thing simply didn't happen to overweight policemen. But it was happening. For whatever reason the most beautiful woman in town was giving him the night of his life. He knew one thing, he wasn't going to last more than three seconds with her. Another thing he knew, from experience, was that whisky gave him extraordinary longevity.

'Alright, let's drink,' he said.

It was going to be a hell of a night. They drank, they listened to music, they smoked cigarettes, and they teased each other relentlessly. When the moment finally came for them to fall into bed, hot and drunk, and embrace each other, it was the greatest singular sensation his body had ever experienced.

CHAPTER 31

William Rain groaned and rolled onto his back. His face and clothes were muddy and his rib was hurting worse than before. He held it tight with his right hand and stared up at the sky. It was still dark. There were stars up there, thousands and thousands of miles away. A sharp pain shot through him from his chest. The pain caused him to wince and a headache blossomed in his brain. He opened his eyes and it looked like the stars were falling from the sky and were about to pierce his body, like a machine gun peppering him with bullets the size of sugar granules.

This must be what a migraine feels like, he thought. It felt like his head was being squeezed by giant hands. He let his head fall back in the mud and stayed there for a while. He hadn't been in the car accident but he felt like he had. Any pain he felt was self-inflicted. It was from the alcohol and the drugs and falling over, not just now, but countless times over the past weeks.

He breathed out and sat up, clenching his stomach muscles tightly with the effort. He grimaced and held himself upright with his left hand, which almost slipped in the mud. His right hand was still holding his ribcage together. He grimaced and shook his head. Come on William, he thought. You're almost there. How much farther can it be? Twenty miles? Less? He wasn't sure. He knew Shelley Town couldn't be far but he had no idea where he was. He could walk it. He could get to his feet right now, put one foot in front of the other and just keep going until things got familiar.

He got to his knees and gripped onto the metal barrier that ran along the central reservation and pulled himself to his feet. He walked a few paces and stopped.

On the other side of the road blue lights flashed past him, the siren wailing. The pitch of the siren stretched out and warbled as it went by. The Doppler Effect in action, he thought. He turned and watched the police car take the slip road off the dual carriageway and cross the flyover to the eastbound side.

He hadn't realised quite how bad the accident had been until that moment. It hadn't occurred to him that the road beside him had been vacant of passing cars. The whole road was blocked. He could see traffic queuing for miles. Two columns of headlights snaking right back to the horizon.

The police car re-joined the carriageway slowly. Cars and vans moved onto the hard shoulder to let it pass. It drove through the centre of the traffic and stopped as close as it could. Between the police car and William was a mess of twisted and smashed up vehicles. The flashing light of the police vehicle lit up the insides of the cars with every turn. Bodies silhouetted in blue light appeared and disappeared over and over again.

William just stared. He had caused this. It was his fault. His paranoia about Jack Matterson had made him get out of Curt's car and Curt had stupidly followed him.

He watched as the policeman got out of his car. He had a radio mic in his hand, the coiled wire stretched out from the dashboard. He was probably requesting more ambulances and fire services. They'll be cutting off a lot of roofs today. Dragging the dead from their mangled motors.

William looked around for Curt's body and his attention was drawn to a figure on the floor. He could see a left arm stretched out with the sleeve of a chequered shirt. At first William thought it was him and was relieved to see the man on the floor had red hair. Curt's hair was blonde. William couldn't see the rest of the man's body. It was under a van. The driver's side wheel was parked at an angle from the shoulder of the outstretched arm to the bottom of his right ear.

He stared at the man, feeling sorry for him, but also relieved that Curt might still be alive somewhere. The policeman got a floodlight out of the boot of his car and set it down on the tarmac. He turned it on and the beam overpowered the blue light, which was still flashing. The silhouettes of the dead and injured became permanent. The blue light had given the bodies artificial movement, it gave them the possibility of being alive. But this still light did the opposite. It cast them as solid unmoving objects.

William looked back down at the man on the floor. He felt his heart drop an inch and his whole body stooped. It was the physical effect of sudden sadness. The man on the floor didn't have red hair at all. Part of his scalp was missing. Tufts of blond hair poked out from a matted red mess. It was Curt.

How easy it would be to just stand in that spot and never move again. Not until he was noticed by the policeman and taken into custody and questioned. He would be put away for manslaughter and he could just sit in his cell not eating. He could just wait for the rot to set in. He'll be found one day, a malnourished and emaciated corpse in a cement room. That felt like a pretty relaxing way to go. William stood there for some time, just staring at Curt's lifeless body. The policeman didn't see him. He was too busy looking into cars, looking for life.

No, he had to get back. He could walk, that was still an option. He saw something move in his peripheral vision. He looked away from Curt's body. One of the silhouettes in the cars was moving. The policeman was on the other side of the pile-up looking in the van that was parked on top of Curt's body. William looked at him and then back at the moving person. The car looked like it was in fairly good condition. The entire passenger side was crumpled in, like another car had hit it side on, but the windscreen was fine apart from a single crack that ran from one corner to the other.

The driver's side door opened and the silhouetted figure, it looked like a woman, dropped out and fell to the floor. She cried out. William couldn't make out the words from where he was but it was clear she was shouting for help.

The cabin of the van darkened and the policeman came around and stood between the headlights, which were still on.

He stood there like he was listening carefully. There was no sound. His torch fell on Curt's body and the policeman moved around him and knelt to look under the van. He ran the torch up and down Curt's body and shook his head.

The woman cried out again and the policeman looked over. His torch light shone over to the other side of the pileup and lit on the crumpled side of her car.

'I'm a police officer, where are you?'

'Here,' came the relieved voice of the woman.

The policeman ran over and knelt down beside her.

William watched as the officer talked to her. He couldn't be heard from where William was but he guessed he was asking her things like, 'Where does it hurt?' and, 'Can you tell me your name?'

After a moment the officer stood up. The woman had her arm around his shoulder. They walked slowly back through the wreckage to the police car and he sat her down in the passenger seat. He spoke into the handset attached to his radio.

William heard sirens coming from behind him and saw flashing lights in the distance. They were driving the wrong way down the dual carriageway. They must have closed off the road, William thought.

He looked back at the cop. He was facing the other way. One of the driver's queuing up on the other side had given in to his morbid curiosity and the policeman was directing him to return to his vehicle.

If you're going to do it you better do it now, William told

himself.

He ducked down and walked as fast as he could to the open driver's side door of the woman's car. He got in and closed it quietly. The airbags had deployed. William bunched up the bag that had exploded out of the centre of the steering wheel as best he could and tried to stuff it back into its hole.

He looked in the rear view mirror. The policeman was still distracted. He went to turn the key and then had a thought. He turned and looked in the backseat. No dead kids, thank god. He looked forward. The ambulances were visible now but still a mile or so away. He turned the key and the engine started. He was so surprised by this that for a moment he didn't move. Then the car was filled with a moving light. He looked in the rear view mirror. The policeman was shining a torch in his direction. He turned and asked the woman in the police car a question. She shrugged and the policeman started jogging towards him.

William put the car into gear and the car jerked forward and stalled. He was in third. He started the engine again, put it in first, and took his foot off the clutch. The engine was noisy but it worked and the car moved away. There was a loud THWAP THWAP THWAP and the car bumped jarringly as it got more speed. It must have had a flat. In truth two of the tyres were flat on opposite corners. The driver's side and the rear passenger side. It was like making a getaway in a wonky restaurant table.

The policeman stopped running and watched the car get away from him. It left a trail of leaking fluid on the tarmac.

It was a frantic and uncomfortable drive but it was a whole lot faster than walking. The two ambulances were approaching fast. William was driving head-on towards them at an increasing speed. It was hard to work out just how soon they would collide. William moved into fourth gear. He was doing forty-five already and was quickly approaching fifty. He shifted up again. The sound of the sirens grew louder. Their headlights were flashing in time with the strip of blue lights on the roof.

He could see the faces of the paramedics in the front of the ambulances now. The paramedic in the passenger seat of the ambulance that shared his lane was motioning frantically to the driver. The driver slowed down, allowing the ambulance in the lane next to him to get ahead so he could move out of the way. William could hear the manic honking of his horn. They were gaining on him much faster than he had anticipated. The hard shoulder had vanished, as they often do (without apparent reason) on British roads, and William was forced onto the grassy verge. The ambulance got out of the way just in time and William lurched back into the lane.

If they had been police cars maybe they would have stopped and turned around to chase him, but they weren't. They were ambulances and they had injured people to attend to. He knew by now that the ambulance drivers, and the policeman at the scene, would have put a call out about a dangerous driver fleeing the scene of an accident. This wasn't a great plan, William thought.

He came up to a slip road and slowed down as he

approached it. A police car was blocking off the entrance at the other end. William reasoned, correctly, that they had closed the road off so that emergency vehicles could enter the carriageway on the wrong side of the road without worrying about driving headfirst into oncoming traffic. They hadn't considered the possibility that William Rain, the national treasure and renowned games developer, would be driving a banged up motor with one working headlight and two flat tyres at high speed on a road that should have been empty.

William accelerated. He was doing eighty and the car was not happy about it. It was jerking violently. Inside, William was shunted left and then right. He shouted with pain and tears ran down his face. His ribs were killing him. If he ever had any hope of them healing within the next six weeks they were dashed now. He would need a surgeon to get everything back into place. Something beeped and a light came on on the dashboard. It was the fuel light.

'Come on, really?' he said.

A warning sign flashed up on the digital display. TEMPERATURE TOO HIGH. He looked at the temperature gauge. It was in the red. Steam started to rise from the bonnet. It billowed over the windscreen. The engine started to lose power.

'Oh, fucking come on,' he said, banging the steering wheel.

The airbag had fallen out of the hole and rested on his lap. A green road sign flashed past and William just about made out what it said. Shelley Town 18.

'Eighteen miles?' he said, in mild astonishment.

Okay, that's not too far. If he could get off the carriageway and on to the B roads he could ditch the car and figure it out from there.

You got to look on the bright side, right? Thought William. You've been driving for what, five or six minutes at high speed? It might not seem like far but that could have taken an hour or more to walk. Right then, so not a completely idiotic move. And hey, it's a story right? Another one to tell the grandkids. 'Shit,' he said, taking his left hand off the gear stick and clutching his rib as a sharp pain jangled right through him. He couldn't keep this up for much longer. A steady drive in this wreck was liable to beat a man half to death.

Another slip road came up. He slowed down to see if it was blocked. It wasn't. He saw a slip road further on with cars joining the carriageway. There was traffic ahead of him. He had gotten out of the closed-off area. He indicated left, just out of habit, and took the exit.

The car struggled for a few hundred yards and finally ran out of petrol, or overheated, or both, and William managed to coast it around the roundabout. Not far off the roundabout was a bus stop. The THWAP THWAP THWAP of the flat tyres slowed down and William rolled into the bus stop and bumped up the curb. The bumper knocked into a red post box on the pavement and he came to a stop.

He let his head fall back on the headrest. He couldn't stay there long but he was pretty grateful that part of the trip was over. He turned the key towards him and the burping engine died. Steam fled up from the bonnet like a sigh of relief.

He pulled the handle and shoved the door open. He would have been happy just to lean to the right and let himself fall out onto the floor. It might even hurt less than manoeuvring himself out properly. But still, sense got the better of him and he swung his right foot out and turned his body sideways. His left foot joined his right and he used the door to pull himself up with his left hand. His right hand, as usual, was holding his ribs tight.

He left the door hanging open and stood there for a moment. What now? He looked up at the bus stop. He still had no idea where he was and thought the timetable could give him a clue. The bus stop was a three-sided shelter with an overhanging roof. It had a red bench that ran from one end to the other. On one end of the bus stop was a poster. He saw his own face looking back at him. It was advertising the gaming convention and starred him as the special guest. The computer character, Doctor Hammer, whom he had created more than ten years ago, had been superimposed onto his shoulder. The other three members off WWAP were sat on chairs behind him with arms folded and legs crossed. He shook his head. He remembered the photoshoot but it all seemed so surreal. So alien. He looked so healthy then. It must have been a tall wagon because it had been a long fall.

He looked back at the timetable and his attention was drawn by the last stop on the route. The 702 bus to Shelley Town. He almost couldn't believe his luck. He was only a bus ride away. He put his hand in his pocket. No change. Of course there wasn't. The car. He looked over at it. The door was still open, inviting him to search it.

He limped back to the car, with more energy than he'd had all night, and leaned in. He pulled the ashtray open. It was like that scene in Pulp Fiction when John Travolta opens the briefcase and a gold glow lights up his face. There was treasure inside. William clawed it all into his palm and counted the coins. Three pounds and some change. He hadn't caught a bus in a while but he figured that would get him pretty close.

He crawled backwards off the driver seat and returned to the bus stop. There was a digital display at the top of the right side of the bus stop that informed him that the time was three fifty-five and that currently there was NO SERVICE.

He checked the timetable. The first bus is scheduled to come at seven forty. Alright, he thought, in three hours he can be on a bus. And for the next three hours? He looked at the red bench. To his tired body it looked good enough to sleep on. He sat down, put his legs up, and leaned back.

William was fidgeting, trying to get comfortable, when he heard the sound of approaching tyres coming slowly around the roundabout. There was a spurt of blue light and a single bleat of the siren and the car slowed to a stop next to him.

A spotlight on the side of the police car came on and lit on William's back. He was too tired to panic. What good would running do anyway? In the state he was in he wouldn't even get to the end of the bus stop before they grabbed him. He just stayed where he was, back to the car, lying on the bench. The light moved from William and illuminated the car he had stolen.

William listened to the officers get out of the police car and close the doors behind them. He heard the twin footsteps move past him and stop at the side of the stolen car.

'Looks like he ditched it and ran,' said a male voice.

'Do you think he saw anything?' said a female voice, and the torch lighted on William again.

'Can't hurt to ask,' said the male voice.

The footsteps came back to the bus stop, where William was pretending to sleep, and one of the officers nudged him with his torch.

'Hey, wake up. Did you see who was driving that car?' It was the male police officer.

William shuffled but didn't respond.

'Sir, we would really appreciate it if you could tell us what you saw,' said the female police officer.

William shrugged and lifted his head up. He looked at the abandoned car and raised his eyebrows as if seeing it for the first time.

'Right. Some kid dumped it and took off,' he said, and put his head down again and closed his eyes.

'Can you describe the man?' said the policewoman.

William shrugged. 'I don't know. He was wearing a hoodie. Tracksuit bottoms. Trainers. You know the type.'

'Can you give us anything more specific, sir?'

'I wasn't exactly taking notes,' said William, sounding fed up. 'Will you let me sleep?'

'Don't you have a bed for the night?' said the male officer.

'No. Is that a crime?'

'That's a grey area,' he said.

'So just a young man wearing a hoodie, tracksuit bottoms, and trainers. Did you see what colour his hoodie was?'

'No, it's dark,' said William.

'Alright,' said the male police officer. 'Well, this is a crime scene now so you'll have to move along. Here,' William heard the policeman rummage in his pocket and then the sound of change falling on the floor. 'There's a couple of quid. I bought you breakfast. See, I'm a nice guy, right? Now move along, there's another bus stop further along you can sleep on.'

William got off the bench, staying hunched up, and bended to pick up the coins, one by one. He nodded and thanked the officer and then limped away from them.

'Thank you for your help, sir,' said the woman.

William found the next bus stop half a mile down the road. He got himself comfortable on the bench and rested his head. You wouldn't think it, especially not on such an uncomfortable excuse for a bed, but William thought sleep would come easy and that it would come fast. And he was right. It was a hungry sleep. It devoured him.

CHAPTER 32

It was cold in Dirk's room. The kind of cold that creeps up on you and licks the back of your neck. The kind of cold that makes you shudder instead of shiver. The kind of cold normally reserved for dead things.

Dirk rolled over to his side and pulled the duvet up to his chin. His back faced the window. The curtains were open, letting in what little light there was from outside. He could see the outlines of furniture, lit by the moon and the street lights. The bed, the bedside table, the wardrobe, the unit with the TV on top and his collection of video game consoles underneath. He could see the chair in the middle of the room that was mostly used to dump clothes on. During school the chair was tucked under the desk next to his bed for homework purposes. In the summer it faced the bed and slowly got burdened with laundry.

A shadow crossed over Dirk's face and he heard the sound of something heavy settling on something soft.

He opened his eyes and stared at the chair. There was a person sitting there. Watching him. Dirk didn't move. This had happened before. You think you see someone and it turns out it's just the shape of some clothes making the outline of a man.

Dirk stared at it. It really did look like someone was there. He could see the outline of his neck and ears, and thin hair making a shadowy halo around its head. As his eyes adjusted to the light the face came into focus. The eye sockets were dark circles in a grey face. Dirk closed his eyes and began to breathe hard. He listened for movement. There was complete silence apart from the sound of his own heart which had started to echo around his head.

Dirk swallowed and held his breath. He scrunched up his eyes and tried to listen as hard as he could. The person wasn't moving. Dirk couldn't even hear it breathe.

Every second that went by was like a horrible tapping. Like Death was knocking on some invisible door in Dirk's soul. 'Nearly time to die, Dirk,' said the cloaked skeleton in Dirk's imagination. Dirk lay there trying to find the courage to open his eyes. He managed to open one. His vision was blurry from moisture that had been squeezed out of his tear ducts from his eyes being scrunched up so tight. The chair came into focus. The man was still there.

In a fit of movement Dirk threw off his duvet and scrambled for the lamp on the bedside table behind him (the smashed lightbulb having now been replaced by his dad). He turned it on and grabbed it with both hands. He spun back around pointing the lamp at the chair like a gun. 'What do you want!?' he shouted.

A circle of light spotted the chair. It looked like the opening scene in a play. An empty set. A stage waiting for an actor to make his entrance. The chair was vacant. Maybe the actor was stood in the wings waiting for his mark. Any moment now he would swan on and start a clever monologue. Dirk stared with his eyes wide open. His jacket was hung on the back of the chair and his dressing gown was slung on top of that. He moved the lamp around the room thinking maybe the figure that had been there had jumped out of sight in the commotion, but the room was empty. He shone the light back on the chair.

He breathed out and looked at it for a moment. Even with the light on it looked like the outline of a man. He had seen a shape in the darkness and the brain's own inclination to see faces, to make abstract patterns into familiar forms, had created a man where a man was not. Dirk was, essentially, fucking with himself.

He laughed, just one single outward noise of relief, and relaxed. The light dropped away from the chair and Dirk put it back on the bedside table and turned it off.

He got comfortable in bed again and rolled over to his side. He looked at the chair and smiled. Even though he knew the shape that was still in the chair was just an illusion it was still freaky. He thought about turning the big light on and just putting everything away and putting the chair under the desk, but he didn't. He was able to look at the silhouette with curious amusement now that the fear had been extracted from it.

He looked at it. It was amazing the way the edge of the dressing gown curved that way so it looked just like an ear. And the way the light fell on the folds to give it the awkward symmetry of a gnarled face. He knew he would get nightmares if he looked at it for too long so he yawned and closed his eyes. He intentionally thought about nicer things so that his dreams would be okay. He thought about a bright kitchen on a sunny day and cold milk being poured into cereal. It was his birthday in his daydream and beautiful women were lined up around the block wearing skimpy underwear and each holding a present just for him. He hoped when he nodded off his subconscious would take over and the fantasy would become real in that way that only dreams can do. You never question the impossible when you're dreaming.

'Hello Dirk, I've got you something for your birthday, but you have to kiss me if you want it,' said the first girl, coming into the kitchen. She looked like an amplified version of Martha. A skinny waist and huge breasts and Martha's sarcastic and wild eyes. Dirk looked out of the window at the other girls. They all looked like Martha. Some were blonde, some were redheads, some were taller than others, but they all had Martha's face and they were all beautiful.

'Well, Dirk? My lips can't wait forever.'

Dirk closed his eyes. He kissed her. When he opened his eyes again she had the face of Billy. Billy with big beautiful tits.

A noise from the chair woke Dirk up. His eyes shot open and he stared at the chair. His ears were listening so intently it felt like they were trying to pull away from his head. He looked around the room and then back at the chair. Nothing had changed. He calmed down and looked at the false silhouette. He watched the thing and his eyes began to close with the heaviness of real exhaustion. The last few days were dragging him down. He needed rest. He should really get out of bed and just chuck the dressing gown on the floor. That was what was freaking him out. It was the way the face seemed to be staring right at him. But no, he just needed sleep.

The head of the man that wasn't there moved.

'Hello?' said Dirk, quietly, and absurdly.

He wasn't scared for some reason. Not like last time. He wasn't about to jump up and scream. Not twice in a row for the same reason. But it *had* moved, hadn't it? Or maybe the light changed outside making it look like it moved.

Dirk looked at the head. He could see the outline of a jaw. It was as if the face had turned away from him and was now looking out of the window. Looking at the house across the road.

Dirk was breathing slowly. A pungent smell of rancid meat, the sweet smell of old chicken and the sulphuric smell of rotten eggs, filled Dirk's nose. He coughed and held his hand over his mouth. He reached behind him, without taking his eyes off the still figure in the chair, and turned on the bedside lamp.

The shape of the man didn't reveal itself to be a dressing gown as it had before. Dirk could see teeth exposed through flesh, jutting out of the side of a dirty surgical mask. He saw hollow eyes that seemed to be caked with pus. He saw patches of hair, brown with dirt, on a scalp that looked like it had the texture of fish skin.

Dirk switched the light off again.

The man didn't move. Dirk started to shake. He put his arms under his duvet and pulled it up to his face leaving only his eyes exposed. He stared at the ceiling.

He looked out at the moon through the window. He wished he could reach up and push it along the sky. Fast forward the night. He would pop the moon over the horizon and the sun would spring up on the other side, bringing the day with it. Bad things don't happen in the daytime.

But maybe that wasn't true anymore. The rules had changed. You turn the light on and the scary thing disappears, that's what's supposed to happen. Now it was safer in the dark. At least in the dark you can pretend it's only your imagination.

Dirk looked away from the window, and its slow moon, and looked back up at the ceiling. He dared himself to glance to his left and to if the monster was still there. It was easy to believe that the whole thing was some kind of hallucination. Like a dream that has spilled over into the wrong side of reality. A dream that has taken a wrong turn and found itself in the conscious part of the brain.

But then, things had happened. Things that don't usually happen. The thing that happened in Billy's treehouse. The game. Mario. The buried bits of somebody's body.

His eyes darted left and then looked back up. It was still there. Just looking out of the window, like it was thinking about something.

Dirk wanted to close his eyes and sleep. Just nod off and to hell with what happened.

All of his senses were on edge, turned up to full. The pupils of his eyes were huge so they could take in as much light as possible. He could see the figure in his peripheral vision. His eyes were wet with tears. They weren't the sobbing kind, not the kind that rolled down your cheeks. They just filled his eyes, covering them like a glaze. It had the effect of magnifying his pupils so they appeared even bigger than they were.

He closed his eyes and the tears beaded up and rolled down the sides of his face, wetting the hair around his ears. He kept his eyes closed and listened. It was silent. He couldn't hear any breathing, but maybe that was because dead people didn't breathe. He couldn't hear it move either.

He was tense but after an hour of listening hard and not hearing anything he became exhausted and he relaxed. He still didn't open his eyes but he had managed to convince himself that his already overactive imagination was on overdrive thanks to a lack of sleep and the nature of the day's events. I mean, how would you expect a kid his age to react? He thought. It's just a bad reaction.

It was still another hour before the darkness quietly crawled over him and slid him off into a dream. Sleep, oh blissful sleep. And not a nightmare either, he dreamt of girls and ice cream and spaceships and all sorts of surreal and horny things. The dreams of a teen.

The sun came up and Dirk's alarm started to beep. He stirred and opened his eyes. The room was yellow with the morning light. A bird was chirping outside. Relief filled him. He had survived. The whole sleepless night just felt like a bad dream.

The morning air smelled like hot road kill. A festering stench of bile and shit.

Jack Matterson's loose skin had peeled away from the edges of his eye sockets. The surgical mask had become stuck to his face like ghastly papier-mâché, stuck to his mouth by the soft decaying flesh of his lips and cheeks. The gunge caked under his eyes was dry and textured, like Dijon mustard. The back of Jack's eye sockets were a thousand miles away and full of unimaginable horrors. Right there, in full daylight, he was far worse than anything in the shadows.

Dirk rolled onto his side and stopped. His breath caught in his throat. Jack Matterson was staring into his eyes. His eyes were dark holes and Dirk saw what was in them. There were people, so many people, and they were all screaming.

Jack moved forward and Dirk lurched backwards and smacked his head on the corner of the bedside table. Jack Matterson span away and so did the rest of the room. Dirk's eyes rolled in his head and he felt sick. The room spun around him again. The chair span past. Jack Matterson was standing up. Dirk lost track of him when the room went for another circle around his head. He could see stars, it was just like a fucking cartoon, he thought. A spinning room and stars. When the room came around again Dirk couldn't see the chair, Jack was leaning over him, blocking the chair from view.

Dirk's eyes rolled back in his head and everything went dark.

CHAPTER 33

Martha slept in the lounge area of the caravan. The caravan was a Bailey Unicorn. Twenty two feet long. Walk in the door and you would find a kitchen to the right and a lounge area to the left with two couches facing each other. Beyond the kitchen was a bedroom with a double bed and a wardrobe and beyond that was a shower room and toilet.

It never felt like a caravan in there. It was a home. It was a pad. It was a bohemian shack.

The bottom of the couches in the caravan slid out and by rearranging the cushions you could turn it into a second double bed. The bed was permanently made and the whole area had been partitioned off by a big dark blue curtain. This was Martha's bedroom and she was sleeping there now.

Hopkirk was padding around the kitchen area with his tongue hanging out. He was panting and looking around with youthful excitement. Dogs have clocks in them. Martha was sure of that. Thirty seconds before your alarm goes off you can be sure the slobber of a dog will wake you first. Dogs know. The excitement gets too great and that last thirty seconds is too much to handle. Hopkirk's face appeared between the blue curtains. There she was. Martha. The great and brilliant Martha. Hopkirk started panting faster and his mouth seemed to broaden into a smile. He jumped up onto the bed and walked in a circle. Not sure why. Trying to get his bearings maybe. All dogs do it. They can't even take a shit without walking around in a circle first.

He was big, as far as puppies go. St Bernard's are heavy dogs. He stood on her chest and stared at her. She didn't wake up. Martha was dead to the world. A warm slither of drool hung down from Hopkirk's jowl. It stretched and then dripped onto the side of Martha's open mouth. It sat there for a while and might have dripped harmlessly down her cheek, had she not moved. Hopkirk's hot breath made her turn her face away. The slobber rolled into her mouth and ran down her tongue. She coughed and woke up. The moment her eyes opened Hopkirk barked.

It wasn't the first time she had been woken in this way but that didn't prevent her from jumping out of her skin and almost punching Hopkirk full in the face. He barked again and started wagging his tail ferociously.

'Take him out, Martha,' came her dad's voice from the bedroom.

'In a minute,' she said, pushing the dog off of her.

Hopkirk barked excitedly again.

'Martha,' shouted Pete.

'Okay, I'm doing it.'

She threw off her duvet and looked the dog in the eye. Her hair fell over her face in a matted mess. 'You're a prick,' she said, and Hopkirk started panting harder as if joyfully agreeing.

'Are you going to watch me get dressed or can I have some privacy?' she said.

Hopkirk jumped off the bed and sat on the other side of the curtain. Martha could sense him staring up impatiently at the gap.

Why are all my friends so fucking weird? She asked herself, pulling on a cotton shirt that used to be her dads. She climbed off her bed and reached underneath where she had discarded yesterday's jeans. She pulled them on and picked up Hopkirk's lead.

'I'm taking him to Billy's,' she said.

'Have you brushed your teeth?' came her mother's voice.

Martha looked around the side of the kettle and behind the sugar pot. There was a packet of mints there. She took one out and put it in her mouth.

'Done,' she said.

'Okay, have fun honey,' said her mum.

'Okay mum. Bye dad.'

'Bye Marth. Have fun with your boyfriend.'

'Not my boyfriend, dad.'

'I know. Just joking. Don't forget to feed the dog.'

'I won't. Love you. Bye!'

'Love, love, love,' said her parents together.

Martha turned into the square. The front wheel of her bike kicked up small stones. Hopkirk ran along beside her, panting happily. It was already warm this morning and the sky was the bright blue of a tropical lagoon.

She peddled fast and swerved into the centre of the pedestrianised part of the square causing pigeons and squirrels to flee, much to Hopkirk's joy. He yapped at a pigeon as it flew over him. She cycled along the path that ran through the centre of the green and slowed down when she came to the other side. She saw Ryman's police car parked outside of Billy's house and rode past slowly. She dropped her bike in Billy's drive and looked through the living room window. She was expecting to see a couple of policeman in there talking to Billy and his mum but the house was empty downstairs. Best not to ring the doorbell and wake Eunice up, she thought.

She went around to the treehouse and looked up at Billy's window. She picked up a stone and threw it. It clinked off the glass and fell to the floor. She waited. No response. She picked up another stone and threw it just as the window opened. It clattered harmlessly off the window frame and Billy poked his sleepy head out.

'Hi Martha,' he said.

'Snoogle Fargle,' said Martha.

'Blarble Garble,' said Billy, throwing his keys down to her.

She caught them and ran to the front door. This wasn't a particularly unusual way for her to get into Billy's house and there had been talk of getting her own set of keys, it just hadn't happened yet.

Hopkirk followed her in and she closed the door quietly behind them. The house had the usual smell of potpourri and the added scent of cigarettes and lingering whisky. Martha went upstairs, careful not to tread on the squeaky step, third from the top, and went onto the landing. Hopkirk was at her feet, moving stealthily with her.

She saw that the door to Billy's mum's room was slightly ajar. Curiosity got the better of her and she pushed it open an inch and looked in. There was a naked man in the bed with her, the bedsheet not quite covering his body. She caught a glimpse of his exposed penis and almost laughed in surprise. She closed the door and put her hand to her mouth to prevent herself from making any noise. When she was halfway to Billy's door she took her hand away.

'Eunice, you dirty bitch,' she said, under her breath.

She opened Billy's door and went in. He was back under his duvet.

'You lazy fucker,' she said. 'Get out of bed.'

'Five more minutes,' he said.

'You know there's a man in your mum's bed?'

'It's DCI Ryman,' he said, into his pillow.

'No way?'

'Yeah.'

'Did you hear them going at it?'

'Yeah.'

'Really? Tell me all.'

'I'm not talking about it.'

'Shit, what about your dad?'

'I'm not talking about it, Martha.'

'Well, get up then. I want to talk to you about yesterday. Have you seen Dirk?'

'No. Until you started throwing stones at my window I was asleep. I haven't even seen my own reflection yet.'

'Then you are luckier than I am.'

'Why?'

'Because I've already had the displeasure of seeing your face.'

Billy rolled over and looked at her.

'Oh, you're a funny girl. Ha ha. You don't look too hot yourself.'

She was sitting on the end of his bed, smiling at him through her matted un-brushed hair.

Billy laughed. 'What do you look like?' he said.

'I couldn't be bothered to get ready this morning. I think I might stick with this look, what do you think?'

He thought for a minute and shrugged. 'It suits you actually.'

'I thought you said I didn't look too hot.'

'You're as sexy as it gets, Martha.' He said, like he was being sarcastic, but he meant it.

She knew he did too but just smiled and kept it to herself.

'Come on,' she said, patting his leg. 'Get dressed.'

He threw off the duvet, revealing, not for the first time, that he slept in his underpants, and sat up on the edge of his bed.

'What time is it?' he said.

'Coffee time,' she replied.

He nodded. Why not. They had only started drinking coffee the month before but they liked it. It made them feel older than they were and it gave them an exciting buzz.

In the kitchen Billy turned the kettle on. He was dressed but had decided not to comb his hair either. If she could look hot in a mess then he could look dishevelled. He really just looked like a scruffy kid.

He put four spoons of coffee in a Thermos flask and six sugars. He filled it until it was two inches from the top with hot water and topped it up with milk. He screwed the lid on and put it in his rucksack. He put two mugs in there too and grabbed a couple of croissants from the basket on the kitchen table.

'Come on,' he said. And they headed out to the treehouse.

Martha lifted Hopkirk out of the desk drawer and Hopkirk ran off to Den the Third to sleep on the bed, as he usually did, and Billy and Martha sat next to each other on the coach seats.

Billy filled the mugs with coffee and gave Martha one of the croissants.

'So, yesterday was pretty fucking weird,' she said, with a mouth full of pastry.

'You can say that again.'

'So I guess ghosts are real,' said Martha.

'Do you think it's over?'

'I don't even know what *it* was. I'm amazed I was able to sleep last night.'

'I'll be honest. I've been pretty scared. If it wasn't for the noise Mum and Ryman were making I don't think I could have slept. I think I'm in shock a bit. It's like my brain has decided to just not think about anything. I don't even have the energy to think about Mum cheating on Dad.'

'You know, you never told me what happened between your parents. Did they break up?'

'I don't know. I think so. I think maybe they're on a break or something.'

'Sorry you have to deal with that shit.'

'It's okay. Being attacked by a ghost is a pretty good distraction.'

'Yeah, I guess. It's all about unfinished business with ghosts right? So maybe it's all over. He just wanted us to find his body and we did.'

Billy nodded and drank from his coffee cup. Martha did too and had another bite of her croissant. Her eyes fell on the console that was still plugged into the television with the game, Shelley Town RPG, in the cartridge slot.

'Do you think it still works?' she said.

'I'm not sure I want to find out,' said Billy.

'Let's turn it on,' she said.

'No fucking way,' he said, and he shuddered at the thought of it.

The television turned on with an electrical CLUNK and a light came on on the console. They both froze and stared at it. The screen went blank and the words SHELLEY TOWN RPG came up on the screen.

'Okay, fuck this, I'm getting out of here,' said Billy, putting his coffee down and standing up.

The screen resolved into a pixelated sky view of Billy's

house with the treehouse in the garden. There were gamer tags over the roof indicating that MIRTH and BRAIN were in the treehouse.

'Wait,' said Martha. 'Look.'

Standing on the pavement, in the game, on the other side of Billy's garden fence, was a third character. It looked like Doctor Hammer from their parent's game. The gamer tag above the sprite read, JACK MATTERSON.

Billy didn't move. Martha crawled over to the entrance of the treehouse and looked out. There was a man wearing a doctor's coat and a surgical mask standing by the fence, staring up at her. She recoiled and knocked into Billy.

'What's out there?' said Billy, his voice quivering.

'I don't know. A man. He's just standing there.'

Something moved on the screen and they looked to see what it was. The character sprite that was called JACK MATTERSON was walking along the pavement to Billy's driveway.

'We have to look,' said Martha.

Billy nodded and got down on his hands and knees. They crawled to the entrance of the treehouse and looked out. The man in the doctor's coat was walking down the drive.

'Holy shit, what the fuck is that?' said Billy, moving backwards out of sight of the thing. 'Why does he look like that?'

Martha looked out again. She could see the gaping holes where his eyes should be and the patches of hair on a rotting scalp. He was walking across the garden towards the treehouse.

Martha shuffled backwards. 'We have to get out of here now,' she said.

The sprite on the screen got to the tree house and started to climb the ladder in a basic two-frame animation. They heard the sound of hands on wood. Not a sound that would normally frighten them. Just a light pat, one after another. It normally indicated the arrival of Dirk, and they would expect to see his head pop up in the entrance any minute.

'He's climbing the ladder,' said Martha.

Billy ran forward and looked down. Jack was closer than Billy had anticipated. A hand, a familiar hand, a hand that Billy had seen just the day before buried in the dirt in a shoe box, grabbed onto the third rung from the top.

Billy ran to the television and picked it up. It was an old television and it was heavy. He yanked it and the plug came away from the socket. But the screen stayed on and the game flickered. He struggled with it but got to the entrance quickly, dragging the games console along with it. He dropped it just as the hand of the dead man landed flat on the inside of the treehouse. Jack Matterson was looking upwards when it hit him, causing his jaw to break even more than it already was. He slid backwards and fell. The TV followed him to the floor. He hit the ground and a split second later the TV hit Jack. It crushed his chest and stayed there, pinning him to the ground.

Billy stared down at him. The exact scene he could see was displayed back at him in the television. There was the treehouse, pixelated but exactly recreated, the sprite of JACK

MATTERSON was lying on the grass with a television on top of him, almost comical looking with its basic graphics. The television in the game flickered off and then the television in real life did the same.

Jack's left arm reached up and pushed the TV aside. It rolled off him easily. He sat up, his chest was caved in and his surgical mask was hanging off one ear. His jaw hung open, split diagonally by a decade old axe wound. He stared up at Billy and started to get to his feet.

Billy had a killer urge to piss in his pants. He didn't know why but his body seemed to think that would help the situation. He managed to keep his bladder under control and shouted back to Martha.

'Grab Hopkirk, we have to go now.'

She nodded and ducked through to Den the Third. Billy followed her. He could hear the sound of the ladder being climbed again.

CHAPTER 34

The bus stop was bright in the morning sun. A woman, wearing a coat three times too big for her, with short white hair and a face full of resolute age, squinted at the timetable. She thought about prodding the man sleeping on the bench with her walking stick. She wanted him to wake up and go somewhere else so she could sit down. But then, there was some part of her that just wanted to watch him start at her prod and fall off the bench. Maybe the vagrant would hurt himself and a bus would come before he had a chance to retaliate. She would get on the bus, tutting. But she didn't jab him with her cane. She just leaned against him as she studied the timetable, hoping to stir him more gently, but he didn't wake. She knew when her bus was coming, she just wanted an excuse to be affronted by a stranger so she could scold him. It was one of the few joys she had left in life. She gave up on her quest for a morning squabble and stood at the edge of the pavement. Purposely too close. Maybe she could shake her stick at the bus driver when the bus got a bit too near to her.

William was deep down, far away from the bus stop. A hole had opened up in the ground and he had fallen in, just like Alice. A blackness that was soft and comfortable at first but then thickened around him. It grew hard like he was being cast in pitch tar. Images were forming in the darkness. At some point in the night he had stopped his slow descent of unconsciousness and settled into his usual dream position. He always dreamed in the same way. It was as if he was sat in a comfortable chair watching the dream unfold in front of him like a movie. He rarely got involved. Only this time the chair was made of marble, and it was cold against his back, and his whole body was being restrained by a tight-fitting harness.

His eyes were wide open against the darkness. Shapes began to appear. A face. It grinned and then stopped. William found that he couldn't talk. The face grinned again only now he was closer. So close that William had to force his head back to stop them from touching. He recognised the face, as close as it was, it was unmistakable. It was Jack Matterson. Just as he had been in 1992 on that terrible day in the basement.

As he thought it, the basement crawled out of the darkness. It formed in blunt shapes at first and then details emerged. The coarse texture of the cement floor. The splintered steps leading up to a door. A ceiling light that was on but dim. The far wall moved forever backwards and the worktops were littered with stars. Jack stood in the middle of it all.

Something in William's peripheral drew his eyes down to the floor. Jack's daughter was lying prostrate with her face turned awkwardly upwards against the wall. Her little feet, in black shoes, were on their tiptoes with her ankles turned away from each other. Her neck was broken and blood was running out of her ears. The blood had run so much that the whole floor was covered. William looked down at his feet. The blood was welling up above the laces of his shoes.

He looked up at Jack. He was still grinning. Something moved in the wall to the right, above Jack's daughter. A figure, devoid of a third dimension, was pulling itself out of the wallpaper. It was like an image projected onto the wall. Its fingers moved down and dug in, it strained to gain form. With a gasp a thin man in a tweed suit and waistcoat breached the surface of the wall and heaved a great hacking breath. The man sagged as if the effort was too enormous and then strained again. For a moment his human façade disappeared. The effort required to break into William's dream must have been too great to keep the effect up and the man's face rolled away. The tweed jacket peeled and floated into the still air like paint chips. The fingers that were dug into the wall lost their colour. They changed and became sharpened grey bone with black mouldy skin, torn at the knuckles. The demon's face was like a twisted balloon made of tyre rubber. Its mouth yawed open showing sharp black teeth. It strained and coughed like it had lungs ravaged by an eternity of cigarette smoking. It spat and something dark and phlegmy landed in the blood and floated slowly across the floor.

A foot splashed in the blood and was suddenly covered with a shoe. They were made of brown leather. William looked up. A man was standing there adjusting his collar. He cricked his neck.

'Do I need to introduce myself?' he said, not looking at William.

William couldn't talk.

Cacophini looked at Jack with curiosity. He stepped next to him and waved his hand in front of his face.

'He must be busy elsewhere,' he said.

Jack came to life and almost fell. He stumbled and corrected himself. He looked around, realising where he was. He looked at Cacophini and then at William.

'Were you busy, Jack?' said Cacophini.

Jack thought for a moment and then gave a nod. He smiled grimly.

Cacophini stepped in-front of Jack and looked William in the eye.

'Your time is nearly up William. You had ten years. It's you or Billy.'

William tried to shout but his lips were either glued shut or missing.

Behind Jack two more people emerged from the dim shadows of the basement. William recognised them and was more startled at the sight of them than he had been with Jack and the demon, Cacophini. It was Walter and Penny.

They stepped forward and stopped either side of Jack, a step behind him.

'What are you looking at?' said Cacophini, and turned around. He was more surprised than William.

Walter and Penny quietly raised their arms and pointed at the back of Jack's head. Their hands were in the shape of guns. The index finger and the middle finger together, the wedding finger and the pinkie closed, and the thumb up.

'What is this?' said Cacophini.

Jack started to turn. Walter and Penny closed their thumbs and there was a loud hissing sound. The basement shot away. It was like the whole scene had been attached to a taut bungee cord and someone had just released it, snapping back into a black emptiness.

William opened his eyes and the brightness of the sun dazzled him. The breaks of a bus hissed and it came to a stop. William flailed and shouted some incoherent noise. He fell off the bench and groaned.

'Serves you right,' said the old lady.

The bus doors opened and the old lady stepped on.

William looked around and blinked. He patted at the floor with his right hand as if checking to see if it was solid. He looked up and saw the bus. Ah, there it was, reality, right where he had left it.

'Hold on,' said William calling up to the bus driver.

'You got money?'

'Yeah, just let me get up.'

He got to his feet and got his balance on the wide flat pavement. His legs were spread apart and his arms were out at his sides, as if he were balancing on an unstable foot bridge. He took a wide step to the edge of the curb and pulled himself into the bus.

'Everything alright, fella?' said the driver.

'You never know if the floor is just going to open up and swallow you, you know?'

'Not really. Where are you heading?'

William blinked at him. 'Right, where am I going?'

'Yes. I need to know so I can give you a ticket.'

'I know. Sorry, I'm still waking up. Shelley Town.'

'Return?'

'One way.'

The bus driver pressed a few buttons and the fare came up on a digital display. 'Two pound seventy please, mate,' he said.

William rummaged in his pocket and counted out the right number of coins. He held his bunched hand out towards the driver.

'Don't give it to me, mate, just drop it in there.'

'Right, okay. I haven't caught a bus in a while.'

William dropped the money in a tray and the driver pressed a button. A thin strip of paper started printing jerkily out of a slit above the tray. When it finished printing William tore it off.

'Thank you,' he said.

The driver nodded and moved the gearstick into first. The doors unfolded and closed and the bus lurched forward. William stumbled back and grabbed onto a yellow hand rail next to the steps to the upper floor. The bus got to its natural speed of eighteen miles per hour and William regained his balance. He walked to the back, holding onto the seats as he passed to keep himself upright.

The eyes of the other passengers watched as he made his way to the back. He slumped down in a spare seat, second row from the back, and sighed. He stared forward. A teenager on the back seat was watching him. He recognised William but couldn't quite place him. It just looked like a homeless guy. If he had realised it was the great William Rain he would have lost his shit. He would have phoned all his mates and bragged about who he saw on the bus.

William wouldn't have noticed the kid even if he was sat in the chair in front of him, craning back to stare at William face on. His eyes had glazed over. His mind had wandered back to that dream. He felt something grey and cloud-like whirling slowly behind his heart. Some kind of panic. Walter and Penny had been there. He shouldn't have slept. He should have stolen another car. Got there faster. Maybe it was just a dream. Maybe it meant nothing.

He looked out of the window. It wouldn't be long now. He'll get there in time. He'll fix this mess. He leaned against the side and let his head rest on the window. The pavement was rushing past. It looked like so much grey sand flowing by like a river. The vibration of the engine and the wheels on the road gently rattled the window against his head. It was soothing. He watched the people with their shopping bags vanish by. He watched the shops come towards him and then rush past. Pampered Pets, Blockbuster, Woolworths. Whoosh, whoosh, whoosh. He was moving, and that was good. He would be in Shelley Town soon enough.

CHAPTER 35

Billy and Martha were in Den the Third. Hopkirk was growling at the tunnel entrance that led out to the main den. Jack Matterson was in the treehouse. They heard his heavy footsteps cross the den to the entrance of the tunnel and stop. There was a pause and then a shuffling sound.

'What the fuck are we going to do?' said Martha.

Billy was at the back wall trying to find a loose board that he could prise free but his dad had done too good a job putting the thing together.

'That's going to take too long,' said Martha.

Billy turned around. 'The chest. Help me lift it.'

'And do what with it?'

'Shove it in the fucking tunnel,' said Billy, a bit too aggressively.

Martha nodded and leaned down to pick up one end. Billy grabbed the other and they lifted it off the floor. Hopkirk's growl lowered to a deep rumble. A hand slapped on the ground a few feet from the entrance and Hopkirk barked.

'Shit shit shit,' said Martha, stepping backwards towards the approaching thing.

'Drop it,' said Billy.

They let go and the chest landed in front of the tunnel. Billy got on the floor and put his feet against the chest. He pushed and it slid into the hole. He scooted closer and kicked it further in. He felt it collide with the thing that was after them and it jutted back out. He kicked it again, as hard as he could and scrambled to his feet. He pulled the mattress away from the wall and lifted one end. He tried to fold it in half and lost his grip, and it sprang back down.

Martha saw what he was trying to do and picked up one end of the mattress and folded it over. They spun it sideways and dragged it to the entrance. The chest jutted out again and Billy kicked it hard. It went back in, not far but it was enough to wedge the mattress in after it. Martha got behind it and pushed. Billy joined her. It was a tight fit but it went in.

There was a tremendous bang and the mattress sprang out of the tunnel and the chest skidded after it and caught Billy in the leg. He fell onto his back and hit his head on the floor.

Martha grabbed Billy by the arm and pulled him away from the entrance just as Jack breached the threshold into Den the Third. His head leered out, rotten and horrible. Martha ran forward and kicked him hard in the face. Jack's head whipped back and one of his teeth fell to the floor.

Billy's head was throbbing and his back was grazed but the adrenaline shunned the pain aside. Adrenaline has one vital purpose. It is a big red banner in the mind that flashes bright. It has the word RUN on it in big black letters that flash hard and fast. It has another setting, one that says FIGHT. Billy was ready to do both. He got to his feet and grabbed the fire extinguisher that leaned against the back wall. He swung at the side of Jack's head, denting his skull. Billy stared at the injury he had caused, shocked by his own act of violence. A part of Jacks skull fell inwards leaving a gap where it had been. There was no brain underneath the skull. No blood to bleed out. The bit of skull that had broken away rested on a mush inside. It was like an apple that had been left on a window sill in the sun for a week. It was squishy and brown.

Billy looked away and swung the fire extinguisher upwards. It smashed against the roof of Den the Third and for a moment the whole thing lifted up and then fell again. He spun around and swung upwards again. The muscles in his arms were screaming. Martha covered her head with her arms. He caught the roof on the edge, just above the wall, and two planks split outwards. Billy stepped over and started hitting the plank next to the two that had already split with the butt. It broke on the third blow. His arms gave in and the fire extinguisher dropped to the floor and landed with a THUD between his feet. He pulled the trigger pin from the top and aimed it at Jack. He squeezed the trigger and a burst of white foam exploded from the nozzle and shot across the floor. It caught Hopkirk on the hind legs and he yelped and jumped out of the way.

Billy angled the extinguisher upwards. Jack was almost out of the tunnel. His knee was bent out and his foot was planted squarely on the floor. He was looking right at him. Billy only looked into those dead empty eyes for a single heartbeat and then lifted the nozzle and filled them with white foam.

Martha picked up Hopkirk and shoved him through the hole in the roof. She lifted herself up and squeezed through, scratching her chest on the splintered wood as she pulled herself up. She grabbed onto the branch that ran along the apex of the pitched roof and pulled herself out. She turned and looked back inside.

'Billy, come on.'

Billy chucked the extinguisher at Jack and it cracked against Jack's knee and fell to the floor. He pulled himself up into the hole and grabbed Martha's hand. She leaned back and pulled Billy halfway out. He let go of her and grabbed on to the branch. He pulled his legs free from Den the Third and climbed up onto the roof.

Jack's arm, in its bloodied white doctor's sleeve, came out of the hole. His head followed and he looked out at Billy and Martha. He grabbed for Martha's feet and she edged backwards. Jack twisted trying to get his other arm through the gap. He struck the roof from the inside and the whole roof shifted sideways a few inches.

Martha stumbled and found her balance. Billy picked Hopkirk up under one arm and grabbed onto a branch. He stepped carefully around onto the roof of the tunnel. Martha followed him and got over just as the roof of Den the Third was shoved off its supporting walls and smashed to the ground.

Billy leapt onto the roof of the main treehouse and lied flat on his front, still holding Hopkirk. He held the puppy over the edge and swung him into the entrance of the treehouse. He swivelled his legs around and dropped down. He put Hopkirk in the lift and pulled the rope free. The lift descended quickly and Hopkirk jumped onto the grass just before the drawer hit the floor.

'Martha?' shouted Billy.

'I'm right behind you,' she said.

Her legs came over the edge and Billy helped her down.

'Ladder,' said Billy.

'No shit,' said Martha, and started down the ladder.

Billy went down after her. They got to the bottom and ran to the driveway. They picked their bikes up off the floor and cycled out onto the road without looking back. They cycled hard and fast. Hopkirk ran gallantly along beside them.

CHAPTER 36

Dirk stirred. His left arm and leg were hanging off the edge of the bed. The corner of his Zelda patterned duvet was wrapped around his torso. The tangled duvet was the only thing that kept him from falling off the bed and hurting himself further. He had dreamt in the night but his dreams were grey and soundless. They were the dreams of the concussed.

He winced. It had taken him a while to climb all the way to consciousness but now he was there he regretted it. With wakefulness came pain. His head was throbbing. He touched the back of his head and pressed down. It had the softness of a bruise. He imagined a pulsing red bump, like in a Looney Tunes cartoon. He checked his fingers, expecting blood, but found them to be unstained. With his condition it was remarkable that his whole skull had not simply shattered to pieces like a dropped snow globe.

He sat up on the edge of the bed and held his head in his hands. The room span for a moment and the sensation scraped against the inside of his skull. He opened his eyes and looked up at the window. The sun came into the room like it was searching for life. Like a big light-filled eye was pressed against the glass. It cast a shadow of the window frame onto the floor and the corner of the bed. In the sheet of light a million dust particles swarmed. Dirk knew what dust was mostly made of. It was a cloud of dead skin. Dirk squinted at them through the pain of his headache. The bright sun was making it worse.

He got to his feet and found his balance. The sun glanced over him and lit up his blue pyjamas. He looked out of the window at the empty street below. The police tape was still up around the garden of the Matterson house. How did I hurt my head? He thought, and then stopped. Frozen in the sunlight. The chair was behind him, on the other side of the bed. There was a man in it wasn't there? Dirk felt the eyes of the man on his back. He remembered his face. The dead skin and the empty eye sockets.

He turned around slowly, keeping his breath held hard in his lungs. He stopped, with the sun on his back, and stared at the chair. It was empty. He breathed out with a grateful sigh. It was just a bad dream. He walked around the end of his bed and opened his bedroom door. The smell of breakfast filled the house and he breathed it in. Hot toast. Fresh coffee. Crispy bacon.

'Save some for me,' he shouted over the banister, making his way sleepily down the stairs.

He jumped off the second step from the bottom and landed catlike on the floor. The smell of breakfast can really bring life back to you. The thumping ache in his head was falling away. He walked into the kitchen and stopped.

The room was painted red with a dripping veneer of blood.

The walls, ceiling, worktops. It dripped off the edges of the table. Black smoke fled from the grill like an upside-down waterfall.

The focal point of the decor, the stars of the show, the cherry on the cake, was the bodies of his dead parents.

Dirk's bottom lip curled up. His eyes turned down. He fell to his knees. And started to scream.

His mother's face had been smashed repeatedly into the open edge of the refrigerator door, which had a hard wooden façade. Now she hung there, like a raincoat on a hook. Her nightgown was wet against her body. Her knees were slightly off the ground. Her toenails were spit and broken from her frantic attempts to get away before the insides of her head had emptied over her body and she'd stopped moving. One of her eyes, split jaggedly across the pupil, looked up at her from its vantage point on the floor, next to some split eggs that had fallen out of the fridge.

Dirk's screams had turned to snotty wide eyed sobs. Tears ran down his cheeks. He coughed and shook where he knelt. He blinked and a vision of Jack filled his imagination. He saw him towering over his mother, the back of her head grasped in his hand. Hitting her pretty face into the corner of the fridge. Her eye socket cracking. Jack pulling her back and hitting her face into the sharp wooden edge again, and again, and again, smashing it inwards until the sound was less like bone knocking on wood, and more like feet treading in grapes.

Dirk gagged and threw up some bile.

Dirk's father was on his back under the kitchen table, like

a discarded ragdoll. His face had been smashed in by one of the table legs which now stood in his head, resting against the back of his skull. The bottom half of the table leg was red with blood spatter. There were brown handprints on the corner of the table top. The mouldy handprints of Jack.

Dirk tried to stop his imagination from playing out the scene. Jack Matterson there, in the morning light of the kitchen, violently murdering his parents. The images came anyway. He imagined Jack lifting the corner of the table over his dad's terrified face, and then slamming it down, his head bursting inwards like a watermelon.

Dirk crossed his hands over the back of his neck and pulled his head down between his knees. He scrunched his eyes up and tried to get out of there. He started crawling backwards out of the kitchen, leaving smeared handprints on the bloody floor.

The front door flew open and banged against the wall. Dirk screamed and turned around. He put his arms over his face to protect himself.

'Dirk!' shouted Billy. 'We have to get out-' he stopped talking.

'Dirk get up,' said Martha, running over to him.

Billy tapped her on the arm and she looked up at him. 'What?'

Billy pointed into the kitchen.

'Oh my god,' she said, with quiet shock.

'Dirk, your parents,' said Billy.

Dirk was crying. It was a drooling erratic sob.

Billy and Martha looked at each other. Billy grabbed Dirk by the arm.

'Get up,' he said. 'We don't have time to react to this now. We have to move.'

Martha looked at him with open wet eyes. Shock had momentarily stilled her.

'Grab his other arm and get him outside,' he said.

She nodded and grabbed him under the armpit.

'Get to your feet, Dirk,' said Billy.

'I can't.'

'You have to.'

They managed to lift him to his feet and drag him outside.

Martha let go and picked up her bike.

Hopkirk was stood at the end of the driveway peering down the road. He was growling. His ears were down and his tail was straight and still.

Billy hooked Dirk's arm around his own neck and walked him quickly to his bike.

'You have to sit on my handlebars. We don't have time to get the Dirkmobile.'

'I can't do this,' said Dirk.

Billy picked up his bike and looked right, towards his house. Jack Matterson was walking diagonally across the road towards them.

'There's no time for this, Dirk.'

Dirk saw Jack and started to tremble. 'He's real. This is all real.'

'Dirk, please get on the fucking handlebars! Martha, get out of here.'

She ignored Billy. 'Dirk, honey, listen to me. We are in danger and we can't leave you here. You don't want us to get hurt do you?' she said.

Dirk shook his head. The front of his pyjamas were wet with urine. His knees and hands were wet with blood.

'So get on my handlebars,' said Billy.

Dirk nodded and started to move. Billy kicked the pedals back and stopped them from spinning with his left foot. Dirk pulled himself up and leaned back so his shoulders rested against Billy. Billy leaned forward. He pushed down on the pedal and cycled out of the drive just as Jack stepped onto the pavement a few feet away.

Martha was quick after them. Hopkirk barked once at Jack and then shot off after Martha in a bounding gallop.

'Where are we going?' said Martha, cycling as hard as she could.

'The convention centre,' shouted Billy, turning his head so the words would travel behind him. He caught a glimpse of Jack Matterson. He was walking steadily after them. They could outrun him easily, thought Billy. We just need to keep moving.

'Why there?' said Martha.

'Because it will be busy,' he shouted back.

CHAPTER 37

The convention centre had been a church once, but you wouldn't think it now. It had been turned into a gamer's heaven. Stalls were packed with merchandise. They were staffed by mostly unshaved men and women with colours in their hair. They wore brand new polo shirts with laminated lanyards hung around their necks.

Every other stall had some kind of tech demo or new game to show off. There were food stands already filling the air with the smell of popcorn and hotdogs and Chinese noodles and a host of other foods. One stall sold pancake pizzas, and they looked great. The stage had two single chairs on it. They were good chairs too, brown leather wingback Chesterfields. It would surprise no one if a lord were about to interview an esteemed novelist on stage. But that wasn't the case. The floor to ceiling screen at the back of the stage read:

10:30
Pete and Amelia Chaplin talk on the art and history of Doctor Hammer.

11:30

> Celebrating ten years of Doctor Hammer (presented by Paul Rose - aka Mr. Biffo from Digitiser).
>
> **12:30**
>
> Doctor Hammer Speedrun Championship. (Introduced by Billy Rain).
>
> **14:00**
>
> Interview with William Rain, Walter Chaplin, Amelia Perry, and Pete Perry.

There was music coming out of the PA speakers. Right now it was the Tetris theme but there were about twenty five classic game themes playing in a loop. The music was quiet. Not so quiet that you couldn't hear it, but not so loud that it was annoying. It was loud enough that someone might stop mid conversation, point at the ceiling, and say, 'Hey, it's Pac-Man.'

Chris checked his watch. He felt like he had checked it every thirty seconds in the last ten minutes. Time was dragging. It was the anticipation. There was a megaphone on the floor next to his feet. Becky stood with him in front of the main doors. On the other side of it were hundreds of eager geeks and nerds. The best kind of people, as far as Chris was concerned.

'Are you ready for this?' said Becky.

'Shitting myself, mate.'

'How long?'

Chris checked his watch again. 'Two minutes.'

'Fuck it, let's open the door now,' said Becky.

Chris nodded. 'Alright, let's do it.'

He pulled the bolt out of the latch in the great oak church doors and held onto the cast iron ring in the middle of the left door. Becky grabbed onto the one on the other side.

'Ready?' said Chris.

'Yep.'

They pulled and the doors swung inwards. There was a cheer from outside. Chris picked up the megaphone and stepped through the open doorway.

Martha and Billy, with Dirk on his handlebars, cycled into the carpark of the convention centre and stopped. Chris saw them over the crowd of people and waved. Martha saw him and waved back. It was a rushed wave, like she had seen someone she didn't have time to deal with right now. Chris watched them drop their bikes on the floor. Billy and Dirk almost fell over as they dismounted. Hopkirk was running excitedly between Martha and Billy, barking occasionally. They left their bikes where they fell and ran into the swell of waiting WWAP fans.

Becky stepped behind Chris and looked out at the people.

'Wow, look at them all,' she said.

'It's crazy, isn't it?' said Chris.

There were probably twenty or thirty people dressed normally, the vaguely disinterested parents of eager children, but everyone else was dressed in cosplay. Some were just chucked together last minute, or bought from costume shops, while others had spent hours and hours over many weeks, building and painting, and sewing, and creating such incredible outfits that Chris thought they ought to be getting paid for their skills by big production companies in Hollywood. No doubt they were just ordinary folks with ordinary jobs that had a passion for gaming and a desire to dress like their heroes.

Chris raised the megaphone to his mouth and pressed the trigger. The loudspeaker crackled and his voice came out, loud and clear. 'Ladies, Gentleman, and other lavatories,' he said. It was a joke he had been conflicted about ever since he decided to use it. The last thing you want is a pause expecting laughter but only having silence returned to fill the void. But it didn't matter, the joke got lost in the general noise of the gathered. Everyone turned and looked at him. The talking turned into a murmur and then into silence.

'At least you got their attention,' said Becky, patting him on the back. 'I'm going to get behind my console and turn the music up a notch.'

'Okay,' said Chris. He smiled and took a casual step forward. He put his free hand in his pocket and put the megaphone to his mouth.

'I'm Chris King, the organiser of this event.'

Everyone cheered and Chris found himself blushing. That hadn't happened since he was a kid. He remembered a particularly attractive teacher at his school had told him he was handsome and he turned bright red, right there in the middle of the class. This felt the same but instead of embarrassment he felt pride.

'I want to welcome you to The Retro Gaming Convention 2002. The first of its kind in Shelley Town. Hopefully it will be the first of many. I will be hosting some conversations on stage later with all of the members of WWAP.'

The audience cheered and a woman screamed with hysteric glee, another joined her, and a few wolf whistles rose from the crowd. Holy shit, thought Chris, it's like Beatlemania out there.

Chris put the megaphone to his lips but stopped short when something fluffy and slobbering burst from between someone's legs and bounded up the stairs. It was Hopkirk.

Someone in the queue said, 'Hey, what do you think you're doing?' and stepped out of the way to let someone pass. The queue begrudgingly let three youngsters barge their way to the front. Billy ducked under the rope at the bottom of the stairs and was stopped by a security guard.

'Hold on there, kid,' he said, putting his hand on Billy's chest. 'You've got to wait like everyone else.'

'That you, Billy?' said Chris.

Martha squeezed through and stood next to Billy, Dirk looked over her shoulder. Martha was holding his hand, keeping him close.

'Yeah, hi. Can we come through?'

'Of course, get the hell up here.'

The security let them through amidst a few boos and quite a bit of speculative murmuring.

'Stand up here with me,' said Chris.

Billy walked up the steps and stood next to him. He turned and faced the crowd. Chris put the megaphone to his mouth.

'Ladies and gentlemen, Billy Rain, Martha Perry, and Dirk Chaplin.'

Everyone screamed. A woman at the back shouted, 'WE LOVE YOU BILLY!'

'Alright, calm down, they're just kids,' said Chris. 'They will be helping out with various things throughout the day. Billy will be hosting a speedrun challenge. Maybe we'll see a new world record time on Doctor Hammer, and-'

But he couldn't finish. He was overwhelmed with more excited shouting and hollering.

Billy looked over the audience, ignoring their gleeful faces and frantic attempts at catching his attention by waving and jumping, and reaching, and screaming, and saw a man standing at the entrance of the carpark, staring right at him. He was wearing a white doctor's coat, covered in red stains, and a loosely fitting surgical mask. From this distance his features were undefined. His skin was brown-grey and he was naked apart from the coat.

Billy glanced at the cheering audience, thinking he should warn them, not knowing what to say, knowing there was no time. Hopefully Jack would leave them alone. It was Billy and his friends he wanted.

He stepped backwards out of sight. Martha and Dirk had already edged past the doorway and were well into the main hall of the convention centre.

'There he goes,' said Chris. 'Alright ladies and gentleman, calm down.'

'WOOOOOOOOO!' shouted a man dressed as the Big Ben boss at the end of the Doctor Hammer game.

'Okay, we're going to be removing the rope and letting you in, in just a minute. There's a lot for you to experience and enjoy inside. We have games you can play, industry people you can speak to about getting into game development, we have food and drink stalls, we have new tech demos. You can try out the new virtual reality gear that is still in its early stages but is set to be the next big thing in gaming. The Nintendo Game Cube came out in May this year, and I'm sure many of you already have one. But we have early access to the much anticipated Metroid Prime game, and you can be some of the first to play it in Europe.'

The crowd cheered. The music coming from inside the convention centre stopped and the plucky theme tune of Doctor Hammer started. Becky moved a slider up on her mixing desk and the music got louder.

'You hear that?' said Chris.

'Doctor Hammer!' someone shouted, and more cheering followed.

'I guess that's my cue,' said Chris. 'The convention has begun!'

The security guard reached over and un-hooked the rope. Chris stood aside and greeted everyone as they filed past him. The room slowly filled up with wide eyed adults and children, some dressed as Doctor Hammer, some as other characters.

One kid was dressed as the cup of coffee that you collected in the game to gain health. There were other characters there too. There was an adult size Kirby and a little girl done up as Sonic. One guy was dressed as Batman. There's always a Batman. And of course there were Star Wars characters. Darth Vader can always be found at a convention, regardless of the theme.

Billy, Martha, Dirk, and Hopkirk, had run straight to the back of the hall to the main stage and were now making their way around back to the organisers area. They hadn't had time to get their guest lanyards but they were well known enough as the kids of WWAP to get past security, who just greeted them cordially and let them through.

'My parents will already be here somewhere,' said Martha. 'We need to find them and tell them what's going on.'

'They're never going to believe us,' said Billy.

'Do you have a better idea?' said Martha.

They were in a back corridor, lined with empty black trunks, which once housed the lights that hung above the stage. Dirk sat down on one and stared blankly at the wall opposite. Billy and Martha stopped and looked at each other. They walked back and sat on either side of him. Billy put his hand on Dirk's back and Martha put a hand on his knee. Hopkirk sat on the floor and looked up at him.

'You okay, Dirk?' said Billy. It was a stupid question, but what else could he say?

Dirk shook his head. 'My mum and dad are dead.'

They expected him to cry but he just kept staring. The

scene in his kitchen was still vibrant in his mind, projected onto the wall opposite him. Every blood-soaked detail.

Billy thought about his own mum then. What if something had happened to her too? No, it wasn't worth thinking about. No point in getting in a panic about things that might not have happened.

'Martha?' came a voice down the hall. They all looked up. It was Pete.

'Dad!' shouted Martha.

She got off the trunk and ran to him, almost knocking him over with her embrace. He put his arms around her and threw a quizzical look at Billy. Billy didn't reply in any way.

'What's up kid?' he said.

'I'm so happy to see you,' she said.

This was the most affection Pete had seen her betray since she was a little kid. Martha was not the lovey-dovey type.

She looked up at him. 'Walter and Penny are dead.'

Dirk burst out crying.

CHAPTER 38

The bus pulled up on the road that ran past Shelley Town square and William Rain thanked the driver and got off.

It was hot. He felt like he could light a match and the air would catch fire it was so dry.

There weren't many people around in the square. In fact it was eerily empty. William swallowed but his tongue just clicked in his mouth. Maybe it was him that was dry. Dehydrated needed a new word. He was completely desiccate of moisture.

He walked down to Finnegan's tobacconist and went in. The bell above the door tinkled.

'Hey, Finnegan,' said William, to the big man behind the counter.

The man behind the till looked at William with a smile that showed he was willing to greet any customer with a smile but didn't particularly recognise this one.

'Do I know you?' he said, still smiling, but now with a slight frown.

'Come on, Finnegan, it's me.'

He frowned more but then recognition dawned on him and he almost laughed.

'What the fuck happened to you?' he said, with a wide mouth and just as wide eyes. 'You look like you belong in a Charles Bukowski novel.'

'I've never read any of his books,' said William.

'I thought you were speaking today at the convention?' he said.

'Yeah, I guess I'm heading that way. I don't have any money on me.'

'What do you need?'

'A drink.'

'Help yourself,' said Finnegan, directing William to the fridge behind him with a nod of his head.

'Thanks.'

William grabbed a bottle of water and noticed the beer bottles on the bottom shelf. He looked away and picked up a can of coke.

'Sure you don't mind?' said William.

'No, that's alright. So what's going on, man?'

William put the can of coke on the counter and opened the water and drank deeply. When the bottle was empty he screwed the cap back on and put the empty bottle down next to the coke. He thought for a minute. 'It's hard to explain.'

'I ain't goin' nowhere,' said Finnegan.

William looked down at the glass-covered counter. Next to the penknives and the Zippo lighters was a long barrelled revolver. He looked at it and visions from his nightmare flashed on the surface of the glass counter, like it was a transparent television set.

JACK'S GAME

Jack Matterson was smiling at him. Walter and Penny stood behind and raised their hands to the back of his head like they were pointing guns at him. Finger guns, like they were playing a game. Their thumbs came down, like they were shooting, and the glass of the counter exploded outwards with a loud CRASH. William stumbled back and raised his arms over his face.

Finnegan leaned forward and grabbed William by the arm to stop him falling back into the fridge. He had pretty good reflexes for an older guy.

'Woah there, man, what's the deal?'

William lowered his arms enough to peer over them and looked at the counter. It was fine. Not even a crack. He let his arms down and apologised.

'I'm sorry, I, I thought I saw something.'

'What do you think you saw, William?' said Finnegan.

'It doesn't matter. I need that gun.'

'I'm not sure that's a good idea.'

'I thought it was illegal to sell guns in England, anyway,' said William, not taking his eyes off that grey piece of violent metal.

Finnegan sat back down. He had a concerned look on his face. 'You're allowed to sell guns that are above a certain length. It's to stop people selling handguns and other concealable weapons. So some bright spark just started making the barrels longer and adding a counterweight to the handle. Looks kinda cool doesn't it? Like something out of an old western.'

'How much is it?'

'What do you need a gun for, William?'

'I think Billy's in danger,' he said, looking away from the gun and directly at Finnegan.

Finnegan looked into his tired heavy eyes and knew he was telling the truth.

'Why, what's happened to Billy?' he said, and found to his surprise that anger welled up from his belly and caught in his throat. 'If anyone harms that kid I'll kill them myself,' he said.

William was taken aback by his reaction. 'I didn't know you knew him that well?'

'He's been coming here every day for years, you know that.'

'Right, for Eunice.'

'Right.'

'You going to give me the gun, Finnegan?'

'Give it to you?'

'I can pay you later but right now I just need the gun. I need you to trust me.'

'Tell me what's happened to Billy.'

'I can't.'

'Why not?'

'Because it sounds fucking crazy. That's why. Just give me the fucking gun, Finnegan!'

Finnegan stood up. 'You better get a handle on yourself, William. We go back but I don't let anyone come in here and just start demanding things.'

'Alright, you're right. I'm sorry.'

William took a step back from the counter. 'Can you spare a cigarette?'

'Sure. What's your brand?'

'Any.'

Finnegan reached behind him and grabbed a packet of Sovereigns and threw them on the counter.

'Thanks,' said William, picking up the pack and peeling off the film sleeve. He opened it up and that familiar dry tobacco smell rose up from the pack. He took out a cigarette and put it in his mouth. 'You got a lighter?'

Finnegan motioned to a large round object on the counter with a brass lever on top. William pulled it down and it clicked, the sound of a spark being generated, and a two inch flame danced out of the top. William raised an eyebrow and put the end of his cigarette into the fire and sucked. He blew out a lung-full of smoke.

'Do you mind if I smoke in here?'

'Sure, if you tell me what's going on?'

William opened the coke can with a fizz and drank from it. 'Ah, Christ, I forgot how much I hate that shit,' he said.

'Here, I can fix that for you,' said Finnegan.

He poured some of the coke into the bin on the floor next to him and picked up a half empty bottle of whisky from under the counter. He poured it into the can.

'Bit too early?' said William.

'I would say so, but by looking at you, I reckon that sort of thing hasn't been bothering you recently.'

'Yeah, you would be right there,' he said, picking up the

can and taking a drink. 'That's much better.'

'So what's going on?' said Finnegan.

'Alight, I'll tell you, but then you have to give me the gun, and no questions. And bullets too.'

'Alright, whatever you say. What's going on?'

William drew on the cigarette and it burned down a good inch. He let out the smoke and had another drink from the can.

'I think Jack Matterson is going to kill my son.'

Finnegan rolled his eyes. 'Jack's dead, William. You killed him yourself.'

CHAPTER 39

Ryman's phone vibrated off the bedside table and fell to the floor with a thump. Ryman's eyes sprang open. The phone vibrated again and jiggled across the hard surface.

Ryman looked left. Eunice was fast asleep next to him. Her hair in a mess, her mouth slack open, drool dribbling onto the pillow. Ryman frowned at her, trying to place just who the hell she was. He looked down at his naked body and then up at the ceiling and at the room around him. Just where the hell was he?

He looked at the woman again. The sheet barely covered her. One of her breasts was free and a long leg was inelegantly exposed. Her legs hung open and she had one arm up on the pillow over her head and the back of her other hand rested on her cheek. Christ, thought Ryman, she sleeps like a bloke.

He sat up on his elbows and closed one eye and raised the eyebrow of the other. Well, he was hungover, that was for sure. A memory was beating at a door in the back of his mind. He opened the door and peaked in.

'Shit,' he said, and swung his legs over and sat on the edge of the bed.

Eunice snorted and woke up. She stared at Ryman and

then looked quizzically around her. She's just as hanging as I am, thought Ryman.

The night before came back to him. Or patches of it did. Pretty good patches.

'Eunice?' he said.

'Why are you awake?' she said, putting her head back down on the pillow.

'What time is it?' he said.

She shrugged and closed her eyes. His phone vibrated again and clattered along the floor. He leaned forward and picked it up. He didn't recognise the number so he let it go to voicemail. It probably wasn't best to answer right now, at least not until he was sure he could speak and think right. The phone stopped vibrating and returned to the home screen. He had never seen the screen on his phone so busy with notifications. The phone was a Nokia he'd had since early 2001. On the top of the screen was a picture of an envelope, next to it was the voicemail symbol, next to that was a phone with a line through it. In the centre of the screen was a rectangle with the words 25 Missed Calls written in it.

He looked around for his clothes and only found a sock.

'Eunice, wake up,' he said, pulling the sheet off her.

'Woah, what's the deal?' she said, grabbing for it and missing.

'Where are my clothes?'

She began to answer and then paused. She thought for a moment. 'In the living room?'

He nodded, remembering, and went to the door.

Eunice listened to him run down the staircase and start knocking around in the lounge. God, he's a noisy one, she thought, rolling out of bed. She picked up the sheet and draped it around her. She walked to the window and pulled the curtain open. She looked at the tree just beyond her bedroom window. She tilted her head and considered it for a moment. Something was different. The roof was gone off the area the kids called Den the Third. She couldn't understand it. She peered down at the ground and saw broken planks of wood on the grass.

She frowned. Had there been a storm? She looked over at the drive. Billy's bike wasn't there. She went on tip toes and tried to look over the wall into Den the Third. The bed was half up against one wall and the chest was at an angle in the middle of the room. The most curious thing was the foam. There was white foam everywhere.

A terror ran down her spine. A maternal pang. Her gut rose up and she stepped back from the window.

'Ryman,' she shouted.

She dropped the sheet and ran out of the room into the hall. She pushed Billy's door open and looked in. Billy was gone. Something had happened.

'Ryman!' she shouted again.

She could hear him on the phone downstairs. She ran down them as fast as she could, holding onto the banister and descending two steps at a time.

'Ryman, Billy's in trouble,' she said, stopping in the

doorway to the living room.

Ryman put a finger to his lips and then pointed at the phone he had held to his ear.

'What do you mean it's not there?' he was saying. 'Uh huh? She's dead?' he had one leg in his trousers and was hopping around trying to get the other one in. 'So, what are you saying? Someone killed Freemont and took the body parts we dug up? How did she die?' He pulled his trousers up and looked around for his other sock. 'How can you not know, you're a forensic pathologist aren't you?'

Eunice walked carefully around Ryman and picked her own clothes up off the floor. She put on her pyjama bottoms and looked around for her top. Ryman watched her absently and tucked the phone between his cheek and shoulder so he could do his belt buckle up. She was bent towards him looking under the coffee table for her top. He breasts hung freely and her firm belly creased where his would have flopped. His memory flashed back to the bedroom last night. He couldn't believe his luck to bag a girl like her. He put the phone back to his ear and picked his shirt up off the end of the couch.

'Her face is gone? Alright, I'll be there as soon as I can. I'm leaving now.' He hung up and put the phone in his pocket.

'I have to go,' said Ryman, buttoning up his shirt.

'I'm coming with you,' she said.

'You're coming? You can't come, there's been a murder. I thought you never left the house.'

She found her top hanging off the back of the stereo and slipped it on. 'Billy's treehouse has been destroyed and I don't know where he is,' she said, locking eyes with Ryman. 'Dead bodies can wait, that's what they're good at.'

'Why are you so sure something is wrong?'

'I can feel it in my gut. It's a mum thing,' she said.

He was sat on the edge of the sofa now pulling a shoe onto his socked foot and the other one onto his bare foot. 'Your gut?'

'I know it sounds silly. But please, will you just take me out and see if we can find him? Pretty please.'

It's not silly, he thought, and it's not a mum thing either. His gut knew things too. He pulled his shoe laces tight and put his head in his hands for a moment. He let out a slow breath.

The hangover was grinding through him. He breathed in and slowly let it out again. His gut flickered and he thought of Billy. If you really want to know what your gut thinks, flip a coin. He really believed that. People misunderstand the logic of it. You don't flip a coin to let it choose, you flip it to find out what side you're hoping for just before it lands.

He flipped a coin in his head and imagined it spinning up from his thumb. Heads it's Billy, tails it's Dr Freemont.

He watched it arch up, flashing in his mind, and land on the floor. It bounced once and stopped. He felt the urge in his heart. He wanted it to land on heads.

'Okay,' he said. 'Let's go find your son.'

CHAPTER 40

Jack Matterson's white doctor's coat stuck to his back like the meat underneath was wet. The back of his head was brown and black with rot with patches of hair sticky with blood, clumped in places. A large chunk of the skin around the back of his skull was missing entirely. You could see the yellow of the stained bone underneath. There was a hole at the top of his head where Billy had struck him with the fire extinguisher.

He walked steadily towards the two security guards, Richard and Grant, at the entrance of the convention centre. The crowd had all filtered inside now and the two guards looked at Jack with blank looks on their faces.

'It's not a horror convention, mate,' said Richard. But his voice wasn't quite jeering. There was a nervousness to it.

The other guard, Grant, stepped back and tripped. He fell and scraped his back on the edge of the top step. Richard looked down at him.

'Ooh, that sounded a bit painful, you alright?'

Grant didn't answer, he shook his head slowly, not taking his eyes off the man in the doctor's coat.

'Not scared of a fancy dress costume are you?' said Richard, looking back at the approaching man.

'What's that supposed to be then? Doctor Hammer Two, Back from the Dead? Know what I'm saying?' He was smiling broadly at his own humour, lacking though it was. He looked down at the guard on the floor and shook his head and let out a short laugh. 'You look terrified, mate,' he said, and looked back up at the man in the coat, who was now at the bottom of the three short steps and stepping onto the first.

He looked into the man's eyes and his grin fell away. 'What is that?' he said, his voice trailing away. It was like there was a movie being projected into the back of Jack's eye sockets. It was a black and white horror film. People were clawing to get out, as if they could crawl right out of his eye sockets. They had fear in their faces and they were screaming. So many of them. As far back as the guard could see. The whole universe was in there and it was full with people. So many people.

Jack hit Richard in the chin with the palm of his hand with such force that his teeth shattered. His head shot back and struck the wall behind him. His eyes rolled and he collapsed, limp, to the floor.

Jack looked down at Grant. He was cowering and trembling. He was shaking his head as if trying to plead for Jack to leave him be. Jack reached down and nicked his neck with a jagged fingernail. The man flinched. Jack stood up and watched him. Grant put his hand to his neck and felt the back of it get wet with something warm. He took his hand away and looked at it. It was dripping with blood. It was like it had been dipped in hot red wax. He looked down and saw a red puddle cascading down the steps. He put his other hand to his neck and felt the pulsing of blood pumping out of the jugular. He felt a coldness spread through his body. It started at his feet and went up his legs. Then his hands went cold. They tingled. It moved up his arms. His neck and the back of his ears went cold and he felt his face whiten as the blood ran out of his system. Jack watched. The guard's eyes closed and opened again, as if he was dozing off. He rested back but his arms were too weak to hold his weight. His elbows gave way and his head hit the hard top step with an audible thud. His eyes closed and his body relaxed. Jack looked away from him and stepped into the main hall of the convention centre.

A few people looked at him and then looked away. This guy was taking it too far. A woman wearing a tight fitting Lara Croft outfit looked him up and down and almost gagged. A teenage boy went past wearing a Halo suit with the helmet under his arm. 'Cool,' he said, and stopped to take a picture. Then he walked on.

Jack stayed where he was and looked at the faces of all the people in the hall. He couldn't see Pete or Amelia, or any of the WWAP kids anywhere among them.

He walked slowly through the river of people. He was mostly ignored. One woman held her nose when she went by and gave him a look that said, 'You could have had a shower before you came out in public, mister.'

Jack walked on and people generally got out of his way. In fact, for the most part, people seemed to be avoiding eye contact. He was being treated the same way as his house was. Don't look. If you don't acknowledge the impossible thing, then it isn't real. You never saw it. It's not there.

There was a queue of kids at the VR stall. Jack watched an over-weight thirty-something man push to the front of the queue and step over the rope.

The stall was run by a small development company called MG Games. The MG stood for Michael and Gavin, the two owners of the company, who were both present today.

'Hey,' said the kid at the front, as the man knocked him out of the way.

'I'm sorry, sir, we're not quite ready yet,' said Michael.

'It's alright, I'm a programmer,' he said. 'Tom Gordon.' There was something in the corner of his mouth. It looked like powdered sugar. That's what it was. This ignorant man has just stuffed his face with a donut and now he's going to start touching things with his sticky fingers.

'Sir, please, we just need a few more minutes,' said Gavin, motioning for him to step back over the rope.

'It's alright I know what I'm doing,' said Tom.

'But it's my turn to go first,' said the kid at the front of the queue who had been nudged out of the way. His eyes were wet with tears. His little sister was standing next to him.

'Yeah, and then it's my go,' said the girl.

'Oi mate, did you push in?' came the voice of a parent outside of the queue.

'It's alright, I work here,' said Tom Gordon.

'Like fuck,' said Michael, under his breath so the kids couldn't hear.

The fat man wiped his fingers on his trouser legs and

picked up the VR headset.

'Come on, you can't just pick that up.'

'Chill out, I know what I'm doing.'

He pulled the headset over his head, squeezing it down. 'God, it's a bit tight guys, who designed this?' he said, with a punch-me-in-the-face smile.

'I'm not sure the problem is with the hardware,' said Michael.

'Just run the demo, let's get this guy out of here,' said Gavin.

Michael hesitated and then typed a command into a laptop.

The whole back wall of the stall was a six foot by six foot screen, made up of nine smaller square LCD displays. The MG Games logo that had been there disappeared and turned black. Some code in white letters scrolled up the screen for a second and was replaced with the word, LOADING... It went away and a three dimensional room appeared on the screen. First walls loaded in, then a virtual table, and then some objects appeared on the table's surface.

Tom Gordon turned his head and the room moved around on the screen, like you were seeing what Tom was seeing.

'Cool,' said one of the kids in the queue.

'Alright, I'm going to put something in your right hand now, Mr. Gordon. Okay?'

'Yeh,' he said, still looking around. He craned his neck up to look at the ceiling, and the screen showed the table fall out of view and the ceiling come into shot. He looked down again.

Michael put a basic controller in Tom's right hand. A

handle with a trigger attached.

'You can use this to interact with items in the virtual environment,' said Michael. 'Why don't you try and pick up one of the items on the table.'

Tom looked around and stepped closer to the table that wasn't really there. He put his left hand down as if he was going to bump into it and one of the kids laughed. Tom smiled too. This was pretty fun.

Jack saw the man and stopped. The ignorant man was wearing a WWAP t-shirt. A t-shirt that was far too small for him and caused his love handles to bulge out into the open for all to see, blotchy and pasty like uncooked chicken skin. On the back of the t-shirt was a black and white image of all four of WWAP standing in odd positions. The first two, Pete and Amelia, were standing the same way, with their hands positioned like they were playing air guitar. Then William was there with one hand down by his side and the other at a forty-five degree angle pointing at the floor. Then there was Walter, one arm directly up in the air and the other in a ninety degree angle, pointing at William's head. They were spelling WWAP in semaphore. All four of them. Four. FOUR OF THEM! And what about Jack? Where was Jack on the WWAP t-shirt? One, two, three, four, five. JACK! Rage filled Jack until he felt like his head was going to burst open. If his vocal cords worked he would have screamed at the man. But instead his anger came out in a more abstract and hard to explain sort of way. The stars, in the galaxies deep in his eyes, seemed to brighten.

Tom Gordon stopped moving. The screen at the back of

the stall turned to loud static and Michael and Gavin instinctively covered their ears from the noise. Tom Gordon took a step back like something in his VR headset was scaring him. 'No, no no no,' he muttered. His voice caught in his throat. He tried to scream but howled instead. He grabbed the headset and tried to remove it from his head. Blood started pouring from beneath the goggles. Jack stood still and watched as the WWAP logo on the front of the shirt was erased with the man's blood. The man stopped howling and coughed. Blood fell from his mouth and he fell to his knees. A trickle of blood rolled over his right shoulder and seemed to form the shape of a fifth man on the back of his t-shirt. And then he collapsed onto his front and stopped moving. Air left his body and he defecated audibly.

Michael and Gavin ran to him and rolled him over onto his back. They pulled off his headset and recoiled at what they saw. His eyes were gone. There were just two scorched blackened holes. Every inch of his face was wet with blood.

Gavin grabbed the fleece from the back of his chair and covered Tom's face with it. All the children who witnessed the event, without exception, were screaming. Parents were picking them up and hurrying them away. Most had tears streaming down their faces.

Pandemonium erupted in the convention hall.

'Hey hey hey, let's not be hasty,' came a voice over the PA system.

A few people stopped and looked up at the thin man on the stage. He was wearing a tweed suit and waistcoat and brown leather shoes.

'My name is Cacophini and I am here on behalf of Hell. Upon your deaths I would like to cordially invite you to join us there. The weather is always nice and the pain will rip through your scared little bodies like buzz saws through butter. We amp up your nervous system to eleven so you can experience pain up to twenty times greater than you feel it here. Who's been good? Are you on Santa's list? You know, I once put my foot on that fat man's forehead and ripped his beard clean off his face with both hands. I say clean. It tore holes out of his cheeks. But hey, that's what you get for breaking and entering. Ho ho ho. Hey kiddie, you want to see what it feels like to swallow hot metal? It glows bright yellow and moves real slow. Your throat will light up like a lantern and then the blood in your heart will boil and that blood will travel around your body sizzling in your veins. And when you die, why, we'll just bring you right back and try out some other fun ways to hurt you. You want to come? Sign up now. Jack's mad and he's going to kill you, baby. Oh yeah, mother dear, I'm talking to the sack of skin and bones in your pram. I bet I can turn every bone in his body to powder with the right touch of the right hammer and keep him alive through the whole thing. And then, when he's all soft, I'll squeeze him in a big loving hug, and see if he doesn't pop like a balloon!'

Cacophini went on. Jack didn't even glance up at him. He walked by a stall and something caught his eye.

The stall sold reproduction props from films, cartoons, and games. They had the ThunderCats sword, and the He-Man sword. They had Han Solo's blaster. All kinds of interesting and unique things. The Lament Configuration from Hellraiser, Freddie Kruger's glove, a black taxidermy cat on a Pet Sematary sign post. There was a Mega Man helmet next to a Metroid helmet. But the thing that caught Jack's eye was right in the middle of the table at the front. It was Doctor Hammer's hammer from the game.

It was essentially no different to a normal hammer. It had a wooden handle and a metal head. Only the proportions were exaggerated. The handle was thicker and slightly shorter, making it look stumpy, and the head looked like it had been inflated. It was a heavy object. Jack looked at it, lying there on the felt-covered table. The hammer from the game he had created. He picked it up by the handle and felt its weight in his gnarled decaying hand. Of course, he couldn't really feel the weight. If he wanted to he could pick up a bus and hit you with it, but where's the fun in that? There's just no intimacy on the grand scale of things. He held the hammer at his side and walked towards the back of the hall. If he was going for the Doctor Hammer look, his cosplay was complete.

If he had bothered to look around he would have seen that the convention hall had emptied quite a bit. People were hiding behind tables and arcade machines. The staff in the food stalls were ducked down behind their counters. A mum was holding her daughter close, with her back to a pillar, trying to hush her crying.

There was one kid still out in the open, Stephen Amis, completely oblivious to the dead thing in the white coat, with the eyes that seemed to stare inwards at the infinity of hell. He was playing on an arcade machine with his headphones on. The game was Street Fighter II. He was playing as Chun-Li, a girl in a blue Chinese dress. She was fighting against Blanka, a green beast with orange hair.

Jack made his way to the door at the side of the stage. He walked past the boy without looking at him. The kid was doing quite well in the game. He was about to give Blanka a final blow with a high kick when the characters stopped moving. The music stopped and then started playing backwards, slowly.

'What the hell?' said the kid, and he kicked the arcade machine.

Chun-Li turned her head and looked at him. The kid stared at her. His heart caught in his throat. 'What's going on?' he said.

Chun-Li's face turned angry and she leapt towards the screen, turning as she did, her foot outstretched in a roundhouse kick. The screen exploded outwards and Stephen's face was torn to shreds by the flying glass. He fell on his back and tried to touch his face but even the slightest glance of his hand caused pain to shoot through him. His face was split in so many places. Glinting shards of glass jutted out of him. His vision was misty with blood and tears. Something moved and he squinted, straining to see through his blurred vision. He could see the vague outline of Chun-Li standing on the edge of the arcade machine. Her long ponytail waving behind her cartoonishly.

'What's happening?' he muttered.

Chun-Li dropped down, her elbow pulled back like she was ready to punch as soon as she landed.

Jack opened the door and let himself through. Behind him he could hear the sound of the kid screaming. There were horrible slicing sounds accompanied by faint feminine cries of, 'Yah, hi-yah, yah!' It sounded like someone was taking a razor blade to an uncooked slab of pork belly. Striking it, again and again. The kid's screams turned to gargled wheezes. He was unconscious now. His face was completely unrecognisable. Shredded to bits by a psychotic Street Fighter character. She had sliced all the way through his face and now punched and kicked and sliced at his brain from the inside. Her whole body was sharp at the edges. Finer than any razor. The kid's head jerked left and right. But not because there was any life in him.

CHAPTER 41

The green room at the back of the convention centre was cluttered with stacks of chairs and empty coat racks. In one corner of the room was the old church pulpit and behind that was a huge cross with a realistic Christ nailed to it. His head hung down, thorns cutting into his head, blood dripping down his face. His hands were limp. Thick nails had been hammered through his wrists. Well-meaning staff at the convention centre had draped a white sheet over it, thinking guests might not want Jesus staring down at them, but the sheet had slipped off and now covered half the pulpit.

The ceiling was twice as high as a normal room. It gave the room a cavernous feeling. It was the kind of space you want to shout the word, echo, just to hear it bounce around the room, like a thought trapped in time.

'Come and sit here, love,' said Amelia, taking a chair off one of the stacks against the far wall.

Dirk sniffed. His mind was a heavy grey place. His bones felt heavy. His face ached from crying. He stood hunched and had become weirdly conscious of his hands. He put them in his pockets but that felt too nonchalant for the circumstances. He folded them but that seemed wrong too. Like he was fed up. He let them fall to his sides and felt dumb, like a caveman. It was absurd. He was so completely distracted by the hand problem he had stopped crying. He had thought that maybe holding his hands to his face would be a reasonable place for them. But then he would look like a bad actress pretending to cry, and besides the tears had already stopped. He stood there looking at them with his palms up. The thing that had happened was too big a thing to process and his mind was reaching. Distracting itself to avoid the big scary thing that was banging on the back of his mind. YOUR PARENTS ARE DEAD DIRK! THEY'RE FUCKING DEAD!

'Dirk?' said Amelia.

He looked up at her and blinked.

'Why don't you sit down sweetheart?'

Dirk looked at the chair and nodded. He sat down and rested his hands on his lap. He stared at the floor just beyond his toes and tried to tune his thoughts to something that would replace the loud greyness in his head.

Billy and Martha were stood by the door, shoulder to shoulder, watching Dirk. Hopkirk was sat behind them, peering around Martha's legs. Pete sat down on the corner of the table next to them.

'What happened?' he said, speaking quietly. Martha and Billy looked at him and then each other. 'You said Walter and Penny are dead. Are they dead? I've tried calling and they're not picking up.'

The grey in Dirk's mind started to fade. Behind it was his kitchen at home. Blood was pouring down the walls. His parents were standing in front of each other, looking... no, they weren't looking, their faces were gone. They couldn't look. They never would again. They were facelessly facing each other. They took each other by the hands and leaned in as if to kiss, only their lips didn't meet, couldn't meet, where they would have normally stopped, their lips having touched, they carried on. The cracked edges of their skulls connected and grinded against each other.

Dirk started waving frantically, trying to wash the vision away, and almost toppled back on his chair. Amelia caught him and shook him gently. His eyes opened.

'Dirk, are you okay?'

Dirk cried and put his arms around her. Amelia hugged him back and looked sideways at her husband. Pete sighed and turned back to Billy and his daughter.

'How did they die?'

'We don't know,' said Billy. 'We were running to Dirk's house to get him and he was on his knees in the kitchen doorway.'

'And what about Walter and Penny?'

'Jack killed them,' said Martha.

Pete didn't respond right away. He stared at her. He opened his mouth as if to say something but couldn't find the words.

'Jack who, honey?' said Amelia, still hugging Dirk.

'Jack Matterson. He tried to kill us and he killed Dirk's parents.'

There was a scream from the main hall and Amelia let go

of Dirk and stood up. Hopkirk barked and then whimpered.

'Did he follow you?' said Pete.

'Follow us? Don't you want to know who he is?'

'No,' said Pete. 'Did he follow you?'

'I don't know. Maybe,' she said. 'We didn't know where to go.'

'Do you know what's happening?' said Billy.

Pete didn't answer. He opened the door a crack and looked out into the corridor. There was a thin man wearing a tweed suit and brown shoes sat on one of the black trunks. He was kicking his legs like a bored child. He turned his head and looked at Pete. He waved and smiled. Pete slammed the door.

'It's Cacophini,' he said, planting his back firmly against the door. 'We have to get out of here.'

'Who's Cacophini?' said Martha.

'You don't need to know,' said Amelia, dragging Dirk up by the arm. 'We need to get you out of here. Was he alone?' she said, looking at Pete.

Pete nodded.

'Jack?' she said.

Pete shook his head.

Amelia ran to the door and pulled the handle down. She peeked out. Cacophini was still there, grinning with razor sharp teeth. She closed the door.

'Pete, get the window open,' she said.

Pete looked at the back wall. There was a window, completely covered by a thick blue curtain, behind all the junk. He ran over and rolled one of the coat racks out of the way. He grabbed five chairs off a stack of fifteen and put them on the ground next to him and then went to grab another five. Billy ran over and pulled a stack of chairs to the ground, letting them clatter to the floor. Pete turned at the noise and saw what he had done. His face was open and blank. Billy had never seen an adult face so full of panic. Pete looked back at the remaining stacks of chairs and grabbed two at once. He pulled them towards him and jumped out of the way, letting them crash to the ground.

Pete pulled the curtains apart and picked up one of the fallen chairs. He smashed the glass with one hard thrust of the chair legs.

'Get out and run straight to Finnegan's, you hear me?' said Pete.

'Finnegan's?' said Billy.

'He'll be able to help, just go there. He'll understand. If we don't make it he can hide you.'

'If you don't make it?' said Martha.

'We'll be fine, just go,' said Amelia.

'Mum, what's going to happen?'

'Please just go, Martha. Please.'

Martha looked into her mother's eyes. They were welling up with tears. She had never seen her mother cry before. Not once. Martha nodded.

'Okay, mum. I love you.'

'I love you too, sweetheart. Now please go.'

She kissed her daughter on the lips and then firmly on the cheek. It was an odd thing, being kissed on the lips by your own mother, but it felt like the most right thing in the world in that moment. Actually it felt like the most terrible thing in the world. It felt like a full stop. It felt like a last kiss.

Billy had a foot in Pete's hands. Pete lifted and Billy climbed out of the window. A jagged bit of glass cut into his leg and he winced. He jumped to the ground outside and turned around. He reached up and pulled the stray shard from the frame.

'Dirk, come on,' he shouted, getting on tip toes and looking back in the room.

Pete was holding Dirk up by the armpits and Dirk awkwardly pulled himself up to the window. He got his legs over and sat on the edge.

'You should have let me go first,' said Martha. 'He'll hurt himself jumping down.'

'I've got him,' said Billy. 'I've got you Dirk, jump down.'

Dirk put his arms out and let himself fall. Billy caught him and lowered him gently to his feet.

'You okay?' said Billy.

Dirk nodded and looked up at the window. They heard Martha say, 'I love you too dad,' and then the sound of a kiss and then Martha's hands grabbed onto the window frame. She pulled herself up and jumped down to the grass. Billy was there ready to steady her if she fell but she didn't need it.

Pete and Amelia looked out of the window at them.

'If you can't get to Finnegan's just run. In any direction. Run and don't stop running. We'll find you when this is all over. Okay?'

They nodded.

'Hold on,' said Amelia. 'You forgot this.'

She disappeared out of site and was back a moment later with Hopkirk. She lifted him out of the window like she was holding a baby up by the armpits. He was panting, with his tongue flopping out, and his tail wagging between his legs.

She dropped the puppy and Billy stepped forwards and caught him. Hopkirk jumped out of his arms and plodded around, sniffing the grass.

Martha stretched up and put her arms around her parents. She kissed them both on the cheeks and let go. 'Why don't you climb out and come with us?' she said.

'Because we have to try and stop him,' said Amelia.

'But you don't know what you're dealing with. Jack isn't human, he's something else.'

'We know,' said Pete.

'He'll kill you. He's too strong.'

The noise from the convention hall got louder and then quieter again, like someone was opening a door and then closing it.

'Go now,' said Pete. 'We love you.'

'Look after her, Billy,' said Amelia.

They disappeared into the room and for a moment Martha just stood there, staring up at the vacant window.

'Come on,' said Billy. 'They know what they're doing.'

'Why didn't they have more questions?' She said, and turned to face Billy. 'They're acting like this is completely normal.'

Billy shrugged. 'I don't know. We have to get moving.'

Dirk started walking away. 'Let's go then. Finnegan's, right?'

'Yeah, Finnegan's,' said Billy.

He put his hand out to Martha and waited for her to take it. She looked him in the eye. Her face said so much. She looked so beautiful to Billy. In her eyes were all her thoughts. I think I just said goodbye to my parents. It's just me and you, Billy. For a moment he thought she was going to brush his hand aside but she didn't. She took his hand and looked at Dirk. She didn't want to talk, she just wanted to go. Lead the way, Billy, she was saying.

Billy walked after Dirk, and then jogged, and then ran.

CHAPTER 42

A woman's scream echoed around the empty convention centre. Stephen Amis's body lay on the floor, a circle of blood pooling outwards from his shredded body. Chun-Li stood at his feet, her chest heaving with exertion. She had torn through his entire body leaving a trench of sliced up mush in her wake. On the screen of the arcade machine Blanka's name had been replaced with Stephens. The scores tallied up and the announcer said, 'YOU WIN. PERFECT.' Chun-Li giggled and jumped in the air in celebration, just like in the game. And then she winked out of existence.

The boy's mother was on the floor, hunched against the wall by the door, shaking and crying. It was her who had been screaming. Blood from her son spread out and touched against her legs and she edged away from it. She looked at Jack Matterson. The blood had pooled around his feet. He appeared ghost-like through her tears.

No one else was left in the hall. It was just Jack, the crying mother, her dead son, and the still body of Tom Gordon in the VR area.

Jack stepped forwards. His feet made a sucking noise when they rose from the blood. He ignored the mother. A part of him wanted to kill her but then he found he derived more than a bit of joy from her visceral outpouring of grief. It made for nice background music, and besides it added an interesting edge to the Doctor Hammer theme tune that was still playing out of the speakers.

He stepped forward and put his hand on the door handle. A part of the skin on his palm slipped off and fell to the ground. He pulled the handle down and it clicked open.

Chris and Becky stepped into the entrance of the convention hall and watched.

'What the fuck is happening?' said Becky.

'You think I know?' said Chris.

'It's your fucking party.'

'He's going backstage. Pete and Amelia are back there. I think that's where the WWAP kids are too.'

'So we better stop him, right?' said Becky.

'Yeah, we should.'

'Like, how?'

Chris gave an exaggerated shrug. 'How the fuck should I know?'

Becky thought for a moment and then grabbed the megaphone from Chris's hand.

'Hey, fucktard,' she shouted.

'You can't say fucktard,' said Chris.

Jack stopped. He let the door close again and turned around.

'Alright, now what?' said Becky.

'Give me that,' said Chris, taking the megaphone back and

putting it to his mouth. 'Listen buddy, I don't know who you are, or who- it's not working.' He pulled the trigger again and tried speaking. 'We've already called the cops and- what's wrong with this thing?'

Becky took the megaphone back and pressed the trigger a few times. No crackle. No amplification. The thing was dead. There was a button on the side that made it sound like a horn. She pressed it. Nothing.

Jack stared at Becky and Chris, with his empty crust-lined eyes, and all the light seemed to flee away from him. Shadows darkened the wall behind him and vomited across the floor. The darkness spurted out of Jack like flames made of antimatter.

'Holy shit,' said Chris, looking up from the megaphone in Becky's hand and finding himself staring at nothing. It was like a black sheet had been thrown over them. He turned around and saw the light in the doorway zip away from him and then twinkle away into the void. The music had stopped. The screaming had ceased.

Becky had turned the megaphone around and put the horn to her ear. She pressed the button and heard a whisper. 'Hey hey hey, it's cold out here, come into the warm.'

'What the hell?' said Becky, and then the darkness dawned on her. How had she not noticed it? She put her hand in front of her face and couldn't see it. She put her arm out to her side and touched Chris.

'That you?' she said.

'Yeah.'

'What's happening?'

The megaphone crackled.

'Jack's got a little surprise for you. You want to hear it? We've got twenty-four carat pain here, we sell it wholesale for a cheap price. As much pain as you can enjoy for as much time as eternity will allow. Admission is one soul, and we've got the best rides in town. Give me a deal and I'll give you ten years, what do you say guys? My gift to you, you can have your dreams. Money, girls, boys, whatever you fancy. Fame, knowledge. You want to know what really happened at Area 51? You can know that and everything else. Hell, you can read thoughts if you want. I'll give you the power to fly. How about it? Tickets are cheap. Act now, warranty guaranteed. Buy now, pay later. That's the deal.'

'Who is that?' said Becky.

'Why, it's me, Cacophini. What do you want more than anything in the whole world?'

Chris was weirdly calm. His heart had gone hard. He knew what he wanted and fuck the consequences. 'If you hurt any one of those WWAP kids I'm going to rip your fucking teeth out of your skull and feed them to you, you got that?'

'Holy shit, man. Yeah, I'm with him. I don't know what the fuck's goin' on here but you ain't getting your hands on my soul. Why don't you turn the lights back on and stop hiding like a fucking coward,' said Becky.

'Well fuck, I didn't realise I was dealing with a couple of brave heroes. I'll tell you what, how about I kill you and chase your souls down when I've got some spare time and see if I can't bag them anyway, huh? What do you say?'

The darkness went like water through sand. The music came back and the blood and the screaming too. They saw the door open at the end of the hall and Jack stepped through it.

The megaphone crackled. Chris and Becky turned their heads and looked at it, blinking like they had just woken from a dream. Becky held it pointed at her face. Cacophini was crouched behind it with his lips to the mouth piece.

'Who-' said Chris, but didn't have a chance to finish.

Cacophini smiled, wiggled his fingers in a camp how-do-you-do and then whispered the word, 'boom.'

The megaphone exploded in Becky's hand, ripping her fingers to shreds, and a white circle of compressed air fired out of the horn. The shockwave rattled the screens in the arcade machines and the sonic boom deafened the mother to her own screams. In the split second it took for the sound to travel from the megaphone, through Becky and Chris, and hit the far wall, blowing the windows out, all of the blood in their heads vibrated violently. Their eyes bulged. Chris managed to get one last thought from the back of his mind to the front. It was the word, 'Fuck.' Their skulls burst open like a glorious ballooning eruption caught in slow motion. Two party balloons full of red paint exploding outwards with a loud CRACK. The blood splattered the ceiling and dripped down around them. Their bodies went limp and they fell to the floor. Cacophini was gone. The cracked horn of the megaphone rolled to a stop, covered in bits of red gunk and white bone.

Cacophini was now back in the corridor, sitting on one of

the trunks. One moment he was whispering into a megaphone, the next here he was. Jack came through the door and looked at him.

'Having fun? I know I am,' said Cacophini.

Jack didn't respond.

'Second door on the right,' said Cacophini.

Jack turned away from the demon and walked along the corridor. The second door on the right opened and then slammed shut again. For that brief moment Jack saw the eye of a woman peer out at him. He passed the first door and kept walking.

CHAPTER 43

Amelia slammed the door and turned the lock. Her chest was heaving. She turned and faced the room, with its high cavernous ceiling, and wished she could climb the walls and hide in the rafters. Her pupils had widened to penny-sized pits. She lurched away from the door like it had burst into flames. Jack's face was imprinted on the back of her retinas. His eyes reflected in hers. It was like all those screaming people had climbed out of him and into her and filled her with their terror.

'Pete, let's just climb out of the window and go after the kids.'

'And then what? Run forever? From Cacophini?'

'It's not Cacophini. It's Jack.'

'Jack is dead, we killed him ten years ago,' said Pete, struggling with the pulpit in the corner of the room. He shifted it forwards and it scraped along the wooden floor. He looked up at Jesus, crucified to the cross. He pulled the cross away from the wall so it was balancing upright. It was heavy, like it was made of railway sleepers.

'He's back, Pete. Cacophini must have bought him back. Ten years right? It's been ten years. That's what he said, ten years. Now he's back and he's going to fucking kill us.'

'Just help me with this,' he said.

'And do what with it?'

The door handle turned and Amelia screamed and ran behind Pete.

Pete strained against the cross and managed to lift it just enough to shunt it forward a foot. He stepped back, moving his hands up the cross, taking its weight, and pushing it upright. He breathed heavily and stared at the door handle.

'What are you going to do?' said Amelia.

'Just wait. And run for the door when I say,' he said.

'The door? Are you crazy?'

The door handle turned and stopped against the lock. It strained and creaked. There was the sound of metal bending and then a sharp crack and the wood in the frame split apart. The door swung open and bits of broken lock fell out of it.

'Holy shit,' said Pete.

'Whatever you're planning to do, do it now,' said Amelia, her voice trembling.

Jack stood there. His white coat clinging to his rotting body. The smell of him wafted into the room. A dank cheesy smell, laced with ammonia and putrid chicken. He held the hammer at his side in his left hand.

He stepped forward and Pete let go of the cross. It fell with weird silence. Jesus belly-flopped towards the hard floor. Its shadow hit Jack first. He stepped back avoiding being struck on the head but not far enough to avoid it completely. The top of the cross caught him on the chest below the right shoulder.

It drove him to his knees, the weight of it pushed down on his ribcage and broke through.

'Now! Run!' shouted Pete.

Amelia hesitated for a moment and then ran, skipping on her tiptoes, to jump around him. Jack pushed the cross aside and it clanked to the floor. The rib cage on his right side hung off. Jack grabbed the loose ribs with his right hand and yanked it free and cast it aside. The exposed lung underneath was completely covered with writhing maggots.

Jack lifted the hammer and struck at Amelia as she skipped past. He caught her in the side of the knee just as her foot was landing next to him. It popped sideways. She howled with pain and buckled over.

'No!' shouted Pete, running to her.

Jack stood up and swung hard at Pete's chest with the hammer. Not hard enough to kill him but hard enough to put him on the floor, winded and unable to move. Pete felt it connect with the hard bone in his chest, the sternum, and his heart wavered. The air fled from his lungs and he gulped several times trying to inhale. He fell backwards clutching his chest, heaving in short breaths.

Jack grabbed Amelia by the back of the head and dragged her to the table. Pete watched. He tried to get to his feet but couldn't. He was starting to see black spots as his body struggled against the lack of oxygen.

Amelia's left leg dangled helplessly and she stepped frantically with her right, trying to get a solid footing. She was crying and pleading for her life.

'Don't kill me. Please don't kill me. I don't want to die. I'm not ready. I don't want to go. Please. Please don't do this.'

Jack slammed her face into the edge of the table and pushed her along. Her bottom lip curled towards her chin and ripped away from the bone. One of her bottom teeth dug into the wood and chipped off. She put her left hand on the top of the table and tried to push herself up and she struck at Jack ineffectively with her right hand.

Pete could only watch. The pain in his chest was like a ratchet tightening around his lungs. His heart was beating slow and hard. Jack watched him and pushed down harder on Amelia's head, forcing her against the edge of the table. Her mouth cracked from the chin to the base of her nose.

'Please stop,' Pete managed to say.

Jack shoved down harder and the bone from the bottom of her nose to her left eye socket cracked and two of her teeth dropped to the floor. Amelia's body started to fit and the table started to creak.

Pete strained and tried to get to his feet. The black spots floating around his vision started to shine around the edges as he started to black out. He stumbled, hardly off the floor and fell back against the pulpit. His head leaned back and the black spots got smaller. He looked at Jack. He looked into his eyes and saw everything. So much pain and torment. A window to Hell.

Jack pushed harder on the back of Amelia's head. There was a loud bang and Jack lurched downwards. Her head burst open and the palm of Jack's hand banged on the table's surface, splitting the wood. Jack moved his hand and Amelia's head slipped off the table and she landed on the floor. She flopped onto her back and her face folded open. Blood was pulsing out of her. Pete stared at her. His mind reached for an emotion but shock had sealed that part of his mind off. He could only stare at her.

Jack took two steps forward and raised his hammer up. Pete watched the hammer come down towards him with complete indifference.

It struck him hard and his face cracked like an egg. Blood poured out of his nose like someone had left the tap on. It covered him in a widening triangle that ran from his chin to his hips. Jack reached back and smacked him again. Pete had become unconscious on the first blow. He was dead with the second. Now Jack was just having fun.

'Jeez, why always the face?' said Cacophini, standing just behind Jack with his arms folded.

Jack dropped the hammer. It was shiny with blood. Jack shimmered with it. Like he had been given a gloss of deep red varnish from head to toe. It dripped from his fingertips.

CHAPTER 44

All of the screens in the convention centre turned to loud static and started flashing frantically. Jack Matterson stood in the middle of the hall. Bloody footprints traced his path back through the door at the side of the stage. Police would later follow them backwards and discover the bodies of Pete and Amelia Perry.

Jack, glistening in the strobing light, turned his head and looked at one of the screens. The flashing and static stopped and silence fell around the hall. He stood there. A dead thing. The light coming in from the windows reflected in the wet coating of blood. He could have been a statue made of blown glass, tinted red.

The words, SHELLEY TOWN RPG appeared on the screens in bold capital letters. It appeared on all of the screens at once. It even appeared, ghostly and faint, in the smashed screen of the Street Fighter II console.

The screens turned to black and then an image formed. It was a top-down view of the old church. It had the convention centre carpark on one side and the old graveyard on the other. At the side of the church three characters and a dog were running towards the graveyard.

Jack clenched his fists and all of the joysticks in the arcade machines slammed left all at once. It made a sound like a rapidly closing blind. Martha stopped.

'You're getting powerful, Jack,' said Cacophini, suddenly standing at Jack's side. 'But you can't control free will.'

The joysticks slowly moved back to their neutral position.

Martha stopped running. Billy's hand slipped out of hers and he stumbled and almost fell. He turned and looked at her.

'What's wrong?' he said.

Her eyes had glazed over. She could have been a waxwork doll of herself. Everything about her had become still. Even her hair wasn't moving.

'Dirk, hold up,' said Billy.

Dirk stopped running and turned around. 'What's going on?' he said, and he put his hands on his knees and started wheezing.

'Something's wrong with Martha,' said Billy.

Billy stepped forwards and looked into Martha's eyes. It was like she had gone into a trance. Her expression was blank. 'Martha, you okay?' he said.

Hopkirk put his paws on her legs and looked up at her. Dirk joined them, getting his breath back.

'Martha?' he said, waving a hand in front of her face.

She blinked and her shoulders relaxed. She looked at Dirk and then at Billy. Hopkirk dropped down but didn't lose the concern in his eyes.

'Why have we stopped?' she said.

'We didn't. You did,' said Billy.

'What do you mean, I didn't do anything. Are we- were we playing the game?'

'What game?' said Billy.

She frowned. 'The game you found.'

'We don't have time for this,' said Dirk. 'We have to keep running.'

Martha shook her head. 'Sorry, I don't- I don't know- are we- where are my parents?'

Dirk felt a horrible anger fill him. 'What the fuck is wrong with you?' he said.

'What?' she said. 'Why are you angry with me?'

Dirk put his hands on his head and started breathing heavily. 'Your parents?' he said. His eyes were looking left and right, searching his mind for some kind of sense. 'Your parents are back there probably having their faces ripped out of their heads!' He coughed and spat phlegm on the floor. The grief that had been finding a way out of him was building like a black fire in his head. It was refusing to let him think rationally. It was like the blood in his veins was made of razor wire. The physical grating of loss. He hadn't had time to process his own parents' death and Martha couldn't even remember where her parents were. He burst into tears and screamed at her. 'How could you just leave them?'

'What? I didn't,' she said, struggling to make sense of him.

'Dirk, I know you're struggling, but this isn't the time,' said Billy.

'The time? When would be a good time for you, huh?

When you're alone with Martha? Maybe we could go and talk to your weird fucking mum,' he stepped back and turned around, looking up at the sun. He put his hands on his face and ran them through his hair. 'I'm sorry. I don't mean what I'm saying. I'm just- It's just hard. I don't understand what's happening. I don't understand why we're running or why it's going to help us. We shouldn't be doing this, we're kids. What the fuck is going on here? Just what the fuck is going on here? Do you understand it, Billy? Does any of this seem normal to you?'

'No it doesn't, but we can't do this now. We just can't.'

'My parents?' said Martha. 'How could we have just left them?'

'Right? How?' shouted Dirk.

Martha looked back along the side-wall of the church. Whatever strange trance had come over her, and momentarily screwed with her memory, was lifting.

'We should go back, Billy. We should be there helping them. They can't possibly know what's coming for them. How could they?' she said.

Billy opened his mouth to say something but couldn't find his words. He shook his head and shrugged. 'I don't-'

'I'm going back,' said Martha.

She turned around and Billy watched her walk away. He turned away for a moment and then looked back at her.

'Martha, wait. Alright, we don't run. But we don't go that way. I have an idea.'

She stopped. 'What idea?'

'He'll be there by now. If we have any chance of killing him we go back through the convention centre and sneak up behind him.'

'And how are we going to stop him?' said Dirk.

'I don't know yet. But we have the same problem going that way, right?'

Martha thought for a moment and then started back. 'He's right. Come on.' She ran past, grabbing Billy by the hand.

The three of them, with Hopkirk keeping pace, cleared the side of the building and ran through the old gravestones at the edge of the carpark.

The old gravestones were like rotting teeth jutting out of the ground. Decaying and old. Dirk felt like the graveyard could fold over and eat him up, crunching his bones, leaving his dead body to mingle with the rotting corpses that were only feet below them. Centuries of death fed the grass that grew there. There were trees here and there. Most were full of leaves but some, at the farthest end of the graveyard, were as dead as the buried occupants. They looked like the hands of dead giants bursting up from the dirt.

They ran through the graves. Martha tripped on an arrangement of flowers on one of the newer marble stones, and sent a flurry of white rose petals into the air like confetti at a wedding. Hopkirk jumped through it and they scattered through the air and settled to the ground in his wake. Martha nearly lost her footing and pulled on Billy's arm. He pulled her back without breaking his stride.

There was a tall hedge that blocked the view of the

graveyard from the convention centre carpark and they had almost reached the open archway at the entrance when Dirk stopped running, putting his arms out to steady himself, as if he had reached the edge of an unexpected cliff.

Martha and Billy slowed down and stopped next to him. He was looking up at something.

'What is it?' said Billy, but his question didn't need answering. He had seen what Dirk was looking at.

Cacophini was sitting, feline-like, in the bough of a tree near the entrance of the graveyard. He had a glass of whisky in one hand and lowered a pipe from his lips with the other. He blew out smoke and looked down at them.

'Going somewhere?' he said, grinning like the Cheshire Cat.

Martha squeezed Billy's hand. Billy stepped forward.

'Who are you?' he said.

'Me? Oh, you don't need to worry about me. I'm just a used soul dealer. Now, here comes a guy you need to worry about,' said Cacophini, and he pointed towards the carpark with his pipe.

The three of them walked forward a few paces and looked through the open gates of the graveyard into the carpark. Jack was standing right there. Not twelve feet away from them, with blood dripping from his hands. His mouth a bloodied gash and his eyes like cigarette burns. His shadow stretched across the tarmac in severe contrast to the shadows from the tree and the gated wall, which fell short from the high sun.

'I hope you're not too fond of your faces, kids,' said

Cacophini, and burst into a hacking laugh.

'What do you want from us?' Dirk screamed.

Jack moved forward, as if Dirk's words had activated him.

Hopkirk started barking. He ran in front of Billy and Martha and stopped. Jack kept moving and Hopkirk stepped back. He backed into Martha's legs and his barks turned into a dark growl. His lips curled back and saliva dribbled to the floor. His teeth were impressive.

'What do we do?' said Martha.

Billy clenched his fists and looked over at Dirk. He had found a branch on the ground by the tree and pulled it free from the overgrowth. It was the kind of branch you see over-enthusiastic dogs dragging along in the vein hope of getting it through a doorway. He picked it up with both hands and held it like a baseball bat. He looked over at Billy. His eyes were wide with excitement. His heart had risen with the adrenaline and for the first time he felt like he could kill Jack. He imagined himself swinging again and again with the new strength that was coursing through him. Pummelling Jack until he was an unmoving mess of broken bones and split skin. He felt like his own brittle bones were made of titanium.

'Throw it to me,' said Billy, holding his hands out, ready to catch it.

'What?' said Dirk.

'Throw it to me.'

Martha had started walking backwards but Billy stood his ground. Jack had stopped walking and was quietly watching Dirk. These children were no threat to him. His body was weak and parts of his skin slipped away at the merest touch, but you could break all the bones in his hand and he would still reach out with his bent and mangled fingers and tear out your throat out like he was pinching candyfloss.

Dirk raised the branch over his right shoulder like a bat and ran at Jack. The memory of his murdered parents burned in his mind. A red hot image that filled him with rage.

'Dirk, don't do it,' shouted Martha. 'Let Billy.'

Dirk swung and the branch hummed as it moved through the air. Jack didn't move. The branch hit him hard across the back and one of his vertebrates cracked. The branch snapped in half and all of the bones in Dirk's wrists shattered.

He dropped the branch and stared at his hands. They fell away from him like loose marionette hands. He fell to his knees and laid the backs of his hands on the floor. He moved his elbows towards him to straighten them out but agony seared through him and he jerked his arms up again. He tried to touch his face in an automatic reaction to the pain and a sharp end of bone that poked up at the skin, without breaking through, touched his cheek. He reeled back at the sensation and stared at his ruined arms. They were folded back like a deflated doll. He felt the backs of his hands against the backs of his forearms and started to shake.

He felt two sets of arms around him and was lifted to his feet.

CHAPTER 45

Ryman and Eunice drove over the tracks back into Shelley Town square. They had checked Pete and Amelia's place and the den in the caravan graveyard but none of the kids were there.

The radio crackled and a voice came through from the control room.

'Ryman, you there?'

Ryman picked up the handset. 'Go ahead.'

'There have been some very strange reports of something going on at the convention.'

'What kinds of reports?' said Ryman.

There was a pause before the person from the control room answered.

'Really fucking strange reports.'

Ryman raised his eyebrows. He had never heard control swear before. He had never even heard a glimmer of personality before now. If you wanted professional no-nonsense protocol, a control room was where you got it.

'Care to elaborate?' said Ryman.

The voice paused again.

'I think you need to get there and see for yourself. It could be a hoax, or a PR stunt, it sounds like one.'

'Alright, I'll check it out.'

'The convention is today?' said Eunice.

Ryman looked at her. 'You didn't know?'

'You lose track of days when you don't go out. That's where the children will be. Do you think they're okay?'

Her eyes were wide and wet. She had her arms wrapped tight around her as if the air itself might harm her. She wasn't officially diagnosed as agoraphobic, and she had convinced herself that she simply didn't like going outside, but now she was out, she felt an irrational panic fill her. Fortunately, the fear she felt for her son overpowered her desire to scream and run back to the safety of her home. A weird case of fear trumping terror.

'I'm sure they're fine,' he said.

He turned to take a shortcut and drove onto the pedestrianised part of the square. It was designed to be wide enough for emergency vehicles. Pedestrian or not. If there's a fire you need room for a fire engine.

The square was unusually empty for a Saturday. Apart from one homeless guy on a bench and some pigeons.

On his left Ryman saw Finnegan. He was walking hurriedly away from his tobacconist. Ryman pressed a button by the gearstick and the driver's side window rolled down.

'Everything okay, Mr Finnegan?'

Finnegan stopped and turned around. He saw Ryman and jogged to the car. 'What in god's name is happening around here?' he said.

'You tell me, what do you know?' said Ryman.

'What do I know? You can't hear that?'

Ryman frowned. 'Hear what?'

'Turn off your engine.'

Ryman did and the faint sound of people screaming came to him from the direction of the convention centre. Finnegan saw Eunice in the passenger seat and was momentarily lost for words. Ryman turned the key and started the engine again.

'Wait,' said Finnegan. 'William's heading that way.'

'William?' said Ryman.

'He's back?' said Eunice.

'Yeah, and he has a gun,' said Finnegan.

CHAPTER 46

Martha and Billy ran with Dirk between them, his arms over their shoulders. His broken hands flapped around freely as they ran. Martha felt something wet and cold on her neck. It squeezed around her throat and she choked.

Jack pulled her back and Dirk felt his arm come away from her. Martha tried to scream but couldn't. Dirk turned his head and saw Jack throw her to the ground like she was a rag doll. Billy let go of Dirk and ran to her. He shoved Jack and his right hand pushed through his soft rotten flesh and connected with Jack's spine. The sensation was horrible. It had the texture of the inside of a slug.

Jack ignored Billy. He leaned over Martha. The blood from her parents dripped off his skull onto her face. She tried to pull away from him, getting as low to the carpark floor as she could, as if she might be able to force herself through the tarmac and hide underneath it.

Jack picked her up by the shoulders and raised her face to his. She stared into his eyes. The backs of his eye sockets were so far away. She could swim away in there. Take off into the abyss. Live amongst the stars, high above the thousands of people that clawed to get out. Miles and miles of terrified faces. All of them screaming and howling.

Billy grabbed Martha by the arm and tried to pull her away but his strength meant nothing to Jack. It was the force of a mosquito trying to steal a grown man's sandwich.

Hopkirk jumped up and bit down on the remaining part of Jack's ribcage. It came away easily. Hopkirk dropped it to the floor and jumped up again, this time clamping his teeth around Jack's heart, which was a shrivelled yellow and black rock of hardened muscle.

He pulled hard, scratching against Jack's groin with his hind legs to get purchase. He was growling through his teeth. He lost his footing and his paw came down hard, tearing some dead skin away as he fell. He didn't let go of the heart. He yanked again, his back legs hanging free, and the heart came away. The arteries snapped and came down with it. It looked like a dead octopus with most of its legs missing. Hopkirk landed hard on his back. His soft white fur had become red and black with Jack's putrid flesh, and the blood of Martha's parents.

Jack paid him no attention. He gripped Martha harder and felt the bones in her shoulders break under his grip. Tears were rolling down her cheeks and her mouth was moving like she was trying to say something, but no sound would come out. Dread had infected her vocal cords and all she could do was mouth her words and croak desperately.

Jack opened his mouth. The bottom jaw was split in two from a decade-old axe wound and it opened at a strange angle. Martha was shaking her head. She managed to get out a word, but it was quiet and shaky.

'Billy.'

Billy jumped up on Jack's back and grabbed his head, crossing his fingers over Jack's forehead. He pulled back, trying to break his neck, but the skin of his scalp slid away from his skull and Billy tumbled backwards landing awkwardly on his neck and shoulders. He screamed in pain.

He felt the sickly flesh in his hand and threw it. It landed a few feet away, hairy and rotten. He looked up at Jack. His skull was entirely exposed.

Dirk tried to get to his feet to do something, anything to help. But there was no time.

Jack's mouth was open unnaturally wide. His top teeth sank into Martha's head, an inch beyond her hairline. His bottom teeth dug into the skin under her jaw.

She was breathing rapidly and kicking with her legs. His tongue forced itself between her lips and ran along her clenched teeth. The back of his throat was clogged with pus. The smell of it made her gag and she threw up into her mouth. She would have choked on it, if she'd had the time.

Jack clamped down on her and she felt her teeth press together with the pressure. There was a horrible crack as her teeth snapped outwards. The vomit spilled out over her chin and pooled in Jack's mouth. Jack bit down harder and broke through her skull. His teeth snapped shut, meeting inside her head, and he jerked his neck backwards and spat her face to the ground. It hit the floor with a cowpat-like SLOP.

Her body fell limp and he threw it to the ground. Blood

flowed out of the hole in her head where her face had been.

Dirk and Billy stared at the face on the floor. It was still recognisably her. Martha. With all her wit and sarcasm. A torn mess in a puddle of blood. The eyes bloodshot and facing in different directions. A few teeth protruding from her once pretty lips.

Billy didn't try and escape when Jack walked up behind him.

CHAPTER 47

William Rain walked into the carpark. He held the gun by his side. The sun glinted on the cylinder of the revolver and the shine ran down the long barrel. His shoulders were loose. Sweat covered his forehead.

There were people hiding here and there. A man sat on the floor with his back to a car. He was shaking his head at William, trying to warn him not to go any farther. There were people hiding down the right hand side of the building. Parents hushing their kids to stay quiet. There was someone at the far end of the graveyard hiding behind one of the gravestones.

William saw Martha's body at the other end of the carpark. Hopkirk was sat next to her with his head bowed. Dirk was shuffling backwards on his elbows. Billy was on his knees, facing William. Jack was standing behind Billy with his hands around Billy's head.

'Dad!' shouted Billy.

Jack looked up. William kept walking and stopped a single car length away. They stared into each other's eyes. The sun was dead centre in the sky, looking down like the eye of God. The heat beat down like a tight snare drum.

Cacophini was sitting cross-legged on the roof of Pete's blue minibus, parked in the carpark just to the left of the action. Best seats in the house, thought Cacophini, looking back and forth between William and Jack.

Jack Matterson. There he was, back from the dead.

William stepped forward again and found himself back in the past. A door opened and he was in Jack's basement, in 1992. The memories that he had been trying to block with alcohol and drugs for so long came back in one hard visceral burst. The carpark went pitch black like some outside hand had flicked a switch and turned off the world. Walls fell into existence around him. Voices that were muffled and confused found clarity and the shapes of people morphed from grey smears to real flesh and blood. William looked left into the eyes of the man next to him. It was Pete. He was ten years younger, and he was gleeful with excitement.

'We launch in three hours, can you believe it?' he was saying.

'What the fuck is this?' said Jack, storming across the basement, dragging his daughter by the wrist. Her face was the image of upset and confusion. Her bottom lip was trembling and her eyebrows were an inverted frown. Jack was holding the game in his other hand and was shaking it at William and Pete. 'Huh? Where's my name? What the fuck is WWAP?'

'Jack, calm down. Let go of Sarah, you're scaring her.'

'Scaring her? Why don't you explain to her why her dad is being screwed by his friends?'

'What are you talking about?' said Pete.

'WWAP, what's that? Your names? Where's my name in this? I'm not even mentioned in the credits.'

Walter and Amelia came down the stairs behind William and Pete.

'What's all this?' said Walter.

'Jack is freaking out,' said William.

'Why don't you sit down so we can talk about this? And how about you let go of your daughters arm, you're hurting her,' said Walter.

'You don't know how much I've given up for this. Everyone I've ever loved. I've given up more than you know, more than any of you. This game would be nothing without me.'

'We just brought you on board to help with the coding, we made the game. It was our concept, our vision,' said Pete.

The four of WWAP were still standing bunched up in the doorway. Jack thrust the game into William's face and clocked him on the chin. Sarah started crying.

'Stop crying,' shouted Jack, and dragged her to the back of the basement. 'Stand against the wall and don't make a sound.'

'You okay?' said Pete.

'Yeah, I'm fine,' said William.

Amelia squeezed past and went to Sarah's side and sat with her. 'It's okay, sweetie,' she said, and held her hand. She turned her wrist over and saw red marks from Jack's grip. She flashed a look at Pete.

The three men walked into the basement and stood

around Jack.

'You have to calm down,' said William.

'You know what I did for you three, huh? I had ten years. That's all I had. I am the best coder who ever lived. I have done things in that game that will make it go down in history as a masterpiece. Do you know what you guys have done? You laughed over your stupid story. A doctor fighting Big Ben. Aren't you smart? You know what I did?'

'What did you do, Jack?' said Walter.

'I made a deal. I gave up my soul. I was given ten years, that's it, ten fucking years. And you know what I did? I spent it all on you. It should be my name on the cover of that game. In big white letters. You're just footnotes in my story. I'm the one that's going to be remembered. Not any of you dull cunts.'

'What are you talking about? You work for us. We could have hired anyone,' said Walter.

'And you weren't exactly easy to work with,' said Pete.

'I am a genius. You couldn't possibly understand. It's all over for me, you know? Today is the day. This is when it ends. Cacophini will-'

'Did someone say my name?'

Everyone in the room, including Sarah, looked at the man who had just appeared at the back of the basement. He was wearing a tweed suit and brown shoes. He was sickly thin and had eyes as black as coal.

'Hello, Jack,' he said, with a strangely effeminate salute of his hand. 'Time's up. How did it go?'

'Wait, not now. I'm not done.'

'Oh, poor boy. Tough shit.'

'Hold on, you fucking snake. You never fulfilled your bargain.'

'What is going on here?' said Amelia.

Cacophini looked down at her. 'Hello my dear. How are you? Well? Good.' Cacophini stepped forward and patted Jack on the back. 'My deal is good. You got what you wanted.' Cacophini put his hand out and William shook it without thinking.

'My name's Cacophini. You are William, you are Walter, and you are Pete. It's so good to make new acquaintances isn't it?'

'You said I would be powerful,' said Jack.

'And you will be,' said Cacophini. 'After you are dead.'

Cacophini clapped his hands and Jack collapsed to the floor. William, Pete, and Walter stepped back.

'Who are you?' said William.

'I already told you. You should pay attention. He'll be back shortly,' said Cacophini, looking down at Jack's lifeless body. 'And you know what? He's going to be mighty upset. I think he'll probably try and kill you all. You know how these things go.'

'Dad?' said Sarah.

'He's dead, grow up already,' said Cacophini, snapping at the girl.

'Hey, she's just a kid,' said Pete.

Jack's body twitched. 'Uh oh,' said Cacophini.

'I don't understand what's happening,' said Amelia.

'William, you seem like a reasonable man. Here's a deal I think you should take. In a few moments Jack is going to violently kill every one of you. I can help you stop him. Give me a soul, I'll give you ten years. In return I will give all of you wealth and fame. You can die tonight or in a decade, what's it going to be?'

'My soul? What are you, the devil?'

'The devil's busy. I'm Cacophini, we've been through this. We shook hands, remember?'

The floor around Jack started to turn black. It was like someone was stood below him and was shining a torch upwards that emitted darkness into the basement. The floor became a patch of night sky and Jack was floating in it. His eyes opened and they were full and bright. He sat up and the darkness fell away. He came to his feet without needing to pull himself up. It was like he had just tilted forwards.

Walter's mind turned to scripture. 'Jesus fucking Christ,' he said.

Jack shot forward and punched Walter in the chest. Walter slammed backwards into the wall and cracked his head. He slumped to the ground. His chest had caved in from the impact of Jack's fist and blood was gushing from his nose. He fell to his side and stopped breathing.

'I can fix that,' said Cacophini.

'Walter,' shouted Pete.

Before Pete had a chance to say anything else, Jack was behind him. He forced Pete to his knees and put a foot on the centre of his back. He pulled Pete's head up by the chin and snapped his spine. Pete fell lifeless to the floor.

Cacophini snapped his fingers and everything stopped.

'I've got a small problem,' said Cacophini.

William looked around. Amelia was frozen with her arm reaching out to Pete. Her mouth was agape with horror and tears were paused halfway down her cheeks.

'You see, I made a deal and I have to stick to it. Looking back it was a pretty stupid deal, but, you know, I guess I got carried away in the moment. It happens. The thing is, I can't really let him go around with all that power, can I? Imagine the problems it would cause. So here's what I'm willing to do. I will give you this axe.'

Cacophini held out an old looking axe with markings burned into the handle. The head of the axe was made of a dark black metal. It was unlike anything William had seen before. It was almost transparent. Only it wasn't the basement he could see through it but some other place. A terrible place, filled with screaming people.

'I think it's the only thing that will kill him,' said Cacophini, admiring the object in his hands. 'I'll bring your friends back from the dead if you make a deal, what do you say?'

William couldn't respond. His mind was an open void. He looked around him at the frozen scene, and the strange object, and the even stranger man. He looked at Jack. His face was a twisted grin.

'I could just unfreeze time of course and let him kill you too. I'll find someone to make a deal with. I can't kill him myself, of course, that would void the deal I made with him.

Fuck it, you know what, I'll let him kill you, I was enjoying the show anyway.'

He snapped his fingers and Amelia screamed.

'No, you fucking monster, what have you done?'

Jack turned on William and flew at him.

'I'll do it, I'll do it,' shouted William.

'I thought you might,' said Cacophini, and he gave William the axe.

William swung immediately and caught Jack across the collar bone. He screeched with agony and crashed to the ground.

'I wouldn't wait around,' said Cacophini. 'Get chopping and I'll go and fix your friends.'

Cacophini walked over to Pete and looked down at him. 'I'll start with this one. He looks easiest to fix. Chop chop, William.'

William blinked and looked down at Jack. Jack grabbed William's ankle and William swung down hard with the axe. It cut clean through his shoulder.

Cacophini flipped Pete over onto his back and pulled the top half of his torso straight. There was a crack and Cacophini put his hand to his mouth. 'Oops,' he said. 'I think I made it worse. Chop, William, chop!'

Cacophini busied himself with Pete's body while William took care of Jack.

Sarah ran to her father's side. William swung back and caught her in the face just above the nose. He turned to see what he had hit and dropped the axe. She stumbled backwards and turned as she fell. Her head caught the basement wall and her neck broke. She slid down and her little body started convulsing on the floor.

'I wouldn't worry too much about her, she was going to die anyway,' said Cacophini. He glanced past William. 'Uh oh, Jack's gonna get ya.' He stood up over Pete's body and brushed off his hands. 'I think that will do it,' he said. 'Wakey, wakey.' Pete groaned. 'Alright, on to the next one.'

Jack twisted into the air, blood cascading out of his wounds. William picked up the axe and swung upwards and caught him across the face. His jaw split open and hung there. Fresh blood fled out of his mouth. William struck him again, swinging upwards. Jack hung in the air as if supported by invisible strings. The axe caught him in the chest and Jack fell to the ground.

'Off with his head,' laughed Cacophini. He was sitting on Walter's face, with both his hands dug into the bottom of Walter's rib cage, he pulled back and they clicked into place.

William looked down at Jack. He pulled the axe out of his chest and took a step back. He held the axe high above him and swung down hard. It cut clean through his neck and took a chip out of the concrete floor. Jack's head came away from his body and rolled onto its side.

'You might want to kick that away,' said Cacophini.

William didn't think to question him and kicked the head clear away from the body. It rolled across the floor and came to a stop under a work bench.

Amelia was slouched against the wall. Tears smeared her

cheeks. Her jaw was going, mouthing incoherent words. Cacophini was still adjusting Walter's body.

'You know what I think I'll do. Seeing as you've been so helpful. I'll take away the emotional baggage that you might all have after today's events so you can enjoy the next ten years, how about that? And you know what, they won't even remember they were dead.' Cacophini looked at Amelia. 'Her crying is pissing me off.' He clapped his hands and Amelia stopped. 'Isn't that better? A crying woman really ruins the ambience, don't you think?'

Walter heaved in a deep breath and sat up. 'And he's fixed,' said Cacophini.

The room was quiet, apart from Walter's heavy breathing. Pete got to his feet and cricked his back. William looked down at Jack's body.

Cacophini stood next to William. 'Gather round everyone,' he said. Nobody moved. 'Alright, I guess you can stay where you are. I'm shooting off now, but before I go, there are some things you need to do.'

William, Walter, Amelia, and Pete, all had the same looks on their faces. A blank open look.

'You've got, what, three hours or so before the launch of your little game? If you want to be ready for that you've got some digging to do. You'll need to separate the rest of Jack's body and bury the parts away from each other. You do not want him to get whole again, believe me. Any questions? No? Good.'

The back wall of the basement exploded open and all the

vacuum of space stood just a few feet away from them. Walter lurched away from it and scurried back a few feet towards Pete. Had he gone the other way he might have toppled in.

Cacophini walked over to Sarah. He reached into her and ripped out her soul. It was a perfect image of her. Lifeless and grey. He walked over to Jack, dragging Sarah's soul along the floor beside him. He reached into Jack's body and tore his soul free too. Jack's soul put up more of a fight and came out jet black and aflame with particles of brilliant light.

'See you in ten, chaps,' said Cacophini, and his body shimmered and broke apart like a handful of leaves in the wind. He shot backwards and scattered into the void. There was a loud PSSHT and a SHTUM and the basement wall was back. Cacophini left two dead bodies and four speechless adults in his wake.

CHAPTER 48

William Rain came out of his memory. It was a momentary thing. A mere blink in real time. The sun was hot on his shoulder and the gun grip was sweaty in his palm.

William and Jack watched each other. Neither of them moving.

'Put the boy down, it's not him you want,' he said.

Jack didn't move.

William used his thumb to cock the hammer on the gun. It moved back easily and a loaded chamber clicked into place.

Cacophini watched.

Ryman drove into the carpark and stopped. He opened his car door and stepped out.

'William?' he shouted.

William didn't answer. Billy's eyes darted to Ryman and then back to his dad. Eunice got out of the car.

'Mum,' shouted Billy.

William didn't turn to look. He raised the gun and put it to his own head.

'It's not him you want, is it? It's me. I killed your daughter, no one else.'

Jack watched on.

Finnegan huffed into the carpark, breathing heavily. He was a long time smoker and his lungs weren't so good.

'William, think about what you're doing,' he shouted. But then he saw Jack. He opened his mouth to say something but found he had nothing to say. What could he say?

'Dad, don't do it, please Dad, don't,' cried Billy. He started sobbing and tears gushed down his face. 'I can't lose you too Dad, please.'

William swallowed and held back every impulse he had to drop the gun and run to his son. Maybe he could grapple him away. But he knew it would be impossible.

'I'm sorry, Son,' he said, and pulled the trigger.

The side of his head burst open and blood sprayed out and glittered in the sun.

'No!' cried Billy.

William collapsed to the floor.

Billy closed his eyes and waited for his death. It would come thankfully. Martha was dead. Martha. The love of his life. His dad was back from his long departure, and now he was gone too.

Death didn't come. He felt Jack's grip loosen around his head and let go.

A pinprick of black appeared behind Jack and the graveyard seemed to warp around it. It was as if someone was pushing a needle into a piece of fabric with the background printed on it. It stretched away from Jack until it reached way back and the needle broke through.

There was a terrible ripping sound and a horrifying

blackness peeled away from the tear. It became a cone of shimmering night. It was endless. There were stars in there.

Jack looked at William's body on the floor and then turned towards the expanding blackness. His body started to fall away as he walked. First his head rolled off, and then his arms fell away. The torso, still draped with the doctor's coat, flopped to the ground. His left leg stepped forward, but the right one stayed where it was and fell sideways. The left leg fell after another step. Now there was just a ghostly image of Jack. Faint against the backdrop of endless dark.

Cacophini jumped off the roof of the minibus and followed Jack into the void, turning and taking a bow before he vanished.

Eunice ran to her son and held him in her arms. She spoke to him but the words were just for them. She held him tight. They were silhouetted against the deafening darkness.

The gap that had opened up, absent of all sensible reality, silently closed.

AUTHOR'S EPILOGUE

So that was the story of Billy Rain. I'm glad you stuck with me all the way through. I guess the weather was good for it. Did you enjoy your stay here in Shelley Town? I guess you'll think twice about coming back. I hope you do though. This town has a lot more to offer. Man, the stories I could tell.

Sit with me for a moment here on this bench. It seems the pigeons have left us for the evening. It's funny isn't it, how calm the square is? With everything that happened today.

You're probably wondering if Billy will be okay. That's a hard question to answer. He'll have good days where he doesn't think about it much, but I suppose there won't be many of them. I suspect Ryman will do everything he can to take care of the boy. That's if things work out between him and Eunice. You know, I think maybe they will.

They're at the house now. You can see Ryman's car there. He's doing his duty, taking a statement. His heart's not in it though. He's not sure how he's going to explain all this.

The sun's almost down now. It's funny how things look different at night. It's sort of romantic. It's strange to me that fear and romance can share the same backdrop, don't you think?

Now, what's this? Here's Finnegan coming out of his tobacconist. And what's that in his hands? Petrol cans? I think they might be. I reckon he's on his way to burn that old Matterson house to the ground. I can't say I blame him.

You know, they never found the body of that girl of Jack's that died in the basement of that creepy old house. I reckon she's still in there somewhere.

Why don't you sit here with me for just a bit longer and we'll watch that old house burn down? I think that would be nice, don't you?

You know, I do believe it's going to rain tonight. That's how it is here in the south of England. You get a few days of sun and you're punished with a day of Rain.

AFTERWORD

The rain started to fall and the grey ashes of the Matterson house turned black. It glinted, like a shimmering oil slick.

A pilot, flying over Shelley Town, thought the remaining embers looked like stars. It was like a patch of space had fallen from the sky. In fact, he could almost see people in there. Deep in the darkness. There were thousands of them, and they were all screaming.

JACK'S GAME

ACKNOWLEDGMENTS

I will do my best to keep this brief. The only people really interested in reading the acknowledgments section of a book are those who are being acknowledged. So let's get to it.

Thanks to everyone who beta read this book over the past few years and gave me incredible feedback and helped shape it into what it is today. Ian Sainsbury, Rob Gregson, Jemahl Evans, Corben Duke, Laura Regan, Spike, Mary, Tom Foot, and Morgan Delaney.

To Mark Stay and Mark Desvaux, hosts of The Bestseller Experiment podcast and everyone in the BXP group on Facebook. Your constant encouragement has been invaluable.

Thanks to my dad, Steve, who I work with. I sat beside him in the passenger seat of the van on many trips as I wrote the first draft of this book. And to my mum, Suzie, for being the earliest reader of the roughest draft and still finding nice things to say about it.

Most of all I have to thank my partner, Rachel Howells. This book simply would not exist without her.

Oh, and I almost forgot, to my daughter, Kassidy, you continually amaze and inspire me. I don't know how many story ideas I have shared with you over the years but I can always trust you to tell me when an idea is bad, and, more importantly, when an idea is good.

Thank you for reading!

If you enjoyed this book please leave a review on Amazon or Goodreads.

As an independently published author I don't have the big marketing budget of a publishing house and so I rely on word of mouth to reach new readers. Tell the world dear reader, tell the world!

If you would like news about future novels you can sign up to my newsletter by going to **www.andychapwriter.com**

You can find me on Twitter and Instagram
@AndyChapWriter

I also have a Facebook group called **Andrew Chapman - Horror Writer** which can be easily found with a search.

Thank you again for reading!

Printed in Great Britain
by Amazon